"What's this

Merry asked. "Have you changed your mind about moving? Is that it?"

He should have shrugged off her questions, but dammit, she had him cornered, and he was tired of hiding his feelings. If Merry wanted answers, then by God he'd give them to her!

"And what if I have?" Nick tossed back at her. "What do you think would keep me here? Or maybe I should ask *who*, dammit! Think about it, Merry. Who could possibly be keeping me in Liberty Hill?"

Caught off guard, Merry just stood there, sure she must have heard wrong. But there was something in his eyes, a frustrated hurt directed solely at her, that set her heart slamming against her ribs and the ground dissolving beneath her feet. Stunned, she shook her head. No. This couldn't be happening. He couldn't be saying what she thought he was saying. There had to be some kind of mistake.

He couldn't mean…

Dear Reader,

Once again, Silhouette Intimate Moments has rounded up six top-notch romances for your reading pleasure, starting with the finale of Ruth Langan's fabulous new trilogy. *The Wildes of Wyoming— Ace* takes the last of the Wilde men and matches him with a pool-playing spitfire who turns out to be just the right woman to fill his bed—and his heart.

Linda Turner, a perennial reader favorite, continues THOSE MARRYING McBRIDES! with *The Best Man,* the story of sister Merry McBride's discovery that love is not always found where you expect it. Award-winning Ruth Wind's *Beautiful Stranger* features a heroine who was once an ugly duckling but is now the swan who wins the heart of a rugged "prince." Readers have been enjoying Sally Tyler Hayes' suspenseful tales of the men and women of DIVISION ONE, and *Her Secret Guardian* will not disappoint in its complex plot and emotional power. Christine Michels takes readers *Undercover with the Enemy,* and Vickie Taylor presents *The Lawman's Last Stand,* to round out this month's wonderful reading choices.

And don't miss a single Intimate Moments novel for the next three months, when the line takes center stage as part of the Silhouette 20th Anniversary celebration. Sharon Sala leads off A YEAR OF LOVING DANGEROUSLY, a new in-line continuity, in July; August brings the long-awaited reappearance of Linda Howard— and hero Chance Mackenzie—in *A Game of Chance;* and in September we reprise 36 HOURS, our successful freestanding continuity, in the Intimate Moments line. And that's only a small taste of what lies ahead, so be here this month and every month, when Silhouette Intimate Moments proves that love and excitement go best when they're hand in hand.

Leslie J. Wainger
Executive Senior Editor

Please address questions and book requests to:
Silhouette Reader Service
U.S.: 3010 Walden Ave., P.O. Box 1325, Buffalo, NY 14269
Canadian: P.O. Box 609, Fort Erie, Ont. L2A 5X3

LINDA TURNER
THE BEST MAN

Published by Silhouette Books

America's Publisher of Contemporary Romance

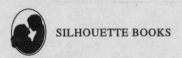 SILHOUETTE BOOKS

ISBN 0-373-27080-1

THE BEST MAN

Copyright © 2000 by Linda Turner

Visit Silhouette at www.eHarlequin.com

Printed in U.S.A.

Books by Linda Turner

LINDA TURNER

began reading romances in high school and began writing them one night when she had nothing else to read. She's been writing ever since. Single and living in Texas, she travels every chance she gets, scouting locales for her books.

IT'S OUR 20th ANNIVERSARY!
We'll be celebrating all year,
Continuing with these fabulous titles,
On sale in June 2000.

Romance

#1450 Cinderella's Midnight Kiss
Dixie Browning

#1451 Promoted–To Wife!
Raye Morgan

 AN OLDER MAN **#1452 Professor and the Nanny**
Phyllis Halldorson

 The Circle K Sisters **#1453 Never Let You Go**
Judy Christenberry

 The WEDDING AUCTION **#1454 Contractually His**
Myrna Mackenzie

#1455 Just the Husband She Chose
Karen Rose Smith

Desire

 MAN OF THE MONTH **#1297 Tough To Tame**
Jackie Merritt

#1298 The Rancher and the Nanny
Caroline Cross

 MATCHED IN MONTANA **#1299 The Cowboy Meets His Match**
Meagan McKinney

#1300 Cheyenne Dad
Sheri WhiteFeather

 The Baby Bank **#1301 The Baby Gift**
Susan Crosby

#1302 The Determined Groom
Kate Little

Intimate Moments

 THE WILDES OF WYOMING **#1009 The Wildes of Wyoming–Ace**
Ruth Langan

 Those Marrying McBrides! **#1010 The Best Man**
Linda Turner

#1011 Beautiful Stranger
Ruth Wind

#1012 Her Secret Guardian
Sally Tyler Hayes

#1013 Undercover with the Enemy
Christine Michels

#1014 The Lawman's Last Stand
Vickie Taylor

Special Edition

#1327 The Baby Quilt
Christine Flynn

#1328 Irish Rebel
Nora Roberts

#1329 To a MacAllister Born
Joan Elliott Pickart

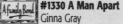 A Family Bond **#1330 A Man Apart**
Ginna Gray

DESERT ROGUES **#1331 The Sheik's Secret Bride**
Susan Mallery

#1332 The Price of Honor
Janis Reams Hudson

Chapter 1

The church dressing room was in chaos. Street clothes were tossed aside and lavender bridesmaid dresses pulled on as the clock on the wall steadily marked off the time. The wedding should have started fifteen minutes ago, but no one was worried about that. They just all wanted to look their best when they finally got the chance to walk down the aisle.

"Has anyone seen my makeup bag? I would have sworn I put it right here with my dress."

"It's on the table with the purses. Lord, these shoes are tight! I knew I should have broken them in but I never could find the time. Now I'm going to have blisters. How am I going to dance? Has anyone got any Band-Aids?"

"Oh, God, I can't believe this! I've got a run in my hose! I've got to get to the store!"

"You'll never make it," Janey McBride told her sister's old school friend, Rose. "The second Thomas gets here, the minister said we could start the ceremony."

"Can you believe Thomas had a flat on his wedding day?" her too-talkative cousin, Stella, said unthinkingly. "Talk about bad timing! It's almost as if fate was trying to tell him something."

Wincing, Janey shot her a reproving look and hoped her words didn't carry to the adjoining room, where her mother and sisters-in-law were helping her sister, Merry, dress. "Since it was fate that brought Thomas back to town in the first place, I don't think we have to look for any hidden messages," she told her cousin quietly, frowning at her before turning back to Rose, who was staring in dismay at her ruined hose. "We can't take a chance on holding things up a second time. You'll just have to wear what you've got."

"But—"

From across the room, a package of hose came sailing right at Rose, who caught it with a laugh. "If you ruin those, I've got six other pairs," Merry said with a grin, her sapphire eyes dancing with happiness as she and her mother and two sisters-in-law, Lizzie and Angel, joined the crowd of bridesmaids. "Plus aspirin, Midol tablets, hive medicine, and every shade of lipstick known to man—and woman."

Already dressed in her wedding dress, her dark hair swept up off her neck to reveal their grandmother's pearls, she was beautiful. With her oval face, fine, delicate features, and elegant looks, everyone had always said she was the prettiest girl in town, but as a bride, she was absolutely breathtaking.

Just looking at her brought the sting of tears to Janey's eyes. Quickly, she blinked them away, but not before Merry saw and frowned in concern. "I'm okay," she assured her thickly, a crooked smile tilting her mouth. "I'm just getting sentimental. You look so pretty, and I don't want anything to ruin this day for you."

Understanding, Merry smiled and hugged her. "It's not. It's going to be perfect. You'll see."

Confident, she wasn't the least bit nervous. After all, what was there to be nervous about? She'd been a bridesmaid so many times, she'd lost count of the number of weddings she'd been in. But at every one, she'd watched and learned the ins and outs, what not to do, how to avoid a disaster. Today was her day. She'd been waiting for it for years, and she had everything planned right down to the smallest detail. Nothing was going to go wrong. She wouldn't let it. Not now that she had found Thomas again.

She and Thomas Cooper had been friends in grade school, sweethearts in high school, then drifted apart when she'd gone to college and veterinary school in Texas and he'd headed east to Harvard for his undergraduate and law degrees. When she'd eventually returned to the family ranch in Liberty Hill, Colorado, to open her own clinic, she'd thought she'd never see Thomas again. He'd settled in Chicago and joined an old, established law firm there, which was just what he'd always wanted. She'd been happy for him, but deep inside, a part of her had longed to see him. Then, unexpectedly, his mother fell and broke her hip. His father had died years before, and he had no brothers or sisters, so it had been left to Thomas to come home to take care of her.

Merry hadn't even known he was back until she ran into him in town. A slow smile curled the corners of her mouth at the memory. It had been just like old times—only better. They'd gone to Ed's Diner for coffee and had Ed's famous chocolate cream pie, and they'd ended up talking and laughing for hours. Just that easily, she'd fallen in love with him all over again, and it had been the same for him.

Still, she hadn't dare let herself even think of a future with him. Her life, her family, her business—everything that was dear to her was in Liberty Hill. And Thomas had only come back to town to see after his mother. It was understood that as soon as she was well and back on her feet, he would return to his law firm in Chicago.

But a month passed, and then another, and even after his mother recovered, Thomas showed no signs of leaving. Then one day, he surprised Merry with the announcement that he didn't intend to return to Chicago. He'd made arrangements with his partners there to resign from the firm. He wanted to set up practice in Liberty Hill and spend the rest of his life with her. He proposed and gave her six months to plan a wedding.

Just thinking about it made her want to laugh, to dance, to sing with happiness. Thomas had wanted a big wedding to show off his new bride, and it had taken six months to get everything ready, but all the work was about to pay off. The big day had arrived, and in less than an hour, she would be Mrs. Thomas Cooper. Finally!

"It's going to be fantastic," Rose chimed in. "The sun's shining, the birds are singing, and there isn't a rain cloud in sight. What could go wrong? The church is full to the rafters, and Thomas is nuts about Merry. If I could find a man who'd look at me the way he looks at her, I'd be walking down the aisle myself. You're very lucky, Mer."

Touched, Merry found her own eyes welling with tears. "I know," she choked. "Sometimes, I have to pinch myself just to make sure I'm not dreaming."

"And this is just the beginning," Angel said, grinning at her. Newly married herself to Merry and Janey's brother, Joe, she knew from personal experience just how wonderful it could be. "You'll settle in together, become a family, have babies—"

"Diapers, colic—"

At her sister-in-law, Lizzie's, droll comment, they all

laughed and the tears that threatened to ruin their makeup disappeared. "I can hardly wait," Merry said with a chuckle. "It's going to be wonderful!"

The others had to agree, and as they finished dressing and the clock ticked toward five o'clock, the rescheduled time of the wedding, they talked about Merry's future with the man of her dreams. Some things were just meant to be, and they all agreed that she and Thomas were one of those things. You only had to see them together to know that they were totally devoted to each other.

Lost in the talk of babies and the nursery she planned to start as soon as possible, Merry didn't notice the passage of time until she suddenly glanced at her watch and gasped. "It's nearly five! Thomas should be here by now."

"He was coming straight to the church as soon as he changed the flat, wasn't he?" Stella asked. "He does know how to work a jack, doesn't he?"

She hadn't thought of that and blanched at the idea of setting back the wedding again. Everyone knew Thomas wasn't mechanically inclined. She should have insisted that one of her brothers go pick him up, but he'd assured her he had everything under control.

"Maybe I'd better call him," she said, stepping over to the phone. "Something must have happened."

She punched in the number of his cell phone, only to get his voice mail when he didn't answer. Surprised, she told herself there had to be a logical explanation. If his cell phone was in the car and he was outside loading the flat tire into the trunk, he wouldn't even hear the phone ringing. Or he'd left the phone on the side of the road and driven off without it. He'd been so absentminded lately that she wouldn't have put that past him.

Or right this minute, he could be lying on the side of the

*road, sick from the same bug that had upset his stomach
last night at the rehearsal dinner.*

She went pale at the thought. Worried, she turned to her
sister. "Janey, what if he's sick? You saw how he was last
night. He was green as a gourd. He said it was nothing, but
what if he's got one of those nasty stomach viruses that
won't go away? He wouldn't have told me because he
wouldn't have wanted to upset me, but he could be in trouble. Maybe the guys should go look for him."

Somber, Janey had to agree that her concern was legiti-
mate. They'd all seen how uncomfortable Thomas was last
night, and he was just the type to keep his illness to himself
so he wouldn't ruin their wedding day. "I'm sure there's
nothing to worry about," she assured her, "but I'll go talk
to the guys. Who knows? He may have called Nick so he
wouldn't have to worry you. I'll find out and be right
back."

"Thank you! If something has happened to him—"

"Don't look for trouble," her mother advised her calmly.
Always the voice of reason when everyone else was falling
apart, Sara McBride was as calm and self-possessed as a
saint as she quietly took charge. "Everything will be fine.
You'll see. While we're waiting, Lizzie and Angel and I
will talk to the guests and assure them everything's okay.
You just stay here and relax and think of how wonderful
your life with Thomas is going to be. I know you'll be very
happy together."

On the verge of panic, that was just what Merry needed
to hear. Tears glistening in her eyes, she took her mother's
hand and squeezed it in appreciation. "Thanks, Mom. How
did you know I needed to hear that?"

"Because I know my children. Don't have a meltdown,
dear. Everything's going to work out just fine. You'll see."

* * *

The room reserved for Thomas and his groomsmen to dress was off the choir room and much smaller than that allotted to the women. Knocking on the door, Janey wouldn't have been surprised to find Thomas inside, scrambling into his tux and cursing the flat tire that had delayed him.

But when her brother, Joe, answered the door and she looked past him into the room, all she saw was their younger brother, Zeke, and the rest of the groomsmen. Already decked out in their wedding finery and standing around with their hands in their pockets, there was something about their somber expressions that had her heart jumping in alarm. "What's wrong? Where's Thomas? He is here, isn't he?"

"Not exactly," Zeke replied grimly.

"What?!"

"He's having trouble getting here," Joe told her tersely. "Nick's on the phone with him in the church office right now."

Confused, Janey frowned. Nick Kincaid was not only the local sheriff, but Thomas's best man. "I don't understand. If he's still having car trouble, why doesn't Nick just send one of his deputies to pick him up?"

"Because Thomas won't tell any of us where he is."

The color drained out of Janey's face at Zeke's curt announcement, and suddenly she understood why her brothers looked so serious. "He's backing out of the wedding?"

"I don't know, but I'm tired of cooling my heels in here," Joe retorted. "C'mon. Let's go see what's going on."

Jerking open the door, he ushered Janey and Zeke out into the hall, only to discover that a number of the guests had grown restless and escaped to the foyer of the church, where they stood in groups of twos and threes, gossiping.

At the sight of the three McBrides, they immediately stiffened and nearly choked on what they were saying. It didn't take a genius to figure out that they were whispering about the delay in the ceremony and the fact that no one had seen the groom all day.

Joe couldn't say he blamed them for speculating among themselves. Thomas's behavior was damned odd, and he intended to tell him that the second he finally showed his face. For now, however, he and the rest of the family would, for Merry's sake, act as if everything were fine.

Nodding to the guests, he forced a smile and said, "Sorry about the delay, folks. There've been a few glitches, but we're getting them straightened out and should start the ceremony any minute."

Not giving anyone time to ask what the glitches were, he led the way to the church office and shut the door as soon as Janey and Zeke followed him inside. Nick, Thomas's closest friend for most of his life, was on the phone and prowling the length of the phone cord. Joe took one look at his scowling face and swore. Whatever breakdown Thomas was going through, Nick had obviously made little progress with him.

Furious, Nick, in fact, wanted to string him up by his thumbs. "Dammit, man, this is just prewedding jitters!" he growled into the phone. "Calm down and think about what you're doing. Think about Merry. I know you love her. You always have. And she loves you. The two of you belong together. Give yourself a chance and talk to her—"

"There's nothing to talk about," Thomas retorted. "I thought I could do this, but I can't. I can't marry her. It would be the biggest mistake of my life."

"You don't mean that. Talk to her—"

"You talk to her. Tell her whatever you like. Tell her I'm sorry. I never meant to hurt her. But I can't marry her.

I can't make her happy. I can't be the person she needs me to be. So I'm going back to Chicago where I belong.''

''No!''

''Goodbye, Nick.''

The phone went dead in his hands, and with a muttered curse, Nick quickly punched in the number to Thomas's cell phone, but he'd turned it off and the call couldn't be completed. Swearing, he slammed the receiver down on its base, and completely forgot he was in church. ''Damn him, I can't believe he's doing this!''

Her brown eyes wide in her pale face, Janey was the first to break the ominous silence that had fallen. ''What exactly is he doing?''

Nick hesitated, wondering how the hell he was supposed to tell Merry's family that the man she loved with all her heart was going to leave her standing at the altar. What could he say that would possibly make sense of this? Nothing, dammit. Nothing at all.

''He's jilting her, isn't he?'' Zeke snarled as Nick struggled to find the words. ''And he's too much of a coward to come here and tell her to her face.''

Nick winced. Like it or not, that pretty much summed it up. ''He's got it in his head that he can't be the man Merry needs him to be, and getting married now would be nothing but a mistake. He's going back to Chicago.''

''The hell he is!'' Joe growled, and headed for the door. ''C'mon, Zeke. You and I are going to have a talk with Mr. Cooper about the proper way a man treats the woman he claims to love.''

Nick wouldn't have blamed them if they'd wanted to do a hell of a lot more than *talk* to Thomas. If it hadn't been his responsibility as sheriff to enforce the law, he wouldn't have minded popping his old friend a few times himself. It was no more than he deserved. But beating the tar out of him wouldn't change anything, and at the moment, they had a much more serious problem to deal with. Merry still didn't know she wasn't getting married today.

Quickly stepping in front of the door, he blocked Joe's path and didn't so much as blink when the oldest McBride gave him a look that could have blistered paint. "You're forgetting Merry," he said quietly. "Somebody has to tell her."

That stopped both brothers in their tracks. Swearing, Zeke tugged off the tie that threatened to choke him and threw it across the room. "This is going to kill her, Nick. She's nuts about the bastard."

No one knew that better than Nick. Best friends with both Merry and Thomas since first grade, he'd watched them fall in love in high school, then again, just last November when Thomas came back to town to take care of his ailing mother. For as long as Nick could remember, Merry had never had eyes for anyone else but Thomas.

"I'll tell her," Joe said grimly. "Something like this needs to come from family."

Nick knew he was probably right. When a woman heard this kind of news, she needed her loved ones around her to cushion the blow. But he loved her, too, dammit! And he'd never been so frustrated in his life. He'd have given his right arm to protect her from this kind of hurt, but it was too late for that. All he could do for her now was break the news as gently as possible and be there for her when she needed a friend.

"I'd like to do it, if you don't mind," he said huskily. "I was the only one who talked to Thomas, and as the best man, I feel like it's my responsibility. I should have seen this coming. I knew something was troubling him, but I thought it was something to do with work and having to reschedule everything so he and Merry could have a month for their honeymoon. If I'd just cornered him and made him talk to me, all of this could have been prevented.''

Her brown eyes kind, Janey patted his arm in sympathy. ''This isn't your fault, Nick. None of us could have predicted this, so don't beat yourself up over it.''

''We all know who the bad guy is here,'' Zeke added, ''and it isn't you.''

''I'd still like to be the one to tell her,'' he insisted. ''She's going to blame herself, and she's not the one who did anything wrong. Thomas is the one with the hang-up, not her. I don't know how I'm going to make her understand that, but I'd like all of you to be there. And your mother, too, of course. She's going to take this hard.''

The three McBrides exchanged glances and came to a decision without saying a word. ''All right,'' Joe said. ''We'll do it your way. Janey, where's Mom?''

''She and Angel and Lizzie were helping everyone get dressed, but Mom said something about talking to some of the guests. They're getting restless.''

''I don't blame them,'' he muttered, pulling open the door. ''I'm a little testy myself. C'mon. Let's go find everyone.''

Pacing nervously, Merry glanced at her watch for the third time in a single minute, worry eating her stomach. What was taking Janey so long? She'd promised she'd be right back ten minutes ago, and she was nowhere in sight. Something was wrong with Thomas, she thought, swallowing a sob. He'd collapsed somewhere and was in the hospital and nobody wanted to tell her. That had to be it. Nothing else but some kind of horrible illness would keep him from her at a time like this. Dear God, what if instead of a stomach virus, he had appendicitis and his appendix had burst? Right this minute, he could be lying on the side of the road somewhere, dying. She had to go to him!

Horrified, she whirled and headed for the door, determined to find her brothers and Nick and make one of them take her to Thomas. But she'd only taken two steps when there was a perfunctory knock at the dressing room door and Nick and her entire family walked in.

At the sight of their somber faces, she paled, her worst fears realized. "Something's happened, hasn't it? He's in the hospital, isn't he?" When no one answered, tears welled in her eyes. "Oh, God! He's not—"

"He's not dead," Janey said quickly, reading her mind. "So don't worry about that. He's perfectly fine."

"Then he's here? Thank God! I've been worried sick."

In spite of the fact that it went against tradition, she would have rushed to the men's dressing room to see for herself that he was really all right, but the grim look that remained on everyone's faces held her motionless where she was. "What is it?" she demanded when her heart started to pound in alarm. "What's wrong?"

For a moment, she didn't think anyone was going to tell her. Then Nick stepped forward and took her hand. "He's not here, Merry," he told her gruffly. "He's gone back to Chicago."

"He has not," she retorted, chuckling in relief. For a second there, she'd thought something was seriously wrong! "We're getting married, silly. Cut the joking. Where is he, really? The minister must be getting impatient. We've got to get this show on the road."

Her hand still in his, Nick tightened his fingers around hers. "I'm not joking, Mer. There isn't going to be a wedding. Thomas had a panic attack and freaked out at the idea of getting married. I tried to talk him out of it, but there was no reasoning with him. He left for Chicago ten minutes ago.''

Stella gasped, and somewhere behind her, Rose murmured, ''Oh, God!'' but Merry never so much as flinched. *No!* She stared up at Nick with large, unblinking eyes, denial echoing over and over again in her head. There had to be a mistake. Thomas wouldn't do this to her. Nick must have misunderstood. This was all just some ridiculous misunderstanding. It had to be!

But there was nothing but sympathy in his eyes, nothing but regret and sorrow in the murmured words of her brothers and sister and sisters-in-law as they gathered around her to hug her and reassure her that everything was going to be fine. Clinging to denial, she submitted to their hugs, wondering all the while when someone was going to spill the punchline to this awful joke. Then her mother came to her, tears glistening in her beloved eyes as she slipped her arms around her and folded her close against her heart, and Merry's defenses began to crumble.

''Mom?''

''I'm so sorry, dear. I know how much you love him. I can't imagine what's going on in his head right now, but I'm sure he never meant to hurt you.''

So it was true. Practically the whole town had gathered to see her marry Thomas, and it wasn't going to happen. Without a word of explanation, he'd literally left her standing at the altar.

The pain hit then, sharp and excruciating, right in the heart. She wanted to cry out, to scream *No!* but her throat closed like a vice. Tears flooded her eyes, and she couldn't seem to blink them away fast enough. Numb, all she could do was hug herself and rock back and fourth as hurt swamped her, threatening to drag her down into the dark void that suddenly yawned at the edge of her consciousness.

Lost in her misery, she suffered the hugs of Rose and Stella and hardly heard the words of condolences that swirled around her. It was like a funeral, she thought dazedly as she sank into the nearest chair and her wedding dress billowed around her. A death, only no one had died. Except her. She should have been wearing black.

Zeke squatted down in front of her, concern lining his face as he took her cold hand. "You don't have to worry about anything, Sis. Do you hear me? Joe and I will talk to the guests and tell them the wedding and reception have been cancelled. Lizzie and Angel are going to go back to the house and help the caterers pack everything up while we wait for everyone to clear out of here. You don't have to see or talk to anyone until you're ready. Okay?"

"As soon as we get the all clear from Angel and Lizzie, we'll take you home," Joe added huskily. "To Mom's house, not yours. There's no reason for you to face Thomas's things tonight. Tomorrow, Zeke and Nick and I will load his stuff into my truck and take it over to his mother's."

Enveloped in misery, Merry just barely held back a sob. She had such a wonderful family. They all had busy lives and didn't always agree on things, but in times of trouble, they closed ranks. And she loved them for it. Unlike Thomas, she could count on them to be there for her through thick and thin and to protect her when she was hurting.

And right now, she was battered and bruised and more hurt than she'd ever been in her life. Like a wounded animal, she wanted to just crawl in a hole somewhere and hide from the world. But she couldn't. Thomas had publicly humiliated her in front of the whole town, and if she didn't face her friends and family now, she didn't think she'd ever be able to look them in the eye again.

The decision made, she blinked away her tears and lifted her chin proudly. "No, *I'll* talk to the guests. They were invited to my wedding, and I should be the one who talks to them."

"Says who?"

"You don't owe anyone anything."

"Are you sure you want to do this, dear? It won't be easy."

Even as her mother cautioned her, Merry knew she understood this was something she had to do. Thomas was the bad guy here, and she wasn't going to hide away like she had something to be ashamed of. The light of battle glinting in her sapphire eyes, she rose purposefully to her feet. "I'm sure. And I'm not cancelling the reception, either. It's already been paid for, and everyone's expecting a party. They're going to have one."

"What?!"

"You can't be serious!"

"Maybe somebody should call a doctor. I don't think she's in any condition to be making these kind of decisions."

Joe scowled at Stella, shutting her up with a single hard glare, and turned to Merry. Struggling to hang on to his patience, he was frustrated and furious with Thomas, and his control snapped. "Dammit, Merry, no one will expect you to go through with the damn reception. It's crazy. So just hush and let us take care of things!"

At any other time, she would have snapped back. This wasn't the Dark Ages and she didn't have to hush and go meekly along with whatever the men in the family wanted. But he was upset and concerned and, like everyone else, more than a little emotional. And for that, she could forgive him. But she was still going through with the reception.

Love squeezing her heart, she pulled him close for a fierce hug, then quickly stepped free before she dissolved in tears. ''I know you're just trying to protect me, and I appreciate it,'' she said with a smile that wasn't quite steady. ''But I've made up my mind and I'm not going to change it. Tell Lizzie and Angel the reception's a go.'' And not giving anyone a chance to argue further, she turned and sailed out of the dressing room with the train of her wedding dress trailing behind her.

Muttering among themselves about the McBride stubbornness that they all had more than their fair share of, there was nothing Joe and the rest of the family could do but follow.

She'd thought it would be easy. Caught up in her determination to do what she considered the right thing, she would march down the aisle, give a no-nonsense explanation to the overflowing crowd, and invite everyone back to the ranch for the reception. But as she started down the center aisle alone in her wedding dress, she could almost feel the shocked surprise that rippled through the crowd. Row by row, silence fell like a stone as people caught sight of her. By the time she reached the spot where she and Thomas were to have stood to take their vows, the church was so quiet, the very air itself seemed to hum. And every eye was on her.

Her heart pounding, she would have liked nothing more than to turn tail and run. But these were her friends and relatives, people she'd known all her life, and she'd kept them waiting long enough.

Gathering her courage, she faced them squarely, with a forced smile that didn't come easily. ''I imagine you've all been wondering what the holdup is, and I can't say I blame you. We had a few unexpected delays, and now Thomas has decided he doesn't want to get married today, after all.''

A collective gasp went up from the crowd, along with more than a few less than complimentary comments about Thomas. But it was the sympathy she saw in people's eyes that almost shattered Merry. Touched, she struggled to hold back tears, but it wasn't easy. Her throat was tight, her heart hurting, and it was several long moments before she could manage to even talk. And even then, her voice was betrayingly husky with emotion.

''I apologize for keeping you waiting, but I was just as surprised by the turn of events as you are. Needless to say, there won't be a wedding, but that doesn't mean you'll have to miss out on a good party. I'll meet you back at the ranch in a few moments, and the reception will continue as planned.''

For a moment, there was nothing but stunned silence, then everyone began to whisper. Suddenly, from the back of the church, one of the cowboys who worked at the ranch jumped to his feet and let out a holler that rattled the church's stained-glass windows. ''Does this mean you're available again, Merry, honey? All right! Can I have the first dance?''

Caught off guard, she had to laugh—she couldn't help it. A wide grin splitting his face and his blue eyes dancing with excitement, he looked like he'd just discovered there was a Santa Claus after all. ''You certainly can, Slim,'' she said with a chuckle. ''I'd be honored.''

''I want second,'' another cowboy called out.

''Hey, I was going to ask her!''

''So what took you so long?''

Flattered, Merry found herself blinking back tears again. ''Don't fight, boys. I'll be happy to dance with all of you. Now if you'll excuse me, I'm going to get out of these shoes—they're killing me! I'll see all of you back at the ranch.''

She hurried up the aisle before the tears could fall and found her entire family waiting for her at the back of the church. Her sisters-in-law, Elizabeth and Angel, had joined the group, along with Zeke and Elizabeth's daughter, Casey, and although they didn't all agree with her decision, they were totally supportive.

Tears glistening in her mother's eyes, her smile tender with love, she said, "Your father would be so proud of you, dear. I know that wasn't easy for you."

"It was the right thing to do," she said simply. "I'm not going to hide away like I did something I should be ashamed of."

"If anyone should be ashamed, it should be Cooper," Zeke said tersely as they all retreated to the dressing room again to wait for the crowd to thin out. "Damn, I'd like to give him a piece of my mind!"

"Don't worry," Joe retorted in a low-pitched voice. "He's going to pay. He'll have to live with this the rest of his life, and he probably doesn't even realize it."

Still furious with his old friend, Nick had to agree. "No, he doesn't. He's not thinking at all—he's panicking. Once he calms down, he's going to regret this, but by then, it'll be too late. It's already too late."

Nick had to only look at Merry's pale, drawn face to know just how badly she was hurting. And there was nothing he or anyone else could do to help her. That, more than anything else, frustrated the hell out of him. Tonight should have been her wedding night, the night she'd planned to spend in some secluded, romantic setting with her new husband. Instead, she would dance the evening away with a bunch of drunk cowboys, then spend what was left of the night alone with dreams of what might have been.

Nick didn't know how she would bear it. No woman deserved that, especially one as kind and caring and beautiful as Merry. She could have graced the cover of any fashion magazine in the world—she was that gorgeous—and Thomas had walked away from her. He must have been out of his mind.

Wishing he could get his old friend alone for just five minutes, he tore at his tie. "I don't know about the rest of you, but I think I'm going to go change out of this monkey suit. This damn tie's choking me to death."

Quickly seconding the suggestion, Janey said, "I think that's an excellent idea. Merry, don't you want to change? With all that bead work, your dress must weigh a ton. Your suitcase is still in my car. Why don't you let one of the guys get it for you so you can put on something more comfortable?"

Merry was tempted. Janey was right—the dress was incredibly heavy—and the most beautiful wedding dress she'd ever seen. She'd fallen in love with it at first sight and hadn't needed to look at any others to know that this was *The Dress,* the one she'd dreamed of wearing when she walked down the aisle to Thomas. But that dream had turned into a nightmare. And the dress no longer represented her hopes for the future with the man she loved, but his betrayal.

And that was why she wasn't taking it off. Not yet. With every step, the weight of it tugging at her would remind her of Thomas and just how close she'd come to making the biggest mistake of her life. God, what a fool she was! She'd loved him, trusted him with her heart and soul. And what had he done? Kicked her in the teeth in front of the whole town.

Numb, she still couldn't believe it. They'd been friends their entire lives—she'd loved him for longer than she could remember. She'd thought she knew him inside and out, better than she knew herself. If someone had told her he was capable of hurting her this way, she would have called them a liar. She would have been wrong.

"No, thanks," she told Janey. "I'll just wear this for now. It can't be returned, so I might as well get some use out of it while I can."

Her eyes sad, her sister said quietly, "You don't have to torture yourself this way, Mer. Why don't you let me take the dress and get rid of it?"

Just that easily, the tears she'd thought she had under control were back, filling her eyes and silently spilling over her leashes. "Maybe later," she said thickly. "For now, I have to wear it. I have my reasons."

Afraid she was going to shatter if she didn't get her emotions under control, she quickly changed the subject and forced a bright smile. "Enough of this. The church has cleared out, so let's get out of here. We've got a party to go to!"

The reception was held at her mother's house, the large, sprawling family homestead that had been added on to by generations of McBrides over the last century. With porches stretching across the front and back of the house and a huge patio under the trees out back, there was more than enough room to accommodate half the county.

Which was a good thing, Merry thought as she, Janey, and her mother approached the house in the limo that had been rented to drive her and Thomas to the reception. Cars lined the drive for a quarter of a mile, and still others spilled onto nearby pastures. Everyone in town appeared to be there, and Merry couldn't say she was surprised. This was a party that no one in their right mind was going to miss.

She'd wanted a wedding that people would talk about

for years to come, and it looked like she'd gotten it. But Lord, she hadn't expected it to be under these conditions! Thomas should be at her side, damn him, with his ring on her finger and hers on his! Instead, he was on his way back to Chicago with his tail between his legs, and she was the one left to deal with the consequences of his cowardice.

Too late, she realized she should have cancelled the reception. She must have been out of her mind to think she could carry such a thing off. People would expect her to smile prettily and graciously accept their hugs and kisses and words of condolences, and she just wasn't in the mood. She appreciated their support, but what she really needed was some time to herself.

Reading her thoughts, her mother said quietly, "You don't have to do this, you know. No one would think badly of you if you thanked everyone for coming, then slipped away by yourself."

"We can handle the party," Janey assured her. "Why don't you go back to your place and have a good cry? You'd feel better."

For all of two seconds, she actually considered it. Then she remembered Thomas's things. His clothes hung beside hers in her closet; his pillow lay beside hers on her bed. Not wanting to have to move into her house after they returned from their honeymoon, when they would both immediately return to work, he'd spent the last week transferring his things from his apartment to Merry's house. Just thinking about facing that now, when she felt like she would shatter at any moment, had her shaking her head in panic. "No, I can handle it. I'm sure I'll be fine."

The limo pulled up before the homestead then, and any time she had to compose herself was gone. Guests started swarming toward the car, and she was left with no choice but to paste on a smile and step out to greet them when the driver opened the door for her. Immediately enveloped in hugs and sympathy, she was passed from one person to the next, then the next, and carried along with the crowd to the back patio, where tables had been set up for the reception. There, even more people were waiting for their chance to talk to her.

Overwhelmed, she felt tears sting her eyes, and in spite of her best resolve not to cry, she couldn't help herself. Horrified that she was going to fall apart right there in front of everyone, she looked around for an escape route, but she was cut off by the crowd at every turn. Then, just when she thought she was going to thoroughly embarrass herself, a drumroll sounded from the band that was set up at the opposite end of the patio.

"Ladies and gentlemen, if I may have your attention, please," the lead singer called out loudly. "The guest of honor has arrived and the band would like to salute her with a song. Merry, this one's for you."

Giving her a thumb's up signal, he turned to the band. With a nod of his head, he and his musicians swept into a rousing rendition of "I Will Survive."

Chapter 2

With one song, the band did what no one else had—they made her laugh. And for the first time in what felt like hours, Merry was her old self, confident and fun loving, the life of the party. One cowboy after another asked her to dance, and she said yes to them all, hoping she could lose herself in the music. And for a while, she did. She two-stepped and waltzed and jitterbugged with the best of them and refused to let herself think. But it couldn't last, not when she was hurting so badly. There was only one man she wanted to dance with, one man she wanted to hold her, and he wasn't there. Try though she might, she couldn't stop missing him.

And she hated herself for it. He'd dumped her, publicly humiliated her, then ran away like an irresponsible jerk. He wasn't worth another tear, let alone a second thought. She knew that, but still, she couldn't get him out of her head. In desperation, she smiled more, laughed harder, and to anyone who didn't know her well, she appeared to actually be having fun. She had, in fact, never been more miserable in her life.

And her family knew it. Standing on the sidelines watching her on the dance floor, they could only watch in pained silence and sympathize. "Somebody needs to do something," Angel said huskily. "Look at her out there, honey. She's got to be hurting."

"Maybe she just needs to get it out of her system," Joe replied, his brown eyes dark with concern as he watched every move Merry made. "At least she's not bawling her eyes out."

"That'll come later," his mother predicted softly. "When everyone's gone home and the letdown hits her. Then she'll cry herself to sleep."

His jaw rock-hard and his eyes narrowed on the cowboy that was holding Merry just a little too close, Zeke growled. "That jackass better watch where he's putting his hands or he's going to find himself picking himself up off the ground."

"Maybe it's time I cut in and gave that clown his walking papers," Nick said tersely. "Excuse me."

The song was just ending as Nick reached Merry and her partner, and with a single hard glare, he sent the other man packing. Merry never even noticed. Giving him a smile that had been known to knock lesser men out of their boots, she walked right into his arms. "There you are, Nick. I haven't seen you in ages. Let's dance."

She melted in his arms as the band swung into the next number, and it wasn't until then that Nick realized she was well on her way to being snockered. Over the years, they'd danced together more times than either of them could remember, and not once all those times had she ever draped herself around him like a limp dishrag. Nick didn't even think he'd seen her dance that way with Thomas. She wasn't into public displays and just didn't do that kind of thing. Or at least, she hadn't before tonight. But then again, she'd never been jilted before, either.

And like it or not, she felt too damn good against him. With no conscious effort on his part, he tightened his arms around her, cradling her close against him before he suddenly realized what he was doing. Biting off a curse, he quickly dropped his hands to her waist and put some breathing space between them.

"Somebody's had a little too much to drink, and it isn't me," he said, frowning down at her when she murmured a protest. "You're going to regret that tomorrow."

Her smile faded, leaving her looking lost and lonely. "I'm going to regret a lot of things tomorrow. What's one more?"

She had a point, but still, it broke Nick's heart to see her this way. Damn Thomas! he thought furiously. Whatever doubts he'd had about getting married, he could have found a hell of a better way to break things off. He must have known weeks ago that he wasn't going to be able to go through with the ceremony, so why hadn't he told Merry then? Why had he waited and jilted her in front of the whole damn town?

"You don't have anything to regret, Mer," he said quietly. "*You* didn't do anything wrong."

Lifting stark eyes to his, she made no attempt to hide her pain. "I'm not so sure about that," she whispered. "It wasn't just anyone that Thomas didn't want to marry. It was *me*. So I have to ask myself…what did I do to drive him away?"

"Nothing! My God, you can't believe you're responsible for this!"

But she did—he could see it in her eyes, in the tears that welled there and started to spill over her lashes. Up until then, she'd been a tower of strength, facing her friends and family with a grace that he couldn't help but admire. But even she had her breaking point, and he had a feeling she'd just reached it. She started to cry, and there didn't seem to be anything she could do to stop it.

Alarmed, Nick knew the last thing she wanted to do was break down with the whole world watching. "C'mon," he murmured, hustling her off the dance floor before anyone noticed there was anything wrong. "I'm getting you out of here."

The crowd closed around them the second they stepped off the floor, and for a second, Nick didn't think he was going to be able to make his way through. But something in his face must have told people to back off because they parted like the Red Sea. Within seconds, he was leading Merry away from the patio and around the side of the house to where the cars were parked out front.

He intended to take her home to her house so she could be alone and cry in private, but she had other ideas. The minute he helped her into the passenger seat of his car, then came around to join her behind the wheel, she sniffed, "I don't want to go home."

In spite of the tears still streaming down her beautiful face, she had that stubborn set to her jaw, the same one he'd seen for the first time when they were both six years old. Over the years, he'd learned all too well that there was no budging her once she stuck out her chin. Still, he had to try.

"C'mon, Merry, don't be that way," he pleaded as he carefully made his way through the parked cars. "It's been a hell of a day and you've had too much to drink. You need to go home and get out of that dress and get some rest."

"This was supposed to be my wedding night," she whispered brokenly, wrapping her arms around herself as if she was suddenly chilled. "Don't make me go home. I don't think I could bear it."

His teeth clenched on an oath, Nick wanted to kick himself. He hadn't thought of that, hadn't considered what it would be like for her when she went home to her lonely house and the empty bed that she'd expected to share with her new husband. She'd have to face the night alone, with nothing but what-ifs for company.

Damn Thomas! He didn't have a clue what he'd done to her, and there was nothing Nick could do to ease her pain...except be there for her as long as she wanted company so the night wouldn't be so lonely. "All right," he said gruffly. "Forget going home. It's early yet anyway. So where would you like to go? Just name it and we're there."

She considered the possibilities for all of five seconds. "I don't know. Someplace quiet, where I don't have to deal with people. Someplace like...the lake! We can watch the moon come up over the water."

It wasn't the place he would have picked—what she really needed was a strong cup of coffee at Ed's Diner—but this was her night to be indulged. "The lake it is," he said easily, and turned north once they reached the highway and left the ranch behind.

Bear Lake was really little more than a large pond, but it was a popular recreational spot for the locals all year round. Ice fishermen claimed it in the winter, and the water-skiers and kids took over the place in the summer. It was the teenagers who came there at night to neck, however, that earned the place its reputation as a lover's lane. Not a night went by, summer and winter, that Nick didn't have to drive out there, clear the young lovers out, and send them home.

And tonight was no different. The kids were there in droves, which wasn't surprising. It was a warm June night, the moon was full, and most of the parents in town were at the McBride place for Merry's wedding reception. And while the cat was away, the mice would play.

Noting the cars that were discreetly parked under trees all around the lake, he couldn't help but grin as he remembered the nights he, too, had sneaked off to the lake with one of the girls from school. Old man Hubbard had been the sheriff back then, and he, too, had made his own nightly trips around the lake looking for errant teenagers. Years from now, Nick imagined, another sheriff would continue the tradition, just as he had. Some things never changed.

"I've got a little official business to take care of," he told Merry, then switched on the spotlight on his car. Reaching for the mike of his radio, he began to slowly drive around the lake. "It's time to go home, boys and girls," he said over his loudspeaker. "The lake is for day use only and closes at nine."

It was the same speech he gave every night, and as usual, the result was the same. There were a few squeals of feminine dismay as his spotlight lit up the interior of several cars, then engines roared to life, and a mass exodus began. Within minutes, the last taillight disappeared down the road, and they were alone.

Satisfied, Nick turned to Merry. "Now that we have the place to ourselves, where would you like to park?"

Her smile flashed in the darkness. "I thought the lake was closed."

Unabashed, he grinned. "It is. And to make sure it stays that way, we're going to stick around for a while. So where would you like to park?"

"Out on the point," she said without hesitation. "Then we can see the moon rise."

It had been their favorite spot when they were teenagers, the place where she and Thomas and he had met to swim and fish and just hang out together. There, they'd talked about their hopes and dreams and how they were all going to one day change the world. It was there that Merry had first kissed Thomas, there that Thomas had given her his letter jacket and asked her to go steady, there that Nick played peacemaker whenever they had a fight.

Driving out onto the point, he parked and cut the engine, then got out of his patrol car to join her at the picnic table the three of them had always called "theirs." It had weathered over the years, but it still bore the initials they'd carved into it the first day of their senior year in high school.

Dropping down to a bench, her wedding dress pooling around her, Merry found the rough letters in the dark and traced them with her index finger. "We had some good times back then, didn't we?" she said with a melancholy smile. "Remember when Thomas smuggled his pet duck into church and it started quacking right in the middle of Reverend Johnson's sermon? I thought he was going to have a stroke right there in front of the entire congregation."

Nick chuckled, his brown eyes dancing at the memory. "He got so upset he pulled his toupee off and the organist fell off her bench! God, I'd forgotten about that."

"And the time Thomas climbed the tree outside my bedroom window and you distracted my mother by pretending you had appendicitis?" she laughed.

"How could I forget," he retorted, grinning. "Joe came home early and caught Thomas hanging from the tree, and I thought we were all three toast."

"What do you mean *all three?* The only punishment you

and Thomas got was a stern lecture from my mother. *I* was
put on restriction and didn't get to see Thomas anywhere
but at school for a month. It was the longest month of my
life.''

Dear Lord, how she'd missed him! And she'd still gotten
to see him every day at school. Now she wouldn't be seeing
him at all. He was gone, out of her life, and he wouldn't
be coming back. Just thinking about it made her want to
lay her head down on the table and cry her eyes out.

But she couldn't. Because if she did, she didn't think
she'd ever be able to stop. Not this time. The hurt was too
raw, too strong, and what little control she'd had earlier
was all used up.

Her eyes burning from the tears she wouldn't allow to
fall, she jumped to her feet, in desperate need of distraction.
''I'm hot,'' she announced. ''I think I'll go swimming.''

Surprised, Nick just blinked at her. ''You can't. The
lake's closed.''

Undaunted, she just cocked her head and mockingly
arched a brow at him. ''Then I guess you'll just have to
arrest me, won't you, Sheriff?''

When she stepped out of her shoes, then reached under
the full skirt of he wedding dress to shimmy out of her
panty hose, Nick told himself she wouldn't actually strip
right there in front of him. She was just playing with him,
pushing his buttons—and, he silently added, doing a damn
good job of it. But she wouldn't really go through with it.
Not Merry. She liked to tease, but that was as far as it went.
The second he called her bluff, she'd back down in a hurry.

Satisfied he had everything under control, he crossed his
arms over his chest and leaned back against the picnic table
to watch the show, daring her with his own arched brow.
A split second later, she reached behind her for the zipper
to her dress.

He stiffened, his gaze narrowing dangerously. "Don't go there, Mer—"

For an answer, the raspy whisper of her zipper growled like a tiger in the night.

Shocked, he jumped toward her. "Dammit, Merry, don't you dare!"

He was too late. Lightning quick, she pulled her zipper down the rest of the way, and with a silent sigh of satin, her wedding dress dropped to the ground. Between one heartbeat and the next, she stole the air right out of his lungs.

He tried to tell himself that the lacy panties and bra she wore revealed little more than a bathing suit, and they'd gone swimming enough in the past that he shouldn't have been impressed. But the last time he'd been to the lake with her, they'd both been seniors in high school. And the woman who stood before him looked nothing like the girl from back then.

Lord, she was beautiful! He'd always known that, but seeing her now in the glow of the moon rising on the eastern horizon, she was breathtaking—there was no other way to describe her. Tall and willowy, with her dark hair swept up off her shoulders and her eyes deep, mysterious pools of sapphire, she looked like a wood nymph there in the darkness.

He wanted to reach for her, to touch, to run his hands over her to see if her skin was as soft as it looked in the moonlight, but he didn't dare move for fear she would vanish right before his eyes. His heart slamming against his ribs, he couldn't get over her total lack of awareness of her own beauty. He'd known other pretty women who used their looks as leverage to get what they wanted out of life, but Merry wasn't like that. Intelligent and loyal, she had a kind, generous heart and, thanks to her mother's teachings, was much more interested in the kind of person you were than what you looked like. And that made her even more beautiful—and even more impossible to resist.

Which was why every single man he knew, including himself, was in love with her.

"Put your dress back on right this minute," he ordered sternly, "before somebody drives in and sees you."

"No," she said obstinately. "I'm going swimming."

"Don't even think about it," he warned.

He might as well have saved his breath. Ignoring him, she turned and headed for the water.

He should have just let her go. It would have been the wise thing to do. It wasn't like she was in any danger. True, she'd had too much to drink, but she wasn't so tipsy that he had to worry about her drowning. She'd be just fine.

But even as he tried to convince himself of that, he found himself turning to follow her. It wasn't until he felt the water lap around the legs of his pants that he realized he was still wearing his tux!

"Damn you, Mer, now you've done it! You owe me for this tux!"

Not the least bit perturbed, she only laughed...and splashed him. Within seconds, they were both playing in the water like a couple of kids.

Later, Nick couldn't have said how long they stayed in the water. Merry was laughing and teasing and seemed to have forgotten, for the moment, at least, what had brought them to the lake at that hour of the night. And Nick had no intention of reminding her. If she wanted to forget, he was certainly giving her the chance to do so. But it couldn't last, and all too quickly, her smile began to fade, her laughter to wane. Just that easily, her tears were back.

It was a warm night, but a gentle breeze against wet skin

soon had Merry shivering. Huddling with her shoulders under the water, she hugged herself and announced through chattering teeth, "I'm cold."

"Hang on," Nick said. "I'll get you a blanket out of the trunk of my car."

He always kept one or two blankets for an emergency, and when Merry rose out of the water like Aphrodite a few minutes later and started toward him, there was no question in his mind that this was an emergency. Silently groaning at the sight of her lacy underclothes plastered to her body, it was all he could do to keep his hands steady and his expression closed as he wrapped the blanket around her slender form.

He could have been a monk for all the emotion he displayed. Then he spoke and gave himself away. "Better?" he asked huskily.

Chilled and caught up in her misery, she didn't, thankfully, notice. "Y-yes. Just give me a minute and I'll be fine."

But five minutes later, she was still trembling. Seated at their picnic table, the blanket wrapped tight around her and her hair dripping on her bare shoulders, she looked absolutely miserable. Nick knew he should have insisted on taking her home then, but he couldn't forget the pain in her voice when she'd told him she didn't want to spend her wedding night alone. And that just gave him one more reason to despise his old friend Thomas. Damn him! How could he have done this to her?

"I'm going to light a fire," he said gruffly. "Maybe that'll help. Sit tight and let me collect some wood."

Within minutes, he had a fire crackling in the fire pit by the table. Sighing in relief as the heat seeped into her, Merry stared into the flames and tried not to think of the cabin she and Thomas had rented for their honeymoon.

They'd wanted someplace private and secluded, where they could completely escape from the world, and the cabin had seemed perfect. A hundred miles away and located high in the mountains on a private alpine lake, it had come equipped with everything they could possibly want, from a hot tub to a fireplace, not to mention enough food to feed an army.

They would have been there by now, Merry thought as she hugged the blanket around her. Thomas would have carried her over the threshold, then built a fire in the fireplace and opened a bottle of champagne. After a toast, they would have spent the rest of the night making love.

But there was no cabin in the mountains, no honeymoon, no lovemaking in front of the fireplace. And no husband.

Emotions pulled at her, tying her in knots. She wanted to rage, to scream, to cry. Then her gaze fell on her wedding dress, which still lay in a heap on the ground where she had stepped out of it. Without a thought, she scooped it up and turned toward the fire.

"Whoa, girl!" Nick cried, startled. "What the hell are you doing?"

"Burning it," she retorted, and dropped it on the flames.

With a muttered oath, Nick made a grab for it, but he was too late. The delicate lace and satin caught fire, and within moments, it had gone up in flames.

"Dammit, Merry, why'd you do that? I know you couldn't have taken it back and got your money back, but you might have been able to sell it. Now it's a total loss."

"Nobody wants a used wedding dress," she said flatly, watching it burn. "And I'll never use it again. It's bad karma."

The dress went up in smoke, and within moments, there was nothing left but a pile of ashes. Just like all her hopes and dreams, Merry thought numbly, staring at the glowing embers. There was nothing left of her and Thomas and what might have been.

Pain squeezed her heart like a fist, and just that easily, the tears that she'd been fighting all evening were back. Only this time, she was too tired, too defeated, to fight them. They welled over her lashes and spilled down her cheeks to drip silently onto the blanket she still clutched around her.

She never made a sound, didn't so much as lift a finger to wipe them away, but Nick must have caught the glint of them in the firelight. With a murmur, he reached for her. "Awh, Merry, don't. I hate to see you hurting."

"I c-can't h-h-help it," she sniffed, burying her face against his wet shirt. "I d-don't understand h-how he c-could do this t-to me. I—I thought he *l-loved* m-me!" What was left of her control shattered then, and with a mournful wail, she collapsed against him, sobbing.

His heart breaking for her, Nick wrapped his arms around her and just let her cry, wishing there was something he could say to explain Thomas's behavior. But he didn't understand it himself. He was best friends to both of them and had watched them fall in love in high school, then all over again when Thomas came back to Liberty Hill when his mother became ill. He would have sworn that Thomas loved her with all of his heart. But if that was the case, how could he have humiliated her this way?

"He does love you," he assured her, and hoped for her sake that it was true. "He's confused right now, but it's only a temporary condition. He'd never risk losing you forever. He just needs some space to get his head on straight and realize what he walked away from. Then he'll be back. You'll see. The two of you will make up; and the next time you walk down the aisle, he'll be waiting for you. Then fifty years from now, when we get together to celebrate your anniversary, we'll all laugh over this.''

Merry knew he meant well, but she couldn't think about the next fifty years when she still didn't know how she was going to get through tonight. And as for laughing, she didn't think she would ever smile again, let alone laugh. Especially over today.

Exhausted, her tears spent, she leaned against Nick and didn't know what she would have done if he hadn't been there to take her weight. ''I'm so tired,'' she said huskily. ''Could we leave now? I don't feel much like swimming anymore.''

''Let me put out the fire,'' he said gruffly, ''then we'll get out of here.''

He took her home with him because he didn't know where else to take her. She'd already made it quite clear that she didn't want to go to her own house, and he was fairly positive that she wouldn't want to arrive at her mother's wearing nothing but her bra and panties. So he took her home, gave her one of his T-shirts to sleep in and showed her to the guest room. When he checked on her fifteen minutes later, she was asleep, but her cheeks were still wet with tears.

Grabbing a beer from the refrigerator, Nick retreated to his favorite chair in front of the TV in the den and didn't even think about going to bed himself. He knew there was little point—he would never be able to sleep. Not when the woman he loved was asleep in one of his beds wearing nothing but his T-shirt.

Staring morosely at the TV screen, he didn't even see the old John Wayne movie that played on one of the cable channels. All he could see was Merry, in a thousand different ways. She was all he'd ever been able to see from the time he was first old enough to appreciate her as a female. And she hadn't known he was alive except as a friend.

Because of Thomas. He'd captured her heart from the very beginning.

Nick ruefully acknowledged that he'd never stood a chance. She was a one-man woman. Accepting that hadn't always been easy, but he'd done it because he needed her in his life any way he could get her, even if it was only as a friend.

Another man might have seen what happened today as an opportunity to further his own relationship with her, but Nick knew he could never take advantage of her when she was hurting so. And it wouldn't do any good anyway. To her, he was just Nick, her old buddy, and that wasn't going to change. Thomas was the one she loved, the only one she'd ever loved. Once he came to his senses and got over his attack of nerves, he'd come running back to her and charm her with roses and heartfelt words of apology. Because she loved him, she'd find a way to forgive him.

And once again, Nick would be on the sidelines.

Which was why, he told himself as he finished his beer, he wasn't going to do anything to try to change the status quo. He didn't want to get hurt, and unlike Thomas, he was smart enough to value the relationship he did have with her. It might not be what he really wanted, but it was better than nothing. So he'd just be her friend. Even if it killed him.

When there was a knock at the door fifteen minutes after Merry went to sleep, Nick didn't have to check the peephole to know it was Joe. Not wanting the McBrides to worry, he'd called the homestead shortly after he put Merry to bed so that her family would know where she was. He'd explained to Joe that she was fine, but exhausted, and would be home tomorrow, but Joe had insisted on seeing her immediately. Nick couldn't say he blamed him. If he hadn't known where she was, he'd have been worried sick about her himself. Resigned, he went to let him in.

"She's all right," he said the second he opened the door to the oldest McBride. "You didn't need to come rushing over."

His rugged face set in grim lines, Joe held up an overnight bag. "Mom thought she might need some things. Where is she?"

"In the guest room. Asleep," he added as Joe strode past him into the living room. "She was pretty wrung out after we left the lake—"

"The lake? You took my sister to the *lake?* At night? After what that jackass did to her?"

"Hey, it was her idea, not mine," Nick defended himself. "You know how headstrong she can be. She didn't want to go home. And it's because of what that jackass did to her that I agreed to go there in the first place. I thought it was better to humor her. Of course, I didn't know then that she was going to burn her wedding dress."

"What?!" Sounding like a parrot, Joe gaped at him. "She burned her wedding dress?"

"I don't think she wanted any reminders of what happened," he retorted. "Can you blame her?"

After giving it some thought, Joe couldn't say that he did. "No. I probably would have done the same thing." Picturing her tossing the dress into the flames, he had to grin. "God, I wish I could have seen that! I guess she was pretty steamed, huh? Good! The quicker she gets mad, the quicker she gets over the jerk."

Hating to disillusion him, Nick knew it wasn't going to be that easy. "She's hurting, Joe," he warned. "She had a pretty hard cry at the lake before we left, then cried herself to sleep when we got here. You need to warn the family she's not going to get over this overnight.''

"Are you saying she still loves the bastard?''

"Would you have stopped loving Angel overnight if she'd stood you up at the altar?''

Put that way, Joe had to admit he had a point. He couldn't imagine a time when he would ever stop loving Angel, regardless of what she did to him. He'd given her his heart, and that was forever. "No, of course not,'' he retorted. "But I would have been forced to admit that we had a serious problem. Whatever trust there was between us would have been destroyed. And without trust, what have you got?''

"Not much,'' Nick agreed, "but Merry's not thinking about that right now. She's hurting and just trying to understand what went wrong.''

"What went wrong is that he's the wrong man for her and always has been,'' Joe replied impatiently. "You'd think she could see that. She's an intelligent woman. She's always been pretty sharp when it comes to people. Except where you and Thomas are concerned.''

Nodding in agreement with everything he said up until that point, Nick stiffened abruptly, his dark brows snapping together in a frown. "What do you mean…where *I'm* concerned? What's any of this got to do with me?''

"Nothing, unfortunately,'' Joe said with a grimace. "And that's what makes it so frustrating. If she'd just open her eyes, she could see that the best man for her, the one who really loves her, has been right by her side all along.''

The surprise that flared across Nick's angular face was almost painful to watch. His expression suddenly as wary as a cornered wolf scenting danger, he didn't so much as blink as his gaze locked with Joe's. "And just who might that be?"

Too late, Joe realized he should have kept his damn mouth shut, but he'd already put his foot in it. Angel was going to kill him for interfering, but personally, he thought it was about time someone said something. If somebody had stepped forward years ago and pointed out to Merry that someone else besides Thomas was interested in her, she might have at least given Nick a chance. Who knew what might have happened then? As it was, they'd never know.

"Look, man, I know this is none of my business, and if you want to tell me to butt out, go ahead. That's your right. I know you love her—"

Shooting a sharp glance toward the hall that led to the bedrooms, Nick hissed, "Who the hell told you that?"

"Nobody. I've known it for years. But, hey, it's nothing to be ashamed of!" he added quickly when Nick started to swear. "I think it's great! The two of you are perfect for each other. I just wish *she* could see it, then maybe she'd tell Thomas to take a hike—"

"Who else knows?" Nick demanded. "Dammit, Joe, how many other people know about this?"

Joe almost told him it had been common knowledge around Liberty Hill for years that there was only one woman Nick Kincaid would ever love and that was Merry McBride. But Nick was already shaken enough as it was, and Joe just didn't have the heart to tell him the truth. A man was entitled to his pride. If Nick realized that the whole town knew and sympathized with him, he'd feel like he was the town laughingstock or something.

Nothing, however, could have been further from the truth. He was well liked and respected, not only for the job he did as sheriff, but for the fact that over the years, he could have tried to come between Merry and Thomas, and he hadn't. He loved Merry enough to want her to be happy, even if it wasn't with him, and Joe didn't know many people who loved that unselfishly.

"No one knows, as far as I know," he fibbed. "But even if they did, they wouldn't fault you for loving her, Nick. Granted, she was a pain in the ass when she was growing up," he added with a grin, "but she outgrew that quite awhile back. Thanks to Zeke and me keeping her and Janey in line, they both turned out all right."

He was teasing and they both knew it, but Nick couldn't manage even a halfhearted smile. God, he'd thought he'd hidden it so well! He'd always been careful to treat Merry just as he did any other friend. He didn't touch her like he longed to or even flirt with her. They were just buddies, pals, their relationship always strictly platonic so that no one would suspect a thing. And all this time, Joe had known.

And if he'd seen through his act, others must have, too. He couldn't help but wonder who. Sara McBride? Janey? *Merry?*

His stomach knotted at the thought. He wouldn't, couldn't, lose her friendship! Not Merry. She was the other half of his soul, dammit, and he wasn't losing her!

"Merry doesn't know, does she? She can't! She doesn't feel the same way, and that would only make her uncomfortable around me."

Personally, Joe thought shaking Merry up a little might be just what she needed, but he kept that information to himself. "As far as I know, the thought's never crossed her mind," he assured Nick. "Anyway, you know Merry. She doesn't hesitate to speak her mind. If she suspected you were in love with her, she'd come right out and ask you."

He had a point, but still, Nick didn't like it. His feelings

were private, dammit, and the less people who knew about
them, the better. "I don't want her to know. I mean it,
Joe," he said firmly when he opened his mouth to argue.
"It wouldn't serve any purpose except to embarrass her.
Merry loves Thomas, and that's not going to change just
because he got cold feet today. So this stays strictly between the two of us. Understand?"

Joe wanted to argue—Merry had a right to know another
man loved her!—but Nick gave him that hard look of his,
the one that kept everyone from disorderly drunks to macho
cowboys to teenagers bent on mischief in line, and he knew
better than to waste his breath.

His own granite jaw as unyielding as Nick's, he grudgingly gave in. "All right, have it your way. But if you don't
want her or anyone else to know you're in love with her,
then you'd better learn to hide your feelings better. Every
time you look at her, it's written all over your face."

Chapter 3

It was Merry's favorite part of the day, right after dawn, when the sun was just peaking over the horizon and most of the rest of the world was still sleeping. The dew was heavy on the ground, the scent of pine sweet and fresh on the morning air, and the sky washed clear of clouds. It was then that she loved to sit on her back porch with a steaming cup of coffee and watch the ranch slowly come awake.

But she wasn't at the ranch this morning, and she found no joy in the sunlight that streamed in through the open window of Nick's guest room. Outside, a robin sang merrily in a nearby tree, but all Merry could think of was last night...when she'd stripped off her wedding dress in front of Nick and waded into the lake.

Groaning, she rolled over and buried her face in the pillow. It was all just a horrible dream, she tried to tell herself, but the memories that marched relentlessly through her throbbing head were all too real. Thomas *had* stood her up, and she'd had too much to drink at the wake of her reception. She'd danced with every cowboy who'd asked her, flirted shamelessly, then completely fallen apart on poor Nick.

Images flashed before her closed eyes, horrifying her in the bright light of day. Standing before Nick in her bra and panties, burning her wedding dress, crying her heart out in her old friend's arms. She was sure she must have thoroughly embarrassed him, and she regretted that. But she didn't know what she would have done if he hadn't been there. All she'd wanted to do was die.

She still did, but life wasn't that easy. Like it or not, she was the talk of the town through no fault of her own, and starting today, she had to face that. But first, she had to face Nick, and just the thought of doing that dressed in nothing but his T-shirt made her cringe. Whatever possessed her to burn her dress? she wondered wildly. She must have been out of her mind.

Left with no choice, she climbed out of bed and only just then spied her overnight bag sitting just inside the room by the door. Relieved, she didn't have to ask how it had gotten there—she knew Nick well enough to know that he'd called her family to let them know where she was and someone had brought her some clothes. He was that kind of man, caring and considerate, and she was lucky to have him for a friend. He'd been kinder to her than the man who had spent most of the last year telling her how much he loved her.

Her emotions all out of kilter, she felt her eyes start to fill with tears and stiffened. No! she told herself fiercely. She would *not* cry! Not again. Thomas was gone, without a word of apology or explanation to her, and she had to find a way to get past that, to get past the hurt that burned like an open wound where her heart had once been. And she couldn't do it by crying. That only made the pain worse.

She needed to focus on today, just today, and what it would take to get her through it, she decided. She had to get dressed, then face Nick. Then tomorrow, she'd go back to work and she could push everything else from her mind. If she was lucky, she'd forget that she'd ever had the misfortune to even meet Thomas Cooper, let alone fall in love with him.

The woman who stepped out of the bedroom twenty minutes later bore little resemblance to the one who'd suffered a serious meltdown the previous evening. Dressed casually in a mint green cotton shift and flat sandals, she'd swept her dark hair up off her neck in a simple twist and kept her makeup to the bare necessities—mascara, blush and lip gloss.

Satisfied that she would do, she had no idea what the sight of her did to Nick. In the process of taking a sip of his coffee when she found him in the kitchen, he very nearly choked.

She was, he thought, shaken, the most amazing woman! He'd known her forever, seen her at her best and her worst as both a child and a woman, and she could still steal his breath just by walking into a room. And it had nothing to do with what she wore or how she had her hair fixed. It was just Merry, the way she moved, breathed, smiled. She had a glow to her, an inherent beauty, that came straight from the heart and a sparkle that a woman either had or she didn't. Even when she was slightly hungover and had every right to be in the depths of depression, Merry had it in spades.

He wanted to tell her that Thomas was a fool, that nothing short of an army would have been able to drag *him* away from the church if she'd been waiting there to marry him, but he couldn't bring himself to take the chance. Not when that would put her in the position of defending Thomas—and irrevocably change the way she looked at him.

Resigned, he swallowed the coffee that seemed to stick in his throat and greeted her gruffly. "Good morning, sleepyhead. How'd you sleep?"

"Much better than I expected," she admitted honestly as he handed her a mug of coffee. "Especially after the way I acted at the lake." Heat climbing in her cheeks, she resisted the urge to stare down into her mug and met his gaze head on, instead. "What should I apologize first for? Stripping in front of you or crying all over you?"

She looked so miserable that Nick had to laugh. "If I remember correctly, you had a bathing suit when you were sixteen that showed a heck of a lot more skin than your bra and panties, so I wouldn't worry about that if I were you. And what's a few tears among friends? After what you'd just been through, I figured you were entitled."

He meant to set her at ease, but the words were hardly out of his mouth when her eyes flooded. "Well, damn!" he swore. "I've gone and made you cry again. I'm sorry, Mer. I shouldn't have said anything."

"It's not you," she choked, swiping at her tears before they could ruin her mascara. "It's me. I swore I wasn't going to do this. I hate crying!"

In all the years that he'd known her, Nick could only remember her crying a handful of times—once, when she broke her arm when she was eight, then again when her dog was run over by one of the ranch hands when she was twelve. That was when she'd decided to become a veterinarian when she grew up. But it was when her father died that she'd been nearly inconsolable. Nick hoped he never saw her cry like that again, but last night, she'd come awfully close.

"There's nothing wrong with crying, Merry," he said quietly. "It's only natural. You're grieving."

She hadn't thought of it that way, but he was right. She was grieving for something that had died—her relationship with the man she loved—and she hadn't even known there was a problem. "I feel so stupid," she sniffed. "This didn't just happen. There had to be signs along the way that something was wrong, and I didn't see them."

"Neither did I, and I'm his best friend," he replied. Pulling out a chair for her at the kitchen table, he sat across from her and confided, "I thought we were as close as brothers, but he never said anything about having any doubts about getting married. In fact, I thought he couldn't wait. These last few months were the happiest I've ever seen him."

"Then what happened? If he was so happy, why did he run out on me?"

He shrugged and could only guess. "I still think he had a bad case of jitters and just bolted in pure panic. You know how he jumps to conclusions—he gets a headache and he thinks he's got a brain tumor. Yesterday, all it would have taken was one little doubt and he'd have convinced himself that the two of you were headed for disaster and he had to do something to stop it. So he gave into blind fear and ran. That doesn't mean he won't come back. He just needs to work some things out and put them in perspective."

She wanted to believe him, but she just couldn't. Not yet. "And how long is it going to take him to do that? A week? A month? Six years?"

That was a question Nick didn't have any answers for. He just wanted Merry to be happy, even if he was nowhere in the picture. If that meant she waited a lifetime for

Thomas to come to his senses, then so be it. "I don't know," he said with a shrug. "That's something the two of you will have to come to terms with. Why don't you let me call him for you?" he suggested. "You need to talk, the sooner the better. I can make a few phone calls, track him down—"

"No!"

"But it's the only way you're going to work this out."

With her chin set at that stubborn angle that meant she wasn't going to budge come hell or high water, she shook her head. "If Thomas comes back to me, it has to be because that's what he wants, not because you or I or anyone else talked him into it."

Nick could understand her reasoning—her wounded pride wouldn't let her accept anything else—but that didn't mean he had to like it. Still, it was her decision to make. "Whatever you say," he said with a sigh of defeat. "It's your call."

Considering how vehement she'd been, Nick had every intention of respecting her wishes. She was the one who'd been left standing at the altar in front of the whole town, and if Thomas wanted to make peace with her, she had every right to demand that he be the one to make the first move. Nick would have done the same thing if he'd been in her position.

But when he took her home a little later, hanging on to that resolve wasn't as simple as he'd have liked. The minute she stepped into her house and looked around, she stiffened, her blue eyes dark with distress. Thomas's things were spread about her living room and the rest of the house—everywhere she looked, she was reminded of him.

She'd known they were there, of course, but that didn't make the situation any less painful for her. Swearing, Nick remembered too late that he and Joe and Zeke had promised to take all of Thomas's things over to his mother's so she could store them for him until he made arrangements to have everything shipped back to Chicago. They should have done that *before* Merry went home, dammit, but with everything that had happened last night, he'd completely forgotten about it. And now Merry was the one having to pay the price for that.

He only had to take one look at the rigid set of her jaw to know that she was hurting.

"Look, there's no reason that you have to deal with this," he said gruffly, moving to step in front of her and block her view of the rest of the house. "Go to your mother's for the rest of the day, and I'll call your brothers to help me pack up Thomas's stuff and get it out of here. You don't even have to see it."

He was giving her an easy way out—all she had to do was politely thank him and turn around and walk out. But she'd never taken the easy way out and she wasn't about to start now. This was her house—and her mess to clean up.

Straightening her shoulders, she lifted her chin. "There's no reason to drag my brothers into this. If you'll help me, the two of us can have everything packed and out of here within an hour."

"You know I'll help," he replied, scowling, "but you don't have to punish yourself this way."

She didn't consider it punishment. "I'm putting my house back in order and reclaiming it for myself. I'll feel better about myself if I have a hand in that."

Put that way, he had no choice but to admit she was right, so they spent the rest of the morning repacking Thomas's possessions in the boxes that were still in Merry's garage. If it had been left to him, Nick would have dumped everything in garbage sacks and hauled it out that way, but Merry would have none of it. She meticulously folded every piece of clothing before putting it away in a box, then wrapped any breakable personal items in newspaper to protect them in transit. And with every box that was taped shut and hauled out to her truck, Merry became quieter and quieter. She was packing away her hopes and dreams and what might have been, and it hurt.

She didn't cry, but the pain in her eyes was impossible to hide, and just watching her made Nick want to throw something. Damn Thomas's miserable hide! He wasn't going to get away with this! The bastard needed to know that the pain he'd caused her hadn't stopped when she'd left the church.

"You're not going with me to Mrs. Cooper's," he said flatly when the last box was carried out of the house and loaded into her truck.

"But you'll need help unloading everything."

"I can handle it."

Not giving her a chance to argue further, he took the keys from her and climbed behind the wheel of her truck. When he drove off a few seconds later and glanced in the rearview mirror, she was still standing where he'd left her in the drive, her shoulders drooping, looking lost and forlorn and so damn lonely that it hurt just to look at her.

It was then that he decided that he was taking matters into his own hands and calling Thomas.

Merry would, of course, be furious with him when she found out what he'd done, but that couldn't be helped. He couldn't stand seeing her so unhappy. If that meant he had to track down Thomas and drag him back to her, then by God, that's what he was going to do. Merry might resent it at first, but that was a chance he was just going to have to take. Once she and Thomas made up, she'd forgive him quick enough.

His mind made up, he drove straight to Mrs. Cooper's. He'd never cared for her himself—she had a sharp tongue and little sympathy for other people—but when she opened the door to him and saw Merry's truck in her drive, her first concern was for Merry. "Oh, Nick, how is she? I wanted to call her, but she was so upset yesterday, and I thought it might be better if I kept my distance."

"She's coming to grips with everything," he said, "but I don't think she feels like talking to anyone yet."

"Of course not. I understand." Looking past him to the truck in the drive, she didn't have to ask what was in all the boxes in the back. "I suppose you've brought Thomas's things."

He nodded solemnly. "Since he gave up his apartment last week, I didn't know what else to do. I was hoping you'd heard from him."

"No," she said regrettably. "I left a message with his old law firm in Chicago in case he went back there, but he hasn't called. I think he's too embarrassed."

After what he'd done, he should have felt a hell of a lot more than just embarrassment, Nick thought irritably, but that wasn't something he felt comfortable telling Maxine Cooper. She was his mother—she had to defend him even when there was no excuse for what he'd done. "If he does call, I'd appreciate it if you'd tell him I need to talk to him. Now, where would you like me to put his things?"

At her direction, he stored the boxes in her garage and worked up a sweat doing it. And with every box, every piece of furniture he lifted, the more his resentment grew. When he'd first realized that Thomas was actually going to jilt Merry, he'd been stunned, but now he had to wonder why he'd been so surprised. An only child born late in life to parents who'd long since given up hope that they would ever have children, Thomas had been spoiled and pampered and indulged from the moment he realized he only had to cry to get what he wanted. And anytime he got into trouble, his mother had always been there to bail him out and make everything all right. This time, however, she couldn't do that. Thomas had to clean up his own mess, and by God, Nick was going to see that he did it!

His jaw set, Nick unloaded the last box, accepted Maxine's thanks, and headed for his office. He'd expected it to take more than a few phone calls to track Thomas down, but he hit pay dirt when he called the manager of the apartment complex where Thomas was living in Chicago when his mother had fallen and broken her hip. Thomas had claimed he'd given the place up once he decided to move back to Liberty Hill months ago, but that, apparently, had been a lie. He still had the apartment.

The son of a bitch! Nick thought furiously. Even then, he'd had doubts. He'd kept a place to go back to in Chicago in case his new life with Merry didn't work out, and he'd never said a word to anyone. All this time, he'd let Merry think he loved her without reservation when nothing could have been further from the truth.

If he could have gotten his hands on him at that moment, Nick wasn't sure what he would have done, but it wouldn't have been pretty. Fortunately for Thomas, he was a thousand miles away, but that didn't mean Nick couldn't tell him what he thought of him. In a matter of minutes, he had his new, restricted phone number.

"You son of a bitch!"

To his credit, Thomas didn't pretend not to recognize his voice. "How'd you find me?"

"It wasn't difficult once I realized you never gave up your old apartment," Nick said coldly. "Do you have any idea what this would do to Merry if she found out about it?''

''You're not going to tell her, are you?''

Infuriated that Thomas even had to ask that, he snarled, ''What do you care? You ran off and left her. At the *church,* for God's sake!''

''I told you why—'' he began.

''But you didn't tell *her,*'' Nick retorted. ''And she's the one who's entitled to an explanation. Dammit, man, call her! She loves you, and I know if you just talked to her, the two of you could work this out.''

For a moment, he thought he'd finally talked some sense into him. Thomas hesitated, obviously considering the suggestion, but then just when Nick thought he had convinced him to do the right thing, he said quickly, ''No! I can't handle talking to her right now. It's too soon. I'm sorry, Nick. Maybe later.''

''Dammit, *I'm* not the one you should be apologizing to!''

That was as far as he got. Without another word, Thomas hung up. Swearing, Nick slammed down the phone. *Jackass!*

Miserable, Merry never knew how she got through the next week. Friends made a point of calling her and asking her out so she wouldn't have so much time to herself, but it didn't help. Even surrounded by a crowd of friends, she'd never been so lonely in her life.

But it was the nights—and the silence of her own thoughts—that nearly drove her over the edge. There was no one to talk to, no one to distract her from the hurt that wouldn't go away. She would lie for hours, staring at the ceiling, her eyes burning from the tears she wouldn't allow herself to shed. And when she finally did fall asleep, she dreamed again and again of a nightmare wedding at a gothic church, where the guests were all corpses and the groom was a skeleton that turned to dust and blew away before her very eyes.

If she hadn't had her work to throw herself into, she didn't know what she would have done. Her clinic was located just next door to her house, which made it easy for her to go in early and stay late. Ruby, her receptionist, warned her she was going to collapse if she didn't quit pushing herself so hard, but the only peace she found was at the clinic. When she worked, she could forget her own pain and concentrate instead on that of the sick and injured animals she treated and nursed back to health.

Most days, she didn't even take a lunch break, but just grabbed bites of a salad in between patients. Frowning in disapproval, Ruby, who never ate anything the color of grass, could only shake her head. "If all you're going to eat are those weeds, at least sit down for a few minutes and give yourself time to digest them. You haven't stopped moving since I got here this morning."

"Can't," she said as she swallowed a quick bite, then started mopping up the puddles left in examining room one by the litter of puppies she'd just examined. "Tawny James will be here any minute with Tiger and Sammy, and this time I plan to be ready for them."

The last time Tawny had brought her cat in for fur balls, her three-year-old son, Sammy, had opened every drawer and cabinet in the examining room and practically destroyed the place. Merry didn't intend to let that happen again. Grabbing the keys, she started locking every cabinet and drawer in sight. "There," she said in relief just as the bell on the front door jingled merrily. "Just in time!"

But the new arrival wasn't Tawny and her little terror but Nick. For the last week, he'd made it a practice to stop by whenever he was in the area. He'd claimed he was just taking a break and wanted to visit, but Merry knew better. He was keeping an eye on her, making sure she was all right, and she appreciated that. But when he walked in with a large cardboard box in his hands and a grim look on his angular face, she knew this wasn't a social visit.

"Whatever it is, bring it in here," she said quickly, pushing open the door to the second examining room. "What happened?"

"Harvey was on call out at Virginia Sawyer's place when he was bit by a fox," he said as he set the box on the examining table. "He had to kill it, but I thought you should take a look at it. He said it ran right at him."

In the process of pulling on gloves, Merry looked up at him sharply. That wasn't normal behavior at all for usually shy foxes, and they both knew. But Nick's deputy, Harvey, wasn't the kind to embellish a story. "You think it's rabid?"

His expression somber, he shrugged. "I don't know. Harvey said it wasn't foaming at the mouth, but it was definitely aggressive. Apparently, it's been hanging around Virginia's place for a couple of days, and that poodle of hers—Boo-Boo—kept running it off. When she heard a noise in her garage, she called the office because she thought it was an intruder. When Harvey saw it was a fox, he gave it plenty of room and thought it would run into the woods, but it came right at him and the dog."

Merry didn't like the sound of that at all. "If it had a den nearby—which it shouldn't have—it might have taken on the dog, but not Harvey, too. Where did it bite him?"

"On the hand. He tried to scare it off, but it just kept coming back at him. He didn't have any choice but to shoot it. He said it was the craziest thing he'd ever seen in his life."

"What about Boo-Boo? Did he get bit, too?"

He nodded. "He gave as good as he got, but the fox tore up his front leg pretty good. Harvey told Virginia she needed to bring him in so you could take a look at him, but she thought she could do it herself. She didn't seem too concerned about rabies. Has Boo-Boo had his shots?"

Merry swore softly. "No."

Every year, she pushed the local citizens to get their pets vaccinated, but since there hadn't been a case of rabies in the county in years, most people didn't see the need. She hadn't been able to convince them that that could change in a heartbeat. If her hunch was right, Virginia Sawyer was about to find that out the hard way.

"I hope he doesn't have to be put down," she said, "but it doesn't look good. He'll have to be quarantined, of course. You told her that, didn't you?"

Nick nodded. "You know how stubborn she is. I tried to convince her that it would be easier on her if she let you take care of that, but she insisted that Boo-Boo would be much more comfortable right there in his own home."

There was no question that the dog would be happier at home, but watching any pet develop signs of rabies was not something Merry would wish on anyone. "I can't force her to bring him in, but I'll call her and explain what she could be facing. In the meantime, I'll send the fox to the state lab this afternoon. Harvey knows he can't wait for the test results to come back to get shots, doesn't he?"

"He's over at the hospital right now," he replied. "The nurses are probably getting a earful. He doesn't like needles."

The situation wasn't funny, but Merry couldn't help but smile at the thought of big, six-foot-four Harvey cringing at the sight of a little needle. "Has he asked for sick leave yet?"

"A week," Nick said with a chuckle. "You know Harvey—he never misses a chance to skip work and go fishing. He probably loaded his fishing gear into his camper before he went to the doctor."

His smile fading as he watched her fill out paperwork for the state lab, he frowned at the dark shadows under her eyes. "So how are you? Sleeping any better?"

He asked her that just about every time he saw her, and her answer was always the same. "Some. And no, I haven't heard from Thomas," she added before he could ask. "I don't expect to."

"You need to get out more. I heard Stella was having a psychic from Colorado Springs at her place tonight and inviting a bunch of women over. You're going, aren't you?"

The question was asked innocently enough, but she'd already told her cousin she wasn't in the mood for a party, and she had a feeling Nick knew it. "Stella called and asked you to talk me into going, didn't she?"

Grinning, he didn't deny it. "It'll be good for you."

"I don't need a psychic to tell me what my future's going to be. I already know it doesn't include Thomas."

"So maybe it includes Tom Cruise. It could happen," he said when she rolled her eyes. "I'm sure your sister-in-law knows him."

Merry didn't doubt that her movie star sister-in-law, Angel, could introduce her to just about anyone in Hollywood worth knowing, including Tom Cruise, but she just wasn't interested. "He's too pretty for my taste," she said with a shrug. "Anyway, why would he look at me when he's got Nicole?"

This time, *he* was the one who rolled his eyes. "You're missing the point, Mer. Nobody's going to take what this woman says seriously—she probably doesn't have a psychic bone in her body. But if you don't want to have your fortune read, then just listen to what she tells the others. The point is to have fun and forget your troubles for a while. I think you should go.''

He had a point. She did need something besides work to distract her from her troubles. And she didn't have to have a reading. Stella would just be happy she came. ''I'll think about it,'' she promised.

Tawny James came rushing in then with Tiger and Sammy, and there was no more time for idle chitchat. Not when Sammy had that little gleam in his eye that spelled trouble. ''Gotta go,'' she said as Ruby showed the three-some into examining room one. ''I'll get back to you with the results from the state lab as soon as they come in.''

From that point on, the day was a madhouse. Miffed by the locked cabinet drawers and doors in room one, Sammy took out his frustration on the waiting room by destroying every magazine in the place while his mother was paying the bill. Then, just as she and Ruby got things set straight, a woman passing through town rushed in with a dog that had been hit on the highway. Merry spent the next hour in emergency surgery and was, thankfully, able to save the dog. That, however, threw her scheduled appointments off for the rest of the day. Normally through by five, it was well after six before she was finally able to close up shop and go home.

Exhausted, she almost skipped Stella's party. She'd already told her she didn't think she would make it, and after the afternoon she'd had, Stella would understand if she passed. She'd call her and tell her what happened and promise she'd come next time.

But even as she reached for the phone, she could hear Nick scolding her for spending too much time by herself. And she knew he was right. It had been a week now since

Thomas had betrayed her, and brooding over it was becoming all too easy. If she wasn't careful, it would become a way of life.

Resigned, she strode into her bedroom and threw open the closet. What did you wear to a psychic party, anyway?

Stella's house was packed to the gills with friends they'd both known all their life, and they were all thrilled to see her. Braced for questions about Thomas, Merry was pleasantly surprised when no one even mentioned his name. She was, she discovered with amusement, old news. No one wanted to talk about Thomas when there was a psychic among them who could tell them about the future instead.

"Do you think she can tell me what my baby's going to be?" Sue Ellen Briggs asked anxiously as she pressed a soothing hand on her swollen stomach. "I really hope it's a girl."

"You don't need a psychic for that, Sue Ellen," Carley Johnson retorted dryly. "Just a sonogram. If you're going to ask the woman something, at least make it worthwhile and ask her for Saturday's lottery numbers."

"Or what really happened to Princess Di," Stella said. "I think she can talk to spirits."

That got the rest of the women going, and before she quite knew how it happened, Merry found herself laughing and enjoying the party much more than she had expected to. Dana, the psychic, was surprisingly good. Sixty if she was a day, with the prim and proper looks of an old-fashioned schoolteacher, she correctly guessed without being told beforehand that Sue Ellen was pregnant with twins, Stella had a secret wish to write, and Carley was going to get an important promotion at work.

"And what about you, dear?" she asked, turning to

Merry expectantly. "You're going to have a reading, aren't you?"

"Oh, I just came to watch," she said quickly. "Please go on to one of the others. I'm sure they still have things to ask."

"Are you sure? You have a very strong aura. Why don't you let me look at your hand?"

"Go on, Merry," Stella coaxed. "It'll be fun. You won't tell her anything bad, will you, Dana?"

"Only if it's something that can be prevented," the older woman replied. "This is supposed to be fun, dear," she told Merry, her blue eyes kind behind the lenses of her wire-rimmed glasses as she smiled at her. "My spirit guides won't tell you anything you don't want to know. They're very careful about that."

Merry didn't doubt that spirit guides were considerate of human feelings—if you believed in such things. She wasn't sure she did, but she didn't have the heart to say anything in front of the others since they were enjoying themselves so much. "Oh, all right," she said with a sigh, giving in. "I guess I would like to know some things about the family. Joe and Angel have been talking about having a baby…"

But when she took a chair at the table where Dana sat and extended her right hand, palm up to her, it wasn't the family Dana talked about. Studying the lines in Merry's hand, she clicked her tongue in sympathy. "You've suffered tremendous heartache recently."

The quiet comment immediately drew startled gasps and turned the mood of the party somber. Stiffening, Merry glanced up at her cousin. "You told her?"

Her eyes wide, Stella was as shocked as she. "No! I didn't tell her anything about anyone."

Not looking up from Merry's hand, Dana said, "The

only thing Stella and I discussed was the time of the party, where it was being held, and my fee.''

''Then how—''

''Your guides, dear,'' she answered before Merry could ask her how she knew anything about her heartache since she wasn't even from Liberty Hill. ''They're very protective of you and want you to know that this is only a temporary condition that could have been prevented if the man in your life had just told you how he felt. He has trouble expressing his feelings now, but he'll learn. And when he does, there won't be a doubt in your mind that you're loved.''

Stunned, Merry could only stare at her. If Dana was talking about Thomas, she was right on the money. Merry had foolishly thought they had the kind of relationship in which they could tell each other anything, but she'd been wrong. When it came to how he really felt about getting married, he hadn't been able to work up the courage to tell her the truth. And because of that, she was the one who'd been hurt.

But according to Dana, this was only a temporary condition, she reminded herself as a spark of excitement flared in her eyes. Once Thomas learned to express himself, they'd work things out—

Suddenly realizing what she was doing, Merry stiffened. Just because Dana had said she'd been hurt didn't mean she was really psychic. Anyone could look at her and see that she was miserably unhappy. And it didn't take psychic ability to predict that her unhappiness had been caused by a man. That was just common sense.

Studying the older woman warily, she said, ''I don't mean to be rude, but so far, you've really only told me generalities. What exactly can you tell me about this man who's supposedly in my life? Can you see what he looks like or what he does for a living?''

Understanding she was testing her skills, Dana took no offense. ''I'll certainly try,'' she replied easily, and turned her attention back to her palm.

For what seemed like an eternity, she didn't say anything. Frowning, she traced the lines in Merry's right hand while the silence in the apartment thickened with expectation. Then, just when Merry thought she was going to admit she couldn't make out anything, she said, ''He's a tall man, around six-two. He's not pretty-boy handsome, but you wouldn't want that anyway, would you?'' Speaking more to herself than Merry, she traced a line down the center of her palm. ''He's attractive, though, and appears to have dark hair and brown eyes. You go well together.''

Her heart pounding, Merry stared at her palm in fascination. ''And his occupation?''

''That's a tough one,'' Dana said with a grimace. ''He's been in your life for a long time, but I'm not sure exactly what he does. He's got a strong sense of justice, which makes me think he's involved in the judicial system somehow, but I don't think he's a judge.''

In the quiet that had fallen over Stella's living room, Merry's voice was husky with emotion. ''No, he's not. He's a lawyer.''

''Then I was close,'' she said simply, not gloating. ''Is there anything else you'd like to know, dear?''

Later, Merry was sure a hundred questions would come to mind, but at that moment, she couldn't think of a single one. ''No, but thank you for what you did tell me. It helped.''

Chattering excitedly, the others pressed forward with more questions about their own future, so Merry gave up her seat at the table and moved to the couch. All around her, the other women laughed over some of the surprising predictions Dana had given them, but Merry hardly noticed. Her thoughts in a whirl, she could think of nothing but Thomas.

He was coming back to her.

Oh, Dana hadn't said that in so many words, but her meaning was the same. If the man in her life was going to learn to express his feelings so that she had no doubt that he loved her, then Thomas obviously had to come back to Liberty Hill. And Merry didn't have a clue how she felt about that.

If someone had promised her the day she was supposed to get married that Thomas would soon come back to her, she would have at least had some kind of hope to cling to. But there'd been no promises, no hope. A week had passed, a long, lonely week in which she'd had a lot of time to cry, to grieve, to think. And not once had Thomas called.

Somewhere deep inside her bruised heart, a voice whispered that none of that mattered if he would just come back and convince her that he really loved her. But in her head, she knew that it didn't matter what he said when he finally returned, actions spoke louder than words.

She would never trust him again.

Chapter 4

The normally gentle and mild-mannered golden retriever lunged at her, his teeth snapping, as she moved to shut the kennel gate and lock him inside a run. Startled, Merry jumped back...just in time to avoid a nasty bite on the forearm. If she'd been two seconds slower, he would have gotten her.

"Oh, Merry, I'm so sorry!" Jack Dryer exclaimed. Lightning quick, he reached past her to slam the gate shut. "Bad dog!" he scolded Lucas. "What's gotten into you, fella? This isn't like you. Have you got a sore paw or something? What's wrong?"

Observing the wild light in the dog's eyes and his unusually aggressive behavior, Merry was horribly afraid she knew, and she didn't know how she was going to tell Jack. An elderly widower who seldom left his house anymore, he depended on Lucas a great deal for companionship.

"He might bite if he were feeling miserable enough and a stranger pestered him," she said quietly, "but he's not going to go after his best friend.'' Nodding pointedly at the sizable bandage on his left hand, she lifted a delicately arched brow at him. ''So how did that happen?''

He shrugged, worry clouding his brown eyes. ''I don't know. One minute, I was throwing his ball for him, and the next, he turned on me and took a hunk out of my hand. I was shocked, and so was he, I think. He hasn't been the same since.''

''He's a yard dog, isn't he? You keep him fenced?''

He nodded. ''Except when I let him out for a run in the morning. You know how he loves the woods behind my house. The second I open the gate, he's off like a shot.''

''And you go with him?''

''I used to—until my arthritis started acting up a couple of months ago and I couldn't keep up with him. Then I started whistling for him from the back porch when it was time for him to come home.''

''And all the times you let him out alone, did you ever notice any bites or scratches on him when he returned?''

Surprised, he said, ''As a matter of fact, I did! He looked like he'd tangled with a cat or something, but he seemed okay. How'd you know? Should I have brought him in? What's wrong with him, Merry? It's something serious, isn't it?''

She hated to tell him, but he had to know. ''Last week, Sheriff Kincaid brought in a fox one of his deputies had to kill when it attacked him and Virginia Sawyer's poodle. I just got word this morning from the state lab that it had rabies.''

He paled. ''Oh, God. You think Lucas has it, too, don't you?''

She couldn't deny it. ''I'm sorry, Jack, but all the signs seem to point to it. I'll keep him quarantined here for a couple of weeks to make sure, but I think you'd better prepare yourself for the worst. He's going to have to be put down. It's the only humane thing to do.''

Giving a pet owner that kind of news was the thing she hated the most about being a vet—it didn't matter how many times she did it, it didn't get any easier. Less than an hour ago, she'd had to tell Virginia Sawyer the same thing about Boo-Boo, who was already displaying serious signs of the disease, then she'd gone into her office and cried her eyes out. When Jack left, she'd do the same thing.

Suddenly looking every one of his eighty-one years, Jack blinked back tears. ''Do what you have to do.''

He walked out with heavy, weighted shoulders, and it was more than Merry could bear. Unable to make it to her office, she leaned her head against the corner post of the dog run where Lucas still watched her and cried.

She couldn't, however, indulge her emotions for long. Not when she had a potential rabies epidemic on her hands. If she didn't want it to get out of hand, she had to get busy. Straightening, she wiped away her tears, then returned to her office. Picking up the phone, she punched in the number to the sheriff's office. ''Nick?'' she said when he finally came on the line, ''we have a problem.''

That very afternoon, she began a campaign to inoculate all domestic animals in the area. It wasn't easy. In spite of the fact that three cases of rabies had been virtually identified, not everyone was convinced the county was on the verge of a crisis. So she held a town meeting the next evening in the VFW hall to explain to people what a threat the disease was to them and their children. Less than thirty people showed up.

Refusing to be discouraged, she went on the local radio station for a call-in show and also printed up fliers that she and Nick posted around town. Busy with her practice during the day, she spent the evenings on the phone, calling everyone in the phone book. Then, when she could find the time, she slipped into the woods and set traps for infected squirrels and foxes.

If she'd wanted something to take her mind off Thomas, she'd found it. For a solid week, she worked from first light to late at night and was so exhausted when she finally fell into bed that she was usually asleep the second her head hit the pillow. Then the next morning, she got up and started the entire process all over again.

Her family was worried about her working too hard, but Merry didn't see any way that she could slow down—not when she thought about all the unvaccinated dogs and cats out there that could not only become infected with the disease themselves, but spread it to their owners. *That* was what scared her. Why couldn't people see the seriousness of the situation?

Frustrated, she didn't know what she would have done if it hadn't been for Nick. He canvassed neighborhoods in town, had his deputies talk to everyone they came into contact with, and even offered to chauffeur people and their animals to and from Merry's office if they needed transportation. Whenever she needed help, he was there.

Finally, they gradually began to make headway. A few responsible citizens brought in their dogs and cats. Then, what began as a trickle of response turned into a flood.

It all happened so fast, Merry didn't have time to anticipate a problem. One moment, she had a handful of patients and their owners in the waiting room waiting to see her, and the next, she had three dozen. And most of the pets didn't like each other at all. Snarling and spitting and ignoring the shouts of their owners, they turned the waiting room into a war zone in a matter of minutes.

Holding back a particularly feisty poodle who wanted to

jump a Great Dane, Merry dragged the stubborn little bit of fluff toward waiting room one. "See if you can track down one of my brothers or Nick," she yelled over her shoulder at Ruby. "We're going to need some help."

The place was a madhouse when Nick walked through the door of Merry's clinic twenty minutes later. The waiting room was packed with what appeared to be half the county's population of animals and their humans, and nobody seemed to be in charge. Every chair was filled and a line was forming outside. At the counter, looking more than a little harried, Ruby was juggling the constantly ringing phones, the cash register, and trying to make herself heard over the deafening uproar of humans and animals.

Sweeping back the red too-long bangs that continually fell in her face, she took one look at him and sighed in relief. "Thank God! Merry needs help in the examining room with Tinkerbell—Mrs. Holly just dropped her off and will be back in an hour to pick her up—but somebody's got to be here at the counter to take care of the bills and the phone. If you want to handle this—"

George Murphy's hound chose that moment to inspect the door to Mrs. Johnson's cat's travel box and got his nose swatted for poking it somewhere it didn't belong. A howl rose to the rafters, followed by a chorus of others, and that was all Nick needed to hear to know that he wanted no part of the scene in the waiting room.

"I wouldn't want to screw the books up," he said quickly. "I'm lousy with numbers. It would be better if I helped Merry."

Not fooled in the least, Ruby only grinned. "Chicken."

Chuckling, he escaped into examining room two, only to find Merry trapped up against a cabinet by a Saint Bernard as big as a small horse. Its front paws draped on Merry's shoulders and a sloppy grin on its foolish face, it licked her cheek and set Merry giggling.

"Stop, you monster!" she laughed, trying to avoid another swipe of its wet tongue. "Get off of me! Nick, don't just stand there laughing like an idiot! *Help me!*"

"But, Merry, she *loves* you," he said playfully, his brown eyes dancing. "Go ahead. Give her a kiss."

Her blue eyes narrowing with promise of revenge, she ruined it all by laughing helplessly when Tinkerbell kissed her again. "Dammit, Nick, what kind of sheriff are you? I'm being accosted here and all you can do is laugh. Where are my brothers? Call them. One of them will help me."

"Not today they won't," he retorted, his grin broad. "They've gone to an auction in Colorado Springs and won't be back until late tonight. Looks like you're stuck with me, sister."

"Wonderful! Now that we've established that, will you get this dog off of me? Aaagh! She got me again!" Laughing, she tried to push the one-hundred-and-twenty-pound fur ball off of her, but Tinkerbell was quite content where she was and only settled more comfortably against her with a happy doggy grin. "Nick! Do something! I don't have time for this. I've been hustling dogs and cats in and out of here for the last twenty minutes, and the waiting room's still full."

"Some vet you are," he teased. "You can't even control your patients. You've just got to know how to talk to them." Demonstrating, he whistled sharply and said. "Come on, Tinkerbell. Let's go for a walk, girl."

For an answer, she just wagged her tail, woofed, and stayed right where she was.

Her lips twitching, Merry said dryly, "Well, you certainly showed her. So much for talking. Now what do you propose to do?"

"Bribe her with a dog biscuit?"

"Nice try, but she's on a restricted diet. No snacks."

"Damn! Then I guess there's no help for it. I'll have to use my brute strength."

He flexed his muscles, making Merry giggle, but Tinkerbell wasn't the least impressed. Thinking they were playing some kind of new game when he tried to tug her free of Merry, she squirmed and tugged and twisted free with ridiculous ease. And all the while, her tail never stopped wagging.

Frustrated, Nick had to laugh. "All right, that's it! No dog is going to get the best of Nick Kincaid. It's time to get rough."

He grabbed the dog around the waist, like a football player making a tackle, and this time, he wasn't letting go. Tinkerbell, sensing the game was up, didn't bother to struggle this time. With a soft groan, she went boneless and collapsed in a heap at Merry's feet.

His grin cocky, Nick held out his hand to help steady her as she stepped over the prone dog. "There you go, princess. All safe and sound."

"Marshal Dillon," she purred, pressing her hand to her heart in a pretended swoon. "My hero." Going up on tiptoe, she kissed him on the cheek.

She'd done it a zillion times over the years, teased him about being the sheriff whenever he called her princess or Miss Prom Queen, and they always laughed about it. But the second her lips brushed his smooth shaven cheek, something changed, something she couldn't put her finger on. Her heart seemed to stumble in her chest, and when she pulled back slightly and looked up at him, there was a flicker of emotion in his eyes that she'd never seen before. Just that quickly, her heart was racing, and for the life of her, she didn't know why.

Confused, she studied his face searchingly. "Nick? What...?"

He blinked, and between one heartbeat and the next, he was the same old Nick she'd known for most her life, and whatever she'd thought she'd seen in his eyes was gone. "This isn't clearing out that crowd out there," he said with a nod toward the waiting room. "Tell me what to do so I can help." When she just stood there, staring at him blankly, he frowned. "Mer? Are you all right?"

Her thoughts jumbled, she jerked back to awareness to discover that she was staring at him like she'd never seen him before. "What? Oh, yes! Of course. I've just got so much to do. Would you put Tinkerbell in the kennel until Mrs. Holly comes back for her? I've got to call the next patient...."

Still flustered, she stepped around him to open the door from the examining room into the waiting room, only to find herself face-to-face with Maxine Cooper. Startled, she stopped in her tracks. She hadn't seen or talked to Thomas's mother since that awful day of the wedding that never happened, and she wasn't sure what to say. What were the rules of etiquette for greeting the mother of the man who jilted you at the altar?

Aware of all the interested eyes trained on the two of them, she forced a smile that didn't come as easily as she would have liked and reached out to pet the Siamese cat protectively cradled in the older woman's arms. "Hello, Maxine. Have you brought Queenie in to be vaccinated?"

As uncomfortable as she, Maxine nodded stiffly, her glance shifting past her to where Nick stood behind her in the examining room, then back to Merry. "Yes, as a matter of fact, I have. I..."

Hesitating, she looked around, noticed that everyone in the waiting room was watching their exchange, and immediately lowered her voice. "I've been meaning to call you, dear, but I didn't quite know what to say. I realize you're busy, but do you think we could talk for a moment in private? I think it would be better if we didn't have an audience."

Her timing couldn't have been worse, but this was a conversation that had been too long in coming. "Of course," Merry replied quietly. Stepping back, she showed her into the examining room and shut the door behind her.

Tinkerbell bristled at the sight of the cat in Maxine's arms, but Nick had the Saint Bernard well in hand. Tightening his hand on the dog's leash, he greeted Maxine with a nod and said, "I think that's my cue to exit. If you two will excuse me, I'll take this big lug to the kennel."

Tinkerbell didn't want to go, but Nick didn't give her much choice, and within seconds, Merry found herself alone with Maxine and not sure where to begin. "So...how have you been?"

The second the words were out of her mouth, Merry wanted to take them back. She didn't have to ask to know that Thomas's betrayal had, in many ways, been worse for his mother than it had for her. Maxine was a proud woman who liked to think of herself as one of the town's social leaders. From what Merry had heard, she'd been so mortified by Thomas's behavior that she hadn't stepped foot in public since the day of the wedding.

"I'm sorry," Merry said quickly. "I know this has been difficult for you, too. Have you heard from Thomas?"

"No," she said with a sigh. "I'm sure he's too embarrassed, but at least we know he's all right. I need to thank Nick again for tracking him down," she said half to herself and never noticed that Merry stiffened in surprise. "I know you had to be mortified by what he did, Merry, but you have to know that he would never deliberately hurt you. He *loves* you. He just panicked. Marriage is a big step, and as a lawyer, he knows better than most the statistics on divorce. Just the thought of the two of you not making it must have scared him to death.''

Her mind still reeling from the news that Nick had actually talked to Thomas and not told her, Merry frowned in confusion. ''Are you saying you think Thomas stood me up at the altar *now* so we wouldn't end up in divorce court *later?*''

''Well, I know it sounds a little extreme,'' she acknowledged, ''but you have to remember how he suffered when his father and I divorced. It's not something he would want to go through again.''

''Then why ask me to marry him at all if he had those kind of fears?'' Merry asked. ''No one held a gun to his head.''

''Because he loves you, dear, and wants you to be his wife,'' she assured her. ''His fears got the best of him, but once he has time to calm down and think, he'll come home to you. He just needs some time.''

She meant well, but Merry wasn't sure she agreed with her. Nearly two weeks had passed. The longer Thomas stayed away, the harder it would be for him to come back and face not only her, but his friends and family. ''Maybe,'' she said with a shrug. ''Maybe not. Time will tell.''

Merry knew that wasn't the response Maxine was hoping for, but that was the best she could do. Whatever faith she'd had in Thomas doing the right thing had died the day he jilted her.

Deliberately changing the subject, she turned her attention to Queenie. ''How'ya doing, girl? Ready for your shots?''

* * *

Maxine had just left when Nick returned to the examining room to see if Merry needed his help. She took one look at him and said, "Why didn't you tell me?"

He didn't have to ask what she was talking about—Maxine had obviously told her he'd tracked down Thomas. And Merry was feeling betrayed—again. Cursing himself for not anticipating that this would happen, he said, "I'm sorry. I didn't want to hurt you. You'd been through enough already."

"You didn't think it would hurt me not knowing where he was? If he was all right? That he'd talked to you, but not to me?"

"He's not ready to talk to you yet, Mer."

The softly spoken words stabbed her right in the heart. "He told you that?"

"Yes."

Hurt, she recoiled as if he'd slapped her. "Well, I guess that says it all, doesn't it? Not only doesn't he want to marry me, he doesn't want to have anything to do with me, either."

"If it'll make you feel any better, I think he wants everyone to leave him alone for a while, not just you. He just needs some time to himself to work things out."

What things? she wanted to cry. *She* wasn't something that should have needed to be worked out, not at this stage in their relationship. He'd asked her to marry him, and she'd accepted, for God's sake! They'd planned a wedding, gotten the license, talked to the minister. The last time she'd seen Thomas, he'd told her he loved her with all his heart and was ready to start their life together. And she'd believed him! Then, the next day, he'd chosen to run away to Chicago without a word to her rather than marry her. What kind of love was that?

Hiding her hurt behind the dignity she pulled around her

like a cloak, she lifted her chin. "He has all the time he needs," she assured Nick. "If he doesn't want to talk to me, I'm certainly not going to force myself on him."

Her pride coming to her rescue, she called in the next patient and, with Nick's help, worked through the rest of the pets in the waiting room. Thomas's name wasn't mentioned again, and for the rest of the day, she was, thankfully, too busy to spare him a second thought.

Everything changed, however, when she closed up shop and went home. The second she stepped inside the house and shut the front door, closing out the world, the lonely silence of her solitary existence slapped her in the face. She'd never felt so alone.

She knew it was because of her conversation with Maxine and Nick that she was feeling so down. She'd thought she was coming to grips with Thomas's betrayal, but the second she saw his mother, all the hurt and anger came rushing back. Then when Nick told her Thomas didn't want to talk to her, she realized she'd only been fooling herself. He'd hurt her in a way no one else ever had, and she wasn't going to get over that any time soon.

Knowing that, she somehow got through the evening, but when her usual bedtime came and went, she knew she was never going to be able to go to sleep. Her heart was too battered and bruised. She'd just lie there and stare at the ceiling and feel sorry for herself.

"The hell you will!" she muttered to herself. "McBrides aren't whiny babies!"

The light of battle sparking to life in her eyes at the thought, she made a snap decision and reached for the phone. Punching in the number to the sheriff's office, she waited impatiently for Nick to come on the line. The man who answered, however, wasn't Nick, but Dean Ziggler, one of his deputies.

"He's out on patrol, Merry," he told her when she asked for Nick. "Is it an emergency? George Rucker headed out your way about thirty minutes ago if you want me to raise him on the radio. I imagine he can be there in a matter of minutes if you need him."

"No, there's nothing wrong," she assured him quickly. "Just forward a message to Nick for me, will you? I'm going to take a ride out to Lookout Point and was wondering if he'd meet me there."

"Lookout Point?" Dean repeated in surprise. "You sure you want to go out there by yourself? It's awfully late. Maybe you'd better wait for Nick."

"I'll be fine. Really," she insisted when he snorted in disapproval. "I just need to get out of the house and thought I'd catch the moon rising from Lookout Point. Tell Nick if he can't make it, not to worry about it. I'll talk to him tomorrow."

She didn't give him a chance to argue further, but simply hung up and grabbed her keys. When the phone rang again almost immediately, she didn't doubt for a minute that it was Dean. Already on her way out, she didn't even break stride. She knew Dean would try to talk her into waiting for Nick, but she couldn't. She'd been pushing herself at work all week, pretending that nothing was wrong, and it had cost her dearly. If she didn't get out of the house and escape from memories of Thomas for at least a few hours, she was going to crack under the strain.

"She did *what?*" Nick sputtered incredulously.

"She went up to Lookout Point to watch the moon rise," Dean dutifully repeated.

"And you *let* her?"

"Well, yeah," he said, surprised. "What else was I supposed to do? She's a grown woman. It's not against the law for her to go up to the Point if that's what she wants to do.''

Nick swore, unable to believe how dense Dean could be at times. ''No, that's true. But she's got no business going up there by herself at midnight! You should have told her to wait for me.''

''I did! But c'mon, Nick, we're talking about Merry McBride. You know how she is—she's just like all the other McBrides. Once she made up her mind, there was no budging her. She was going, come hell or high water, and all she wanted me to do was pass on the message that she'd like you to meet her there if you could. That's what I'm doing.''

Muttering curses, Nick knew Dean was right. When Merry got something in her head, no one was changing her mind. ''I'm sorry I got short with you,'' he apologized. ''I'm just worried about her. She's having a rough time, and I'm afraid she's going to get herself in trouble if she's not careful.''

''She wasn't crying or anything, if that's what you're worried about,'' Dean assured him. ''She's a smart woman, Nick. She's not going to do anything stupid just because Cooper didn't know a good thing when he saw it.''

Nick agreed, but he wasn't taking any chances, not where Merry was concerned. ''I know, but I'm going to head on up to the Point and make sure she's all right,'' he said as he checked his mirrors to make sure no one was behind him on the highway, then swung his patrol car into a U-turn and headed back the other way. ''Holler if you need me.''

With a dark highway in front of him and no cars in sight, he didn't need his siren, but he turned his light bar on so if he did encounter another vehicle, they could see him coming from a long way off. Then he hit the gas.

A drive across the northern section of the county should have taken him thirty minutes. He made it in fifteen. He would have made it in less if he hadn't had to slow down for dead man's curve, but his wheels were hardly touching the ground as it was.

As expected, Lookout Point was pitch black—which was what made it so popular with stargazers, not to mention teenagers looking for a place to make out. The few stargazers that were still there at that hour of the night turned to scowl at him when he came racing up to the observation area with his lights blaring, so he hit the switch to turn off his emergency lights, but not before he made sure the teenagers knew he was there. Within seconds, four cars started up and made a hasty retreat.

Grinning, he made no move to detain them, but headed for the big rocky outcropping that marked the eastern boundary of the observation area. There, at the edge of the rock, the ground fell away to give a commanding view of not only the valley below, but the stars. And there, not surprisingly, he found Merry, sitting on a blanket, staring out at the night sky.

It was a reflective place, one that made you think of your own mortality, and as teenagers, he and Thomas and she had often met there to discuss where they were going in life, what they wanted, their hopes and dreams. It was here that Merry had announced that she was going to become a veterinarian and Thomas had told them of his fascination with the law. And it was here on New Year's Eve, Nick knew, that Thomas had asked Merry to marry him...and she accepted.

That was six months ago, and Nick could still feel the sharp pain that had cut through his heart when they'd told him they loved each other and were going to spend the rest of their lives together. Trying to be happy for them, it had been the worst day of his life. He'd felt like somebody had died.

But that wasn't something he could think about now, not when he knew that Merry, too, was probably remembering that day and hurting.

Cursing Thomas all over again, he parked, then quietly made his way to where Merry sat, watching the moon rise like a huge orange ball on the eastern horizon. He didn't announce his presence, but he didn't have to. She'd known he would come.

Sitting on the blanket, her knees drawn up to her chest and her arms wrapped around her legs, she never took her eyes off the moon as he sat down beside her on the blanket. "Do you remember the last day of summer after we graduated from high school?" she asked huskily.

He nodded. "Yeah. The three of us met here the night before we left for college."

"To say goodbye," she added. "I never told you, but when I went home that night, I cried myself to sleep."

"Why?"

She smiled at his horrified tone, her sad, reflective eyes still trained on the moon, but gazing into the past. "Because everything was changing and I couldn't stop it. It had always been the three of us against the world, and suddenly we were all going off in separate directions. I guess I was scared. You were my best friend, and I was in love with Thomas, and I knew that even if we all eventually came back here some day, nothing would ever be the same again."

"But I'm still your best friend," he pointed out huskily, "and you're still in love with Thomas."

"But Thomas isn't in love with *me*," she stressed as tears welled in her eyes.

And that, Nick silently acknowledged, made all the difference in the world. Because he'd spent most of his life silently loving her, and he knew what it felt like not to have that love returned. It was a hurt that never went away.

Still, he loved her enough that he wanted her to be happy, even if it was with someone else, and he had to help her if he could. "Thomas never said he didn't love you. In fact, I'm not sure that any of this has anything to do with love, at all. I think it has more to do with maturity. His entire life, Maxine was always there to clean up his messes and take care of him, and he never really grew up. He didn't have to. Then, suddenly, he finds himself on the verge of getting married, of being a husband and one day, a father. And I think it scared the hell out of him."

She wanted to believe it—he could see the hope in her eyes. "You think that's the real problem? He's afraid of responsibility?"

"He wouldn't be the first man to bolt at the thought of a ring around his finger," he said dryly. "Marriage is a rite of passage. You can't be a kid anymore."

"And he always was a spoiled brat." A half smile curled one corner of her mouth as memories from the past came streaming back. "Remember the time we both got new bicycles for Christmas and he'd gotten one the year before? He went crying to Maxine that everyone but him got a new bike from Santa, so she went and bought him another one!"

"Maxine always made sure he had the best and the newest," he said dryly, "even when he didn't need it."

"Yeah, like that time she bought him that fancy little sports car when he was sixteen and he almost killed himself when he wrapped it around a telephone pole a week later. My mother was so disgusted with her, she didn't speak to her for a month. But you know, he was always generous with what he had," she added. "Remember the time..."

Lost in the past, she reminded him of times with Thomas

when they were six and ten and seventeen, times that Nick had, in some instances, forgotten about completely. And with every anecdote she told, he couldn't help but hear her pain and loneliness and love for another man. The moon rose high in the night sky as she poured out her heart to him, and she never knew that Nick would have given everything he owned to hear her talk about him just *once* with that kind of longing in her voice.

It wasn't often that Nick came into work with a chip on his shoulder, but on the rare occasions when he did, his deputies knew him well enough to cut him a wide berth or risk getting their heads bitten off. Normally, they only had to take one look at the rigid set of his jaw and they'd duck their heads and scatter. But not the next morning when he stomped into the office like a bear with a sore tooth. He'd barely settled at his desk with the thickest, blackest cup of coffee he could manage to rustle up when not one, but *two* of his deputies came knocking at his door.

Not even looking up from the budget proposal he had to draw up for the city council, he growled, "This isn't a good time."

"I'm sorry, Nick, but this can't wait," Dean said stiffly. "I need to talk to you privately."

His expression somber, George said, "So do I. It's important."

Important or not, Nick didn't like the sound of it. But he wasn't the type of man who made a habit of letting his private life interfere with his job. With a muttered curse, he tossed down his pencil and sat back in his chair. "Then I guess we might as well get this over with. You first, Ziggler. Come in and shut the door."

He didn't have to tell Dean twice. Five seconds later, he sat in the chair across from Nick's desk and announced,

"I've been offered a job in Denver. I've got to take it, Nick. The pay's nearly twice what I'm getting here, and Vicky has family there. She'd kill me if I turned it down."

Stunned, Nick couldn't find fault with that. A man had to do what was best for him and his family. "I'm going to hate to lose you," he said quietly. "I wish I could match the offer, but there's just no room in the budget. When do you leave?"

"Two weeks."

It was the usual notice, but Nick had been hoping for more time. Dean was a good deputy, and finding someone to replace him at the limited salary the county could afford to pay wasn't going to be easy. But that wasn't Dean's problem. Rising to his feet, Nick offered him his hand in congratulations. "Denver's lucky to get you. We'll miss you around here."

Relieved, Dean thanked him for being so understanding and walked out with a broad smile on his face. Two minutes later, George took his place in the chair across from Nick's desk and stunned Nick by announcing that he, too, was giving his notice.

Narrowing his eyes at him, he growled, "Is this a joke?"

"No! Why would you think that?"

"Because Dean just told me the same thing. What the hell's going on?"

Shocked, George swore. "Oh, man, I'm sorry! Talk about bad timing. I had no idea, Nick. He didn't tell me."

"He got a better offer in Denver," he said with a shrug. "It happens. So what about you? Where are you going?"

"Back to school," he replied simply. "You know how much I've always wanted to finish my degree and go on to law school. I would have done it years ago, but I just couldn't afford it with the kids and all. Then I found out my grandmother left me some money when she died last month. Jan and I discussed it and agreed that if I was ever going to do anything, I had to do it now, before the kids got older and we needed the money for their education.''

As much as Nick hated to lose him, he had to admit that some opportunities only came along once in a lifetime and you had to grab them when you could. ''You'll make a damn good lawyer,'' he told him. ''I hope you're going to come back here to practice.''

''Of course. This is our home. But I hate to leave you in the lurch like this, with both me and Dean leaving. What are you going to do?''

Nick was wondering the same thing—in a back-country town like Liberty Hill, good deputies didn't come along every day of the week—but that wasn't George's problem. ''I'll think of something—don't worry about it. Right now, you've got more important things to worry about. Like where you want to go to school and moving your family.''

George had already given that considerable thought, and as he rattled on with his plans, Nick couldn't help but think that everyone was going on with their life except him. And with no warning whatsoever, he found himself in the middle of a midlife crisis.

What the hell was he still doing in Liberty Hill? he wondered as he listened with half an ear to George. There was nothing for him here and never would be. Merry loved Thomas, not him, and in spite of the fact that Thomas had left her standing at the altar last Saturday, she could no more change her feelings for Thomas than Nick could change his feelings for her. And when Thomas finally calmed down and worked up the courage to return to town, Merry would find a way to forgive him. Nick didn't want to be there when that happened. He didn't think he'd be able to stand it.

It was time he left, he decided, and got on with the rest of his life. He had a friend with the FBI who'd been pushing him for years to apply with the Bureau. Maybe he'd give him a call.

Chapter 5

Later, Nick couldn't have said how things snowballed so fast. One minute he'd been talking to Howard Quinn, telling him he was considering applying for a job with the Bureau, and the next, not only was Quinn overnighting an application to him, but Nick had decided there was no use putting things off. As soon as he'd hung up with Howard, he'd advertised for deputies in the Denver, Colorado Springs and Tucson papers. Even if he didn't get the job with the Bureau, he still needed two men to replace Dean and George. Then, before he'd let himself question the wisdom of what he was doing, he'd called Tina Adams, one of the two realtors in the area, to get her advice on selling his house.

What's the hurry? a voice inside his head demanded. *You don't have to do this now!*

But he did. He'd already spent years waiting for Merry to open her eyes and realize that Thomas wasn't the only man in the world for her. Now that he'd actually accepted the fact that that was never going to happen, he couldn't wait another day to get on with the rest of his life. Because if he gave himself time to think about what he was doing, he knew he probably wouldn't be able to leave her.

Convinced he was doing the right thing, he met Tina at his house and watched her go over the place with a fine-tooth comb, examining everything from its street appeal to how big the pantry was in the kitchen. With the help of friends, he'd built the homemade log cabin seven years ago, and he knew every nook and cranny of it better than the lines of his hand. And he loved it. He always had. He never stepped through the front door without feeling a sense of peace and accomplishment.

But now, studying it through Tina's eyes and trying to imagine how a prospective buyer would see it, he couldn't help but be concerned. In spite of the fact that he'd built it from the ground up, he wasn't blind to its faults. There were places where the window trim didn't quite meet and closet doors that had a tendency to stick on humid days. *He* liked the primitive look of the place, the rough-hewn cut of the bare log walls and plank floors, but he readily admitted that not everyone wanted to live like Daniel Boone in the middle of the forest…especially women. And Tina was probably one of them. Her face expressionless, he couldn't tell if she loved or hated the place.

"Maybe I should Sheetrock some of the walls so it doesn't look so much like a log cabin," he said when she frowned at the wall that separated the kitchen from the great room.

Lost in thought, she blinked, then realized what he said. "Oh, no! That's what's going to sell it. What's the point of living in a log cabin if it doesn't *look* like one?"

"That's why I left the logs exposed," he said. "But some people might have a problem with that."

Unconcerned, she shrugged. "There's a market for everything. People who don't like exposed logs won't look at log cabins to begin with, so that's not a problem. What we have to worry about are some loose boards on the back porch, a leaky faucet in the downstairs bathroom, and some general cosmetic work. You take care of those things, trim up the yard and put some geraniums in the flower beds and curtains at the windows, and I think you'll have a buyer by the end of the summer."

Stunned, Nick couldn't believe he'd heard her correctly. "You're kidding! That soon? But I thought the market had slowed down because of the rise in interest rates."

"It has," she agreed, then qualified, "some. But people will always find a way to buy a good piece of property, even when rates are high. And what you've got here is going to appeal to a lot of buyers."

She was one of the most successful realtors in southwestern Colorado and sharp as a tack. That's why Nick had called her. She couldn't make any promises, of course, but if she said the cabin would sell quickly, it was pretty much a given that he'd be looking for someplace else to live by the end of the summer. *If* he decided to sell.

Reading his mind, she arched a brow at him. "So what's it going to be? It's your call. You want to list it or not?"

He should have told her he'd think about it overnight and get back to her in the morning, but his life had been on hold for too long as it was. If he was ever going to get out of this limbo he was in and find happiness for himself, he had to do it now! Making a snap decision, he nodded. "List it. I'll start making the repairs immediately."

Pleased, she snapped open her briefcase and pulled out a contract. "Then let's sign the paperwork, and you'll be all set. An ad will come out in tomorrow's paper."

* * *

Checking the traps she'd set in the woods, Merry didn't know whether to be relieved or worried when she found them empty. There'd been no more new cases of rabies in the county or reports of any kind of aggressive behavior in foxes or any other normally timid wild animals, but she didn't fool herself into thinking that the crisis had passed. Rabies was a silent killer, especially in the wild. It would spread from foxes to coyote to wolves, and there was no way to know just how dangerous the situation was until the rabid animals turned on humans and pets.

Which was why she was determined to see that every dog and cat in the county had its shots, she reminded herself as she climbed back into her Explorer. If she could just convince people to act responsibly and protect their pets, half the battle would be won right there. The problem was that educating people about the disease wasn't that easy. Not everyone understood what all the fuss was about. Some of the good old boys who lived back in the woods didn't see why they had to vaccinate their dogs when they could just shoot all the foxes and coyotes they came across and eliminate the problem that way.

Rolling her eyes at the ignorance of such thinking, she'd spent the last few days going door to door in the more remote areas of the county, talking to people and trying to make them understand why killing innocent animals in the wild wasn't the solution, but she hadn't gotten very far. And she didn't doubt for a minute that it was because she was a woman. Male chauvinism, unfortunately, was still alive and well and thriving in Liberty Hill, Colorado, and there didn't seem to be a damn thing she could do about it. Pets were going to die and people suffer through the agony of rabies shots in the stomach just because men like Junior Reynolds and Dirk Smith couldn't handle the fact that she, a lowly woman in their eyes, knew more than they did.

If they wouldn't listen to her, maybe Nick could get through to them, she thought in growing frustration as she turned onto the county road that wound through the hills north of town and led to his house. He'd told her yesterday that he was working the late shift today. She'd just stop by and see if he could make a few calls while he was out on patrol later. Junior and Dirk might be idiots, but their families had a lot of influence in the area. If Nick could convince them to do the right thing, the other holdouts just might fall in line, too.

Her thoughts still on the vaccination campaign, she didn't notice the For Sale sign in Nick's front yard until she pulled into his drive and cut the engine. Reaching for her door handle, she stiffened, unable to believe she was seeing correctly. There had to be a mistake. Nick wasn't selling his house. He couldn't be. He'd never said a word.

He came around the side of the house then, just as she stepped from her car, his arms loaded down with an array of carpentry tools. "Hey, I wasn't expecting to see you today," he said by way of a greeting, a pleased smile breaking across his face. "What's going on?"

"I was about to ask you the same thing," she said with a frown as she crossed the yard to join him. "What's with the For Sale sign? I thought you loved this place."

Swearing silently, Nick set his tools on the porch and wanted to kick himself for not anticipating that this could happen. He and Merry dropped by each other's houses unannounced all the time. She'd been so busy trying to head off the rabies epidemic, though, that he really hadn't expected her to come by today. Not that he was trying to keep anything from her, he silently assured himself. He wasn't. He'd fully intended to tell her he'd decided to make a career move that would mean leaving Liberty Hill, but only after he'd had time to come up with an explanation that wouldn't lead her to suspect why he was really leaving—because of her.

"I do," he replied, "but I've been thinking about making some changes in my life, and the timing just seemed right."

Her eyes wide in her suddenly pale face, she looked up at him searchingly. "What kind of changes?"

He hesitated, then motioned to one of the two willow rockers on the front porch. "Sit down, Mer. We need to talk."

He hadn't meant to sound so grim, but suddenly, her eyes were swimming in tears. Ignoring the chair he wanted her to take, she reached for him instead. "Oh, God, something's wrong, isn't it? That's why you've looked so sad over the last couple of days. What is it? What's wrong? Are you sick? I'll talk to Janey. We'll get you a better doctor—"

The feel of her hand on his cheek, the worry in her eyes, was nearly his undoing. Dear God, couldn't she see what she was doing to him? How he ached just to hold her, just once, the way a man holds the woman he loves. Didn't she realize...

But she didn't and never would. Convinced more than ever that he was doing the right thing, he took her hand from his cheek and squeezed it before releasing it. "I'm not dying," he assured her with a wry smile. "I just feel like I've been stuck in a rut and I need a complete change of scene. So I'm going to apply with the FBI—"

"What?!"

"You remember Howard Quinn? My college roommate? I talked to him this morning in D.C., and he's pretty sure he can get me into Quantico as an agent. He's overnighting me an application.''

Stunned, Merry felt as if he'd just cut her off at the knees. She'd never met Howard, but she'd heard Nick talk about him enough to know that he was a senior agent with a lot of pull. If he'd told Nick he could get him into Quantico, submitting an application was just a formality.

No, I can't lose you, too! Not on top of everything else. I don't think I could bear it.

The words rose in her throat like a cry of pain, but she caught them back just in time. No, she thought, struggling for control. She couldn't be selfish about this. Throughout their lives, Nick had always been there for her, totally supportive of whatever she wanted to do. She didn't know what had brought on this sudden decision of his, if he was going through some kind of midlife crisis or what, but after all the times she'd cried on his shoulder, the least she could do was be there for him now.

''That's wonderful!'' she said, and tried to mean it. ''When do you think you'll be leaving?''

''It's too early to say. I'll send the application back as soon as I get it, but the background check takes at least six weeks. And I can't go anywhere until I find a replacement for George and Dean.''

Shocked, she blinked. ''They're quitting, too?''

''Yeah. Which is why I won't be going anywhere soon. Good help is hard to find, and I can't leave the county in the lurch with only Harvey to handle everything.''

She tried to take comfort in that, but all she could think of was that he was leaving, going on with his life, and leaving her behind. And it hurt—nearly as much as Thomas's betrayal.

Guilt swamped her at the thought, and she knew she should have been thoroughly ashamed of herself. This was a different situation entirely from Thomas's betrayal. Nick's leaving had nothing to do with her. He'd been offered a wonderful opportunity, and instead of selfishly thinking about herself and how lonely she was going to be without him, she should have been happy for him. He was a good man and deserved all the best things that life had to offer. And she *was* happy for him, she told herself. If her heart broke at the thought of being left behind, that was her problem, not his, and something she would take with her to her grave.

Forcing a smile, she dropped down into the rocker closest to her on the porch. "So tell me everything. I see you listed the house with Tina. She must have been thrilled to get the listing. It'll be an easy sell."

"She seemed pretty confident we'd have a buyer by the end of the summer."

That soon? Hurt pierced her heart, but she remained determinedly enthusiastic. "That's great! You'll be out of here before you know it."

"A lot of things have to come together first. I've got to make some repairs—"

"I can help you with that in the evenings if you need an extra pair of hands," she offered. "I can come over right after work. It'll be fun. I'll bring supper...."

She chattered on as if it didn't bother her in the least that he was moving away, even going so far as to teasingly warn him not to forget his old friends when he got to Washington, and Nick could have cheerfully throttled her. Did he really mean so little to her? Frustrated, he almost asked her, but he wasn't sure he wanted to hear the answer. And in the end, what difference did it make, anyway? Thomas was the one she loved, the one she wanted to spend the rest of her life with. And nothing he could say or do was going to change that. Some things just weren't meant to be.

Accepting that with a heavy heart, he forced a smile that never reached his eyes. "That sounds great. Think you can come over tomorrow night? Tina's going to place an ad in Friday's paper so she can start showing the house over the weekend, and I was wondering how I was going to get everything done by myself."

"Sure," she said. "But what's wrong with tonight? I've got nothing to do and a frozen pizza in the freezer. I'll go home and get it and we can work while it's cooking."

She was gone before he could stop her, driving away with a bright smile and a wave, and Nick couldn't help but think she was damn eager to get rid of him. Still, he knew he would never tell her that he didn't want her help. He might be a masochist where she was concerned, but whatever time he could have with her he was going to grab with both hands. Because this was all he was ever going to have of her when he left, memories of what might have been.

Laden down with brushes and drop cloths and a false enthusiasm that weighed heavy on her soul, Merry was back thirty minutes later and didn't know how she was going to get through the rest of the evening without breaking down. She'd fought tears all the way to her house and back, knowing that if she gave into them, even for a second, the floodgates would open and she'd cry her eyes out. And she couldn't do that, not in front of Nick. He'd never understand.

She really was happy for him, and if this was what he wanted, then she truly hoped everything worked out for him. When it came time for him to leave, she'd wish him well and kiss him goodbye, and he'd never know that inside, her heart was breaking because she was losing everyone she loved and there didn't seem to be anything she could do about it.

Her life was in chaos and she didn't even know how it had happened. One moment, she'd been getting dressed for her wedding, and the next, the man she loved was gone, taking with him the future she'd thought they would have together. And now, Nick, too, was leaving. He'd been her friend for so long, she couldn't remember a time when he hadn't been in her life. How was she going to live without him?

"Mer? You need some help with the ladder?" Nick asked suddenly from behind her. "Here, let me do that."

Lost in her misery when she should have been setting up the ladder so she could clean some mildew off the back porch eave, she snapped to attention and quickly hid her sorrow behind a bright smile. "No, that's okay. I can do it. I was just thinking about my house and the changes Thomas and I talked about making next year. Did we ever tell you about them?"

"Yeah. You were going to add a family room off the kitchen and another bathroom."

His tone was stiff, his expression shuttered, but she never noticed. Without even closing her eyes, she could see the home she and Thomas had planned to create together. "I should have done that when I rebuilt the house last year, but I never even thought about it."

"Why would you? You weren't thinking about getting married at that time. You were dating Bubba Smith, for God's sake!"

He sounded so disgusted, Merry had to bite her lip to keep from laughing. He'd never understood why she wasted her time on Bubba. He'd always seen him as nothing but a lazy, good-for-nothing cowboy whose only ambition was to go drinking with his buddies on Saturday night and date the prettiest girl in the county. Merry couldn't argue with that—Bubba had never pretended to be anything but what he was—but he'd made her laugh at a time when she'd badly needed a diversion, and that was all she'd wanted from him.

Even if she'd wanted a more serious relationship then, there'd been no time for one. A stalker who was fixated with her movie-star-sister-in-law, Angel, had torched her house and clinic—not to mention her brother Joe's house— and all her energy had been focused on rebuilding and keeping her practice up and running. Then, just after she moved back into her house and reopened her clinic, Thomas came back to town and they fell in love all over again. Just that easily, Bubba was history.

"Bubba wasn't so bad," she said as she positioned the ladder under the eave, then grabbed the pail of soapy water she'd made and climbed up to where the mildew marred the wood. "All he wanted was a few laughs and someone to dance with. He wouldn't have looked twice at me if I hadn't been able to two-step."

"Yeah, right, Miss America," he snorted. "Tell me another one."

"Okay," she laughed, "so he has this thing about never going out with anyone who's uglier than he is, and he thinks he's a damn good-looking man—"

"Oh, he doesn't just think it, he *knows* it."

"Well, he is cute, Nick."

"And if he had a brain in his head, he'd be dangerous," he grumbled.

She couldn't argue with that. "True. He's never going to set the world on fire with his intellect, but he was shrewd enough to realize that he never stood a chance once Thomas came back to town. He saw us together at Ed's Diner the first night Thomas was back in town, and he never asked me out again. I think he realized right then it was a lost cause.''

Nick had to give him credit. He didn't care for Bubba, but he'd been a hell of a lot sharper than he, himself. At least Smith had had the brains to get out before his heart was involved, which was more than Nick could say about himself. Like an idiot, he'd hung around for years, falling deeper and deeper in love while he waited for the day when Merry would finally wise up and realize she loved him instead of Thomas. But that wasn't ever going to happen. Somehow Thomas had brainwashed her, and even now, after he'd publicly humiliated her, she still got that dreamy look in her eye whenever she talked about him.

She loved the scumbag, and as much as it hurt Nick to admit it, once Thomas worked up the nerve to call her again, she wouldn't be able to hold on to her anger. All would be forgiven, and Thomas would come running back to her open arms. And when he did, Nick intended to be as far away as possible.

In spite of the For Sale sign in his front yard and his conversation with Merry, Nick still hoped to keep his plans private as long as possible. In a town the size of Liberty Hill, however, where everyone knew the true color of everyone else's hair and didn't mind telling them, he was hoping for the impossible.

''Hey, Nick, what's this?'' Gary Peyton, the postman, asked him two days later when he strolled into his office without knocking. ''You expecting something from the FBI?''

In the process of filling out a report for the mayor on the county's latest crime statistics, he glanced up from the numbers he was scowling at and swallowed a groan at the official-looking letter Gary waved under his nose. Damn

Howard! He'd expected him to send the application to his house, not the office.

Taking the letter and the rest of the mail, he sat back in his chair and gave the other man a chiding look. "You know I can't tell you that, Gary. It's official business."

"Well, hellfire, man, you know I won't tell anyone! I work for the government, too. So what's going on? Did you have them check out that compound those Yankees built out by Bear Falls? I swear they're running drugs out of there."

"Why do you say that? Have you seen something?"

"Well, no…"

"Because there aren't any drugs, Gary," he said quietly. "I know. I checked."

"Well, then, what's that?" he demanded, motioning to the letter Nick had slipped into his desk drawer. "What's the boys in Washington want with you? Oh, I get it," he said suddenly, his eyes widening as he put two and two together. "You've got your place up for sale, don't you? I saw the sign yesterday when I was out that way delivering an overnight package to Dolores Ivy from her son in California. I bet you're applying for a job, aren't you? I knew it! I always thought you belonged in the city, working with the big boys. So when are you leaving?"

Swearing, Nick could already hear the gossip, and that was the last thing he wanted. "Look, Gary, do you think we could keep this just between us? Nothing's definite yet, and until it is, I'd rather not talk about it. Okay?"

"Well, yeah, sure, man, if that's what you want. But people are going to know something's up when they hear you've put your house up for sale."

He had a point, one Nick had already thought of. "I'll just tell them I decided I wanted to buy something closer to town."

"My lips are sealed," Gary promised. "I won't tell a soul."

Nick wanted to believe that, but he knew Gary too well. His heart was in the right place, but he just couldn't resist spreading the news whenever he heard something interesting. And as one of Liberty Hill's handful of mailmen, he heard more than his fair share of interesting gossip. "Thanks, Gary. I appreciate you doing what you can."

"Sure. Anytime."

He was gone with a nod, hurrying out the door and heading, no doubt, straight to Ed's Diner, where he could share his news. Shaking his head, Nick went through the rest of the mail and was surprised to discover three responses to the ads he'd placed for deputies. And they'd come with the same delivery that brought him the application with the Bureau. He had to take that as a good omen. Settling back, he ripped open the letters from the job applicants and began to read.

When Nick stepped out of his office an hour later, things were finally looking up. He was taking charge of his life, and he felt good about it. He'd filled out the application for the Bureau and put it in the mail, then contacted two of the three job applicants who'd sent in résumés for the deputy positions. They'd both be in town on Friday for an interview, and he was keeping his fingers crossed that they'd work out. If they didn't, he'd start the process all over again until he found someone suitable to replace Dean and George. Between the new deputies and Harvey, the three of them could handle things until the mayor was able to find someone to take over the sheriff's duties. Because he was still leaving, Nick vowed, even if he didn't get the job with the Bureau.

He didn't fool himself into thinking it would be easy,

however. Except for the years he'd gone away to college, he'd spent all of his life in Liberty Hill, and its citizens were as much a part of his family as his blood relatives. He cared about them, their kids, and what was going on in their lives. He made a walk through the business district every day just so he could talk to people and see how they were doing. It was one of the favorite parts of his job, one that he knew he was going to miss.

Strolling into Ed's Diner, he wasn't surprised to see Myrtle Henderson and her gray-haired bunko club seated at the large booth in the corner. It was Monday, and they always met at Ed's for coffee and pie after a wild afternoon of bunko. Nodding, he greeted them with a grin. "Ladies. How are you all this afternoon?"

"Heartbroken," Myrtle answered for the group. "According to the latest scuttlebutt, you're quitting to go work for the FBI. Is that true?"

His smile never wavering, Nick wanted to track Gary down and give him a piece of his mind. So much for his promise to keep his mouth shut! "The FBI?" he said with just the right touch of startled appreciation. "C'mon, Myrtle, get real. I'm a small-town sheriff. What would the FBI want with me?"

Old enough to be his grandmother, Myrtle had been around the proverbial block far too many times to be taken in that easily. Giving him a reproving look over the top of her glasses, she chastised, "Don't think you can pull a fast one on me, Nicholas Kincaid! I know what you're up to and why. We all do. You're leaving town because of that girl—"

He stiffened like a porcupine. "I don't know what you're talking about—"

"Oh, yes, you do," she insisted, "and I say it's a darn shame! It's as plain as the nose on your face that you're nuts about her, and she can't see anything but that rat who left her high and dry at the altar. Instead of giving up and leaving town, why don't you grab her and kiss her? That'll wake her up!"

"Or send her flowers," Cheri Sutton suggested. "I remember when I was single, I just *loved* getting flowers from a man. It was so romantic."

Feeling heat climb into his face, Nick struggled for patience and told himself that they meant well. "You've got it all wrong. There's nothing going on between Merry and me—"

"Jewelry," Evelyn Fargate said flatly, interrupting him without batting an eye. A no-nonsense woman who didn't have a romantic bone in her body, Evelyn was a retired schoolteacher who had once been the terror of Liberty Hill High. "If you want to get a woman's attention, spend some real money on her so she'll know you're serious. Otherwise, you're just wasting her time."

The others in the club disagreed with that, and within seconds, they were all jumping into the discussion, sure that they each knew best how Nick could win Merry. Frustrated, he tried to tell them that they were barking up the wrong tree—he and Merry had never been anything but friends— but he might as well have saved his breath. They knew what they knew, and nothing he could say was going to change their minds.

How did they know? he wondered irritably. He didn't wear his heart on his sleeve, for heaven's sake! In fact, he'd always made sure he hid his feelings well. And still, everyone seemed to know, dammit! First Joe, now Myrtle and her *entire* bunko club! And if those chatterboxes knew, was there anyone in town who didn't?

Merry...dear God, had someone told her? he wondered with a groan. All this time when he'd thought she didn't have a clue how he felt, was she just being kind and pretending not to know to spare his feelings? Would she really do that to him?

The answer came to him immediately—he didn't even have to think about it. No. He knew Merry better than he knew himself, and she wasn't capable of that kind of deception. There was nothing they couldn't say to each other, and if she suspected that he loved her, she would have asked him about it long ago. No, she didn't know. *Yet.* And that was what worried him.

Unabashedly eavesdropping on the entire conversation from his position behind the counter that ran the length of the diner, Ed Randolph, the owner of the place, clicked his tongue in disapproval and motioned Nick over. "Don't pay those old hens any mind," he growled as he served him a cup of coffee and a slice of his famous chocolate pie without waiting for Nick to order it. "They don't mean any harm. They just want to see you and Merry happy, and it frustrates them that she can't see what's right in front of her nose. But they would never say anything to her, Nick. You've got to know that. Your secret's safe with us."

Nick wanted to believe that, but it wasn't easy. As he continued on his rounds around town after finishing his pie and coffee, he would have sworn he could hear people whispering behind his back about why he was leaving. And everywhere he went, Merry's name seemed to follow him.

It was enough to give a normally easygoing man ulcers. Convinced she must have heard the gossip going around town about the two of them, he half expected her to confront him each night when she came over to his house to help him finish the last of the cosmetic touch-ups the realtor had recommended, but she'd been so busy with the rabies scare that she obviously hadn't, thankfully, heard anything.

Still, he just wanted the interviews over with as quietly as possible so people would stop talking.

Unfortunately, it didn't happen that way. When Friday rolled around and the time he'd set up to meet with the two applicants approached, he couldn't help but notice that there were an inordinate amount of people hanging around the square on a Friday afternoon. Ranchers who usually didn't come into town except on Sundays for church stood in small groups in front of the shops on Main Street talking to friends and shopkeepers like they didn't have a care in the world. And there, outside Ed's Diner and in full view of the courthouse, Myrtle and her friends had gathered to watch every car that came down the street toward Nick's office.

"Just like they were waiting for a damn parade to start," he grumbled to his dispatcher, Sheri Johnson, as he dropped the blind he'd been peeking through and turned to prowl restlessly around the office. "What the hell's wrong with everybody? You'd think they'd never seen a couple of strangers come into town before."

A kind soul but always one to speak her mind, Sheri never looked up from her typing. "They haven't. Not like these, anyway. Think about it. Two deputies and the sheriff are all leaving as soon as you're able to hire someone to replace Dean and George. Of course people are curious. Your replacement will have the power to make their lives— not to mention, mine—miserable if he's a hard-ass-by-the-book kind of guy, and you won't be here to protect them."

"I wouldn't hire someone like that!"

"No," she agreed, "but people want to know what they're going to have to deal with, all the same. They'll settle down once they realize they have nothing to worry about."

Nick hoped so. Because finding good people was going

to be hard enough as it was without having them think they were walking into some kind of circus. Liberty Hill was a nice quiet little town in a beautiful part of Colorado, but that was about all it had going for it. As far as the job went, the salary the county could afford to pay was hardly generous and the hours were long. Everyone, including the sheriff, pulled whatever duty was necessary to keep the citizens of the county safe.

Then there was the town itself. For Nick it was home. But he readily admitted that Liberty Hill wouldn't, in all likelihood, appeal to everyone. Anyone used to any kind of city life at all was going to be bored out of their mind. There was no nightlife, just Tiny's Pool Hall and Ed's, no elaborate shopping malls, no museums or cultural centers.

Wondering how he was going to find not one, but two applicants who could accept all that, he was still pacing the outer office when a tall, muscular man walked in and looked around curiously. Obviously a stranger, he glanced past Sheri at her desk to where Nick stood at one of the filing cabinets. Seeing the badge on his khaki shirt, he made an easy guess and said, "Sheriff Kincaid? I'm Lincoln White. I hope I'm not too early for our interview?"

"Not at all," Nick assured him, immediately liking the mix of intelligence and easy confidence in his blue eyes. Crossing to shake hands with him, he motioned for him to precede him into his office. "We can talk in here. I see you didn't have any trouble finding us. How was your flight into Colorado Springs?"

Three hours later, Nick had interviewed not only Lincoln White, but Rick Stanley, the other applicant, as well, and he had to admit, he was impressed with both men. White lived in a small town fifty miles north of Salt Lake City, and Stanley, who'd worked in L.A. for the last year, had grown up in a one-horse town in Texas. Educated, but more interested in the quality of life they could have in a small town than the money they would make in a large city, they had their heads on right and their priorities straight.

They were just the kind of deputies Nick was looking for, but when he finished each man's interview, he thanked them for making the trip to Liberty Hill and promised to make a decision within the week.

"I can't believe you let those men get away," Sheri grumbled, turning on him the second the door shut behind him. "I thought they were just what you were looking for."

"And how would you know that?" Nick asked, giving her an arch look. "I never discussed that with you."

"You didn't have to," she said with an insulted sniff. "I know you, Nick, and you're going to hire deputies every bit as good as the ones you've got or you won't hire them. And those men were good. So what's going on?"

"This isn't something I'm going to rush into," he said stubbornly. "It's too important."

She clearly didn't believe him, and he couldn't say he blamed her. This had nothing to do with not wanting to make a mistake, and they both knew it. As long as he put off hiring any new deputies, he couldn't leave Liberty Hill...or Merry.

Chapter 6

"I tell you, Merry, they were perfect! And Nick just let them walk away! Can you believe it? Sheri was stunned. She chewed him out for not snatching them up when he had the chance, but he still didn't call them. I just don't understand it. Everybody knows he wants to leave, so why's he dragging his feet? What's going on?"

"Maybe he's having a midlife crises," Clair Vickers continued before Merry could get a word in edgewise. The owner of the only office supply store in town, Clair did love to talk. Bagging the items Merry had bought for her clinic, she rambled merrily on, quite content to carry the entire conversation by herself. "But he's not that old, is he? He graduated with you and Thomas, didn't he? So that would make him what? Thirty-two? Thirty-three? That seems awfully young to be having a meltdown. Of course, anyone can get stressed out. Why don't you go over to the sheriff's office and see what's going on? You and he have always been close. He'll talk to you."

"Oh, I don't know, Clair," Merry hedged. "We never interfere in each other's business."

"But this affects the whole town," the other woman wisely pointed out. "And if he's stressed to the max, his thinking's going to be screwed up and he's not going to make the soundest decisions—not only for us, but for himself. Just think—he's got a chance to go work for the FBI. The *FBI,* Merry! That's something you don't get an opportunity to do everyday. And if he's not careful, he's going to blow it. Go talk to him. He needs your help."

She should have said no. She didn't want him to go to Washington. As far as she was concerned, he could put off hiring his replacement for the next ten years, and she'd never say a word. But what kind of friend would that make her if he really wanted to leave and just needed a nudge of encouragement from her?

Guilt nagging at her, she reluctantly gave in. "Oh, all right. I'll see what I can do, but don't blame me if he tells me to mind my own business."

She found him holed up in his office, scowling at a file that was open on his desk. From where she stood at the doorway, she couldn't see what he was reading, but she wouldn't have been surprised if the file contained the resumes of the two men he'd interviewed the day before. Clair was right, she realized with a twinge of remorse. This couldn't be easy for him. If he got the job with the Bureau, he would be leaving everything that was dear and familiar, and that would be difficult for anyone. Maybe he did need some encouragement.

Straightening her shoulders, she forced a smile and knocked jauntily on the doorjamb. "Hi!" she said with a smile when he looked up. "I heard you had company yesterday. How'd it go?"

Leaning back in his chair, he gave her a mocking look. "I think we both know the answer to that. Every gossip in the county was standing on the square when they drove out of town. People have been talking of nothing else since."

"They're just curious," she said with an easy shrug. "Gossip's died down about me and Thomas, so they need something else to talk about. Looks like you and your deputies are it. So they weren't qualified?"

"I didn't say that."

Puzzled, she frowned. "I don't understand. If they were qualified and had good references, which I assume they did or you wouldn't have interviewed them to begin with, why didn't you hire them? What was the problem?"

For a moment, she didn't think he was going to answer. He hesitated, then shrugged. "Just because they checked out and interviewed well doesn't mean they're right for the job. Neither one of them is from Colorado—"

"Neither is Dean," she reminded him. "He's from Idaho, isn't he?"

"Yes, but Dean's different."

"How?"

Put on the spot, he frowned. "I don't know. He just is, dammit! He's...he's...he's a family man! He goes to church and likes to hunt and fish and watch football on Sundays in the fall."

None of those things had anything to do with a man's ability to do his job, but Merry wisely refrained from pointing that out. "I see," she said, when she didn't see at all. "And I suppose the men you talked to yesterday didn't like to do those kind of things?"

"I don't know," he said sullenly. "I didn't ask."

It wasn't like Nick to be so nonsensical, and Merry almost laughed. He couldn't be serious, she thought. But one look at his face and any thought she had of laughing died a swift death. She'd never seen him look quite so stressed before.

Concerned, she took a step toward him. "Nick, what's going on? I know you. You'd never leave without making sure the sheriff's department had enough deputies to keep the local citizens safe. So why are you making excuses not to hire these men when they seem perfect for the job? Have you changed your mind about going to Washington? Is that what this is all about?"

He should have shrugged off her questions and come up with a more plausible excuse, but dammit, she had him cornered and he was tired of hiding his feelings. If she wanted answers, then by God, he'd give them to her!

"And what if I have?" he tossed back at her. "What do you think would keep me here? Or maybe I should say *who,* dammit! Think about it, Merry. Who could possibly be keeping me in Liberty Hill?"

He practically threw the questions at her like darts and wanted to kick himself for it. Over the years, he must have imagined a thousand times or more how he would tell her that his feelings for her were much stronger than those of a friend. And not once in all those times had he pictured himself taunting her with how he felt. What the devil was wrong with him?

Disgusted with himself, he sighed. "Look, forget I said anything."

But it was too late for that. Caught off guard, Merry just stood there, sure she must have heard wrong. But there was something in his eyes, a frustrated hurt directed solely at her, that set her heart slamming against her ribs and the ground dissolving beneath her feet. Stunned, she shook her head. No. This couldn't be happening. He couldn't be saying what she thought he was saying. There had to be some kind of mistake. He couldn't mean...

Suddenly afraid of finishing that thought, she backed away from it and him. She couldn't do this, couldn't take it. There'd been nothing but one upheaval after another in her life lately, and it had to stop. She didn't want any more change—especially this kind. Nick was her friend and she did love him—*as a friend*—nothing more. He had to know that, had to know that that was never going to change.

Because she still loved Thomas. Only a month ago, they'd planned to be married. Her feelings weren't something she could turn on and off like a faucet. She couldn't stop loving him just because he'd hurt and betrayed her. It wasn't that simple.

But even as she stubbornly tried to cling to her love for Thomas, she had to wonder who she was trying to convince—Nick or herself? The answer wasn't nearly as clear as it should have been. And that scared the hell out of her.

Pale and shaken, in desperate need of some time to herself, she took another quick step back, then another. "I—I h-have to get b-back to the clinic," she stuttered, already turning to make a run for it. "I'll talk to you later."

"No, wait!" Nick began, rising to his feet to stop her, but he was too late. She rushed out of the main office like the hounds of hell were after her. Swearing, he stared after her and just barely resisted the urge to throw something. Dammit to hell! He'd known that once she realized that his feelings for her were more than those of a friend, she'd never look at him the same again. And that was exactly what had happened.

All too clearly, he could see her face when she'd finally understood what he was trying to tell her. She'd been so shocked, so uncomfortable, that she hadn't even been able to look him in the eye. And he had no one to blame but himself. If he'd just kept his big mouth shut, nothing would have had to change.

But, no! He'd had to tell her, and too late, he realized what he'd done. He'd forced her to look at him in a different light, and by doing so, stripped away the innocence of their relationship. And dear God, he regretted it. With a few impulsive words, he'd ruined everything and destroyed a friendship he cherished more than anything else on earth. And there was no turning back the clock.

She wouldn't forgive him for this, he silently acknowledged. He knew her too well. Because she would no longer be comfortable in his company, she'd avoid him, withdraw into her work, find someone else to confide in, and in no time at all, she'd be out of his life—without his ever leaving Liberty Hill.

Shaken, he realized that as much as he hadn't been able to tolerate the idea of living anywhere near Merry and Thomas once they married, he found the thought of being in the same town with her and knowing that he couldn't be friends with her even less tolerable. If he couldn't see her, talk to her, have her in his life, even as a friend, there was no longer any reason to stay in Liberty Hill. At least in Washington, he wouldn't have to worry about running into her on the street and being reminded of what he had lost.

His mind made up, he reached for the file on his two applicants, found their phone numbers and picked up the phone. The minute Lincoln White came on the line, he said, "Good afternoon, Linc. This is Nick Kincaid. I've given your application some consideration and think you're just what I've been looking for in a deputy. When do you think you could start?"

Confused, her thoughts in a whirl and her stomach twisted in knots, Merry drove right past her clinic without even slowing down and headed for the one person she'd always been able to depend on to keep her head when everyone else was losing theirs. Her mother. She was always calm, always in control, always knew what to do. She would help her.

Ten minutes later, she braked to a stop in the circular driveway of the large rambling rock-and-log home that had been in her family for generations. It wasn't the type of house that would ever make the cover of *Architectural Digest*—over the decades, it had been added onto too many times without regard to maintaining any one particular style—but it was home and she loved it. It was here that the family gathered to celebrate every joy and mourn every sorrow and hold memories dear. And it was here that she and Janey and her brothers came when they were troubled and needed guidance.

Janey still lived there with their mother and had the same room she'd had as a child, but she was at the nursing home, where she worked as a registered nurse, so their mother had the house to herself. Merry only had to follow her nose to find her.

"Mmm. Apple pie," she said with a smile as she stepped into the kitchen and sniffed the air. Sweet with the scent of baking apples and cinnamon, it smelled heavenly. "Please tell me that's not for tonight's church supper."

Up to her elbows in flour as she rolled out pie crust at the kitchen table, Sara McBride chuckled. "Sorry, dear, but I've got to have six ready by five-thirty and I still have two left to make."

"Darn!"

Her blue eyes, so like Merry's, sparkling with amusement, she gave a nod to the counter, where five pies were cooling on trivets. One, larger than the rest, had already been cut into. "I don't know how you kids always know when I'm baking pies—you must have radar or something. Joe and Zeke both dropped in earlier. Luckily, I had a feel-

ing they would and made one just for the family. Get yourself a plate, dear, and sit down and tell me what's troubling
you.''

Merry would have sworn that her expression was un-
troubled, but that had never stopped her mother from knowing when something was wrong. She just seemed to have
a sixth sense where her children were concerned.

Cutting herself a generous piece of pie, Merry took a
seat at the table directly across from where her mother was
working. ''I need some help, Mom,'' she said quietly.
''Something happened today and I don't know how to deal
with it.''

''Tell me about it,'' she said simply.

The words came spilling out then, a jumbled mix of hurt
and confusion and fears and tears that demanded release.
''I feel like the ground just dropped away beneath my
feet,'' she choked, ''and nothing's the way it's supposed to
be. I thought I loved Thomas, but I also thought he would
always be here for me. And he's not. He ran off without
me, and I've just been so lost lately.

''And now Nick…'' Emotion squeezed her throat. ''I
don't know how this happened. I never knew…never realized that he felt…that he wanted…''

Unable to finish, she swallowed thickly and wiped at the
tears that trailed down her cheeks. ''What do I do, Mom?
I just want everything to go back to the way it was before,
but I know that's not ever going to happen. And it hurts. I
don't understand how all of this happened.''

Sara McBride would have given anything if she'd had
the magic words that would take away all her daughter's
pain, but life, unfortunately, wasn't that easy. ''I'm so
sorry, dear. I know this is tearing you apart, but we both
know this isn't something I can help you with.''

The tears that had started to abate welled up again and

spilled silently over her lashes. "Oh, God, I was afraid you would say that! Mama, what am I going to do?"

Her own eyes flooding, Sara had to smile. Merry hadn't called her Mama since she was a little girl. "You have to decide what you truly want and go after it, honey. If that means you think you're still in love with Thomas and want to find a way to work things out with him, then don't let him get away. Go to Chicago, find him and make him talk to you."

"What if he doesn't want to see me? I think I'd just die of mortification."

"But what if he does and he's afraid to contact you?" she countered. "Do you want to take the chance of losing him forever because you don't want to be embarrassed?"

"No, of course not," she said huskily. "But I can't forget what he did to me. No one has ever hurt me like he did. I think I still love him, but I can't be sure. I'm just so confused right now."

Her appetite nonexistent, she pushed her pie away and looked up at Sara with eyes stark with pain. "This thing with Nick has me totally thrown. I know I must have hurt him by running out of his office the way I did, but I was just so surprised that I didn't know what else to do. I never expected this. I thought we were friends—"

"You *are* friends, dear. But that doesn't mean your relationship can't grow into something more—if you want it to."

Startled, Merry blinked. "Are you saying I should...that Nick and I should—"

"I'm not saying anything except that you need to follow your heart," Sara said gently. "That's all that matters here—that you take the time to decide what *you* want. If it's not right for you, it can't be right for Nick or Thomas."

"But I can't have both of them, Mom! Not now. I'm

going to lose one of them, and that's what's tearing me apart. How can anyone expect me to make a decision like that?''

She'd already lost one of them, she just didn't realize it yet. And Sarah didn't have the heart to tell her. ''Your heart will tell you what to do when the time is right,'' she assured her. ''Listen to that, and you'll be fine.''

It was the hardest decision of her life.

For the next three days, Merry avoided Nick like the plague, taking the time, as her mother had suggested, to decide what she wanted. She struggled and fought with it, and even cried. And in the end, there was really no decision to make, after all. At this point in her life, she couldn't think of Nick as anything other than a friend, not when she still didn't know how she felt about Thomas.

Relieved that she'd finally made some kind of decision, even if it didn't change anything, she almost called Nick. She'd missed him, missed talking things over with him as she usually did at the end of the day. But she was afraid he would want to pick up their last conversation where they left off, and she wasn't ready for that. Not yet. So she decided to wait until she ran into him in town.

Instead, *he* was the one who called her.

When the phone rang in the middle of the night, Merry knew it wasn't good news—it never was at three in the morning. Immediately awake, her heart in her throat, she reached for the phone in the dark. ''Hello?''

''I'm sorry to wake you,'' Nick said huskily in her ear, ''but I thought you'd want to know that Maxine Cooper was rushed to the hospital a half hour ago. It looks like she had a heart attack.''

''Oh, no!'' Sitting up abruptly, she switched on the light

and reached for her clothes. ''Is she all right? Has Thomas been notified?''

''I just called him. He's catching the first flight out this morning.''

''Then it must be bad,'' she said somberly. ''I'll be right there.''

Later, she never remembered the drive to the hospital. Maxine Cooper was a possessive mother who had always doted on Thomas, and she hadn't been thrilled at the idea of losing him to a wife. But Merry had found a way to make peace with her and even developed a certain fondness for her. She was the last parent Thomas had left. If she died, he'd be devastated.

Even now, he was on his way to Liberty Hill and would be there in a matter of hours. Merry didn't fool herself into thinking she wouldn't see him. Whatever his feelings were for her, he was a devoted son and this was going to hit him hard. An only child, he had no family to help him through this except for her and Nick. He was going to need them.

Her stomach knotted at the thought.

What was left of the night crawled by. All alone in the ICU waiting room, Merry drank one cup of coffee after another as nurses walked down the hallway on rubber-soled shoes. With nothing but her thoughts to keep her company, she found herself watching the clock and wondering where Nick was. She'd expected him to join her, but he never did, so she assumed he was working the night shift.

Sometime after four in the morning, an intern came in to tell her that she didn't need to stay—Maxine had stabilized and was heavily sedated. She wouldn't wake for hours. For all of ten seconds, Merry considered going home, but she couldn't stand the thought of Thomas's mother being there all alone, with no one to care about her. So she stayed...and waited for Thomas.

She had hours to think about him and how she would feel when she finally saw him again. Somehow, she'd always known that the day would come when they would meet again, and over the course of the last month, she'd pictured that meeting a thousand times in her head. But she'd never imagined it would happen like this, in the hospital, with his mother fighting for her life.

His first concern would be Maxine, she reminded herself, and rightfully so. She was the one whose health was in danger, and any discussion about their relationship—or lack of one—would have to wait. And that, Merry realized, was probably for the best. Neither one of them had expected this. They weren't prepared to talk about the future yet. They could do that later, after Maxine was on the road to recovery and they were free to focus on themselves and what they did and didn't want.

Still, Merry knew that first moment when they came face-to-face was going to be the most difficult. She thought she was prepared for it. But when she heard his footstep in the hall outside the waiting room just after eight in the morning and looked up to see him step into the doorway, it wasn't hurt or confusion or pain that hit her like a fist in the heart and stole her breath. It was fury. Red-hot, blazing fury.

He'd changed little over the course of the last month. Trim as ever in jeans and a green knit shirt that exactly matched his eyes, he looked tired and worried and incredibly attractive. Once, just being in the same room with him would have been enough to turn her knees to water. With his blond hair, chiseled face and boyish smile, he'd always been able to captivate her without saying a word. But not this time.

She should have greeted him and at least told him how sorry she was about his mother's illness, but she was too angry. Afraid that if she so much as opened her mouth, she'd blast him for treating her so badly, all she could manage was a curt nod.

Surprised, he stopped dead at the sight of her, and it was then that Merry realized he really hadn't expected to see her there. The blood drained out of his face, only to rush back into his cheeks with a painful flush. Hesitating, he had the look of a man who would rather be anywhere but where he was.

But he didn't, to his credit, bolt as she half expected. Instead, he seemed to mature right before her very eyes. He squared his shoulders, dragged in a deep breath, and faced her unflinchingly. "Hello, Merry. How are you?"

"Fine," she said stiffly. "Have you looked in on your mother? She's in room 305."

"I know. I just talked to her doctor and checked on her. Have you been here all night?"

To lie would have been pointless. "I didn't want her to be alone. Now that you're here, however, there's no reason to stay."

Her head up and her chin lifted proudly, she would have walked right past him but he quickly stepped in front of her and blocked her path. "Merry, please, don't be this way," he pleaded. "We need to talk. I've thought of you so much—"

She snorted before she could stop herself. "Oh, really? Isn't that interesting? You thought of me, but it never entered your head to pick up the phone to call me. You talked to Nick and your mother and God knows how many other people over the last month, but not me. Not the woman you asked to marry you. Not the woman you stood up at the altar."

"I can explain that," he said quickly, desperately. "I know I acted like a jerk and I handled everything badly, but I was scared. I never meant to hurt you. How could I? I love you!"

"Love me?!" she sputtered, her blue eyes sparking with fire. "How dare you! You don't know the meaning of the word."

"But I do! If you'll just listen—"

"I've heard all I intend to hear right now," she snapped. "Get out of my way, Thomas. I'm going home."

He wanted to argue, but the glare she leveled on him had him backing up in a hurry. "You're right. This isn't the time. You're tired and need to get some sleep. We can talk later."

Angrier than she had ever been in her life, she stormed out without saying a word, her only thought to get away. If Thomas was right about anything, it was that she did need to get some sleep, but she never thought to go home. The minute she climbed into her Explorer, she immediately headed for Nick's.

It was as instinctive as breathing, turning to him when she felt like the world was closing in on her, and she felt guilty about that. It was insensitive of her to go to him about Thomas now that she knew how he felt about her, but old habits were hard to break. They'd always been there for each other, always helped each other with whatever problems life threw their way, and she needed him. Surely, he would understand that.

His truck was in his driveway, just as she'd known it would be. His shift had ended at seven, but he'd no doubt had paperwork to do and had probably just gotten home. This wasn't, she knew, a good time to approach him. After working all night, he'd be tired and in need of sleep, and the last thing he'd want to do was talk to her about her relationship with Thomas.

And she couldn't blame him for that. *She* didn't want to talk about it, either. But she knew Thomas well enough to know that now that he'd faced her and decided *he* wanted to discuss the wedding that hadn't happened, he wasn't going to let her put him off for long. Once he was assured his mother was going to be all right and he'd given her time to calm down, he'd come looking for her, and Merry didn't have a clue what she was going to say to him.

Which was why she had to talk to Nick, dammit! No one was more levelheaded than he was in a crisis, and this definitely qualified as a crisis. He would help her, she told herself as she parked behind his truck and cut the engine. He had to.

She was the last person he expected to find on his doorstep. After she'd run out of his office the way she had, then spent the last few days avoiding him, he'd thought he'd pretty much destroyed their friendship. Yet here she was, standing at his front door with her chin raised defiantly and her eyes glinting with determination. In all the years that he'd known her, she'd never looked prettier, and as usual, his body responded to the sight of her.

Silently swallowing a curse, he stiffened. He didn't know what she wanted, but a voice in his head warned him that if he was smart, he'd send her packing. He was dead on his feet, his defenses down, and she looked too damn good. If she gave him the slightest opening, he was going to do something stupid—like reach for her—and that could only lead to disaster.

But instead of standing his ground and coming up with some excuse to shut the door in her pretty face, he found himself stepping back and inviting her inside. "You look tired. Have you been at the hospital all this time?"

"If it had been my mother, I would have wanted someone with her until I could get there," she said as she stepped inside. "Once Thomas arrived, I left."

"So you saw him."

It wasn't a question, but a flat statement of fact, and just that easily, he knew why she'd come knocking at his door. She was upset and needed someone to talk to. And deep down inside, that hurt. Didn't she realize what it did to him when she talked about Thomas? He loved her, dammit! And she loved another man. Knowing that ate at him like a cancer. Couldn't she see that?

He almost told her then that he didn't want to hear whatever she had to say. He couldn't take it anymore. But the time he had left with her was limited now that he'd set the wheels in motion to leave town. If this was all he could have with her, he was going to take it.

"He wanted to talk," she said furiously. "Can you believe it? The nerve of the man! He disappears off the face of the earth for a month—a whole damn month!—and now suddenly, he needs to explain why he couldn't marry me." Preceding Nick into the living room, she snorted in disdain. "As if I need to have things spelled out to me. When a man jilts a woman, what other explanation can there be? He obviously doesn't love her."

Arching a brow at her, Nick said the last thing he ever expected to hear himself say. "Are you sure about that?"

"Sure about what?"

"Are you sure he doesn't love you?"

Stunned, Merry couldn't believe she'd heard him correctly. "This is a joke, right?"

His expression grim, he met her gaze somberly. "Trust me, I don't find anything about you and Thomas funny. If

I'd have had my way, he'd have never laid eyes on you again.''

With just a look, he reminded her about the conversation in his office and how he felt about her. Her heart suddenly thudding crazily, Merry quickly steered the conversation back to safer waters. ''He hurt me, Nick. And betrayed me. Why should I listen to anything he has to say?''

''Because you *are* hurting,'' he said simply. ''And so is Thomas. Granted, he caused all this with his stupidity, but don't kid yourself into thinking he hasn't suffered for it. He has. And you'll both keep suffering until you find a way to get past this and go on with your life. I think the only way you can do that is to talk to him and air out your feelings.''

If her mother had said such a thing, Merry would have agreed that it was sound advice. But this was Nick. And after knowing him for a lifetime, she suddenly felt like she didn't know him at all. He'd claimed that he'd stayed in town all these years because of her, yet now he was encouraging her to not only talk to Thomas, but to make peace. Didn't he realize that if she did that, she might be opening the door for Thomas to come back into her life? Is that what he wanted?

More confused than ever, she rubbed at the headache that was suddenly pounding in her temple. ''I'll think about it. Later. After I get some sleep. Nothing's making sense right now.''

Feeling like she was going to cry and not knowing why, she thanked him for his help and beat a hasty retreat. She was just tired, she told herself as she headed for home. She'd feel better after she got some rest.

But although she went to bed the second she got home and immediately fell into an exhausted sleep, there was nothing the least bit restful about her dreams. With her defenses down, she was helpless to control the images of Nick and Thomas that flickered through her mind. They tugged and pulled at her heart, then turned and walked away in opposite directions, leaving her all alone and not knowing which way to turn. Crying out, she ran first after Thomas, then Nick, and couldn't catch either one of them. And they didn't seem to care.

She woke up with tears streaming down her face and pain lancing her heart. More confused than ever, she knew she needed to call Thomas, just as Nick had suggested, if she was ever going to get past the hurt that held her in its grip, but she couldn't. Not yet. She wasn't ready for that. She knew Thomas too well. He'd been charming his way out of tight spots for as long as she'd known him, and there'd been a time when that had endeared him to her. But not now. If he flashed that boyish smile of his at her and tried to convince her he loved her with all his heart, she just didn't think she could take it.

So she spent the rest of the day working and thinking of her future and where Thomas and Nick fit into her life. But when she closed her clinic at six, she was no closer to having the answers she needed than she had been when she'd started.

Dejected, unwilling to face the all-consuming silence of another evening alone, she decided to go into town for supper at Ed's. It was meat loaf night, and not even her mother could make meat loaf and scalloped potatoes like Ed. With a slice of chocolate pie for dessert, she'd feel a lot better.

It wasn't until she pulled into the parking lot next to the diner that she realized she probably should have stayed home and eaten leftovers. She wasn't the only one who liked Ed's meat loaf. Through the plate glass windows that stretched the length of the building, she could see that the place was packed. Every booth was taken, and a crowd was bunched up just inside the door, waiting for a table.

Tempted in spite of that, she considered staking out a place at the end of the line, but she knew what would happen if she did. By now, the word had gotten out that Thomas was back in town. The second she stepped inside, people would start asking her if she'd seen him, if they'd made up, if there was a possibility that they were getting back together. And that was a discussion she didn't want to have tonight.

Disappointed—she really wanted meat loaf, dammit!— she started to back out of the parking lot when she spied Nick sitting alone at the last booth near the windows and remembered he was as fond of Ed's meat loaf as she was. Once, she would have joined him without questioning whether she'd be welcome or not. Now that wasn't the case. Gnawing her bottom lip, she hesitated, and that was when he looked up and saw her. For just a second, she thought he was going to nod and turn his attention back to the blue plate special Ed, himself, delivered to his table, but he must have thought better of it. He said something to Ed, and with a sharp move of his hand, the older man was motioning her inside and past the crowd at the door.

A former prison cook who was still hard and rough around the edges, Ed had always had a soft spot for Merry and he didn't care who knew it. His grin crooked as he watched her make her way toward where he still stood at Nick's booth, he teased, "And just what the Sam Hill do you think you were doing? I saw you. You were leaving!"

She couldn't help but laugh. "I forgot how crowded you'd be tonight."

"I'm never too crowded for you. Anyway, didn't you see Nick? You know you never have to wait when he's here. Isn't that right, Nick?"

He didn't hesitate as she had feared, but nodded. "That's right, Ed. Bring Merry the special, will you? That is what you're having, isn't it?" he asked, arching a brow at her. "The meat loaf?"

He knew her too well. "And iced tea," she added as Ed headed for the kitchen. Sliding into the seat across from Nick, she said, "We can talk about pie later."

His brown eyes starting to twinkle, he chuckled. "I don't know who you think you're fooling, Mer. Everybody in town knows you've got a sweet tooth that could keep Hershey's in business. I'll bet Ed cut your pie the second he stepped into the kitchen."

"He did not!"

"Wanna make a bet?"

They grinned at each other, the familiar line a challenge right out of their childhood, and were totally oblivious to what was going on around them...until Thomas suddenly slid onto the booth seat next to Merry. "I figured I'd find you two here," he said with a flash of his dimples when she gasped. "It's meat loaf night, isn't it? I don't know how you two eat that stuff."

"Some of us like it," Merry said stiffly, glaring at him. "What are you doing here, Thomas? You should be at the hospital with your mother. What do you want?"

"Hey," he said, managing to look wounded, "Mother's doing much better. And since when did I have to have an excuse to be with my two favorite people in the world?"

"Since you left me standing at the altar," she snapped. "That's not how you treat someone you claim to love. Or at least, it's not how *I* treat people I care about. *I* actually showed up at the church, which is more than can be said for someone else at this table."

She had him beaten with just a few words, and he knew it. His smile tight, he turned to Nick for help. "C'mon, man, don't just sit there. I'm getting my ass kicked here. Help me. You know I love her. Tell her.''

''Tell her yourself,'' Nick growled, glaring at him with hostile eyes. ''For your information, you're not the only one who loves her. I do, too. And if you think I'm going to help you win her back, you're crazy.''

Chapter 7

Merry hardly slept at all that night. Every time she closed her eyes, she could see Thomas grinning at Nick and asking him to help him win her back. Oooh! The nerve of the man! she thought furiously as she finally gave up all pretense of sleeping and rolled out of bed to do some housework before she got dressed for work. Did he really think it was going to be that easy? That all he had to do was just waltz back into town, flash his pearly whites at her, and she was going to fall into his arms? She didn't think so! Not after what he'd done to her.

Fuming, so agitated she couldn't sit still, she cleaned the house from top to bottom before seven in the morning and found little satisfaction in the task. Damn him! How could she have ever thought she loved a man who was so insensitive? Last night at Ed's, when he'd finally realized that he wasn't going to be able to charm either her or Nick, he'd looked genuinely hurt. As if *he* were the injured party and he couldn't for the life of him understand why they would want to hurt him!

And she'd almost bought into his act! .

And that, more than anything, was what had kept her tossing and turning throughout the night. How could she be so gullible where he was concerned? She, more than anyone, knew just how little he could be trusted to be honest about his feelings, yet for a moment there, when he'd rose from the booth and looked down on her and Nick with wounded, puppy-dog eyes, she'd felt like a heel. He'd apologized for bothering them, then stalked out, stiffly clinging to his dignity, and she'd almost called him back. She had to be out of her mind!

She would *not* let him take her in a second time, she promised herself grimly. And she didn't fool herself into thinking that he wouldn't try again. She'd seen the irritation that had flashed in his eyes when he'd realized that not only was Nick not going to help him patch things up with her this time, but that he was also interested in her himself, and he hadn't liked it one little bit. Despite his injured air, Thomas had no intention of backing off and giving Nick a clear field. He'd just pulled back to regroup and rethink his strategy on how to win her back. He'd try something else, and when he did, she planned to be ready for him.

Relieved that she was finally seeing him for what he really was, she promised herself she wasn't going to let him disrupt her life any more than he already had. She had work to do and she couldn't afford to be distracted. The rabies inoculation plan was in high gear, and she was pleased with the response she'd gotten from the community, but there was still a lot to be done. She had to contact the schools to set up a meeting with students to educate them about the dangers of rabies, then she was going to make house calls to the elderly pet owners she knew who weren't able to bring in their cats and dogs to be vaccinated. By the end of the week, she hoped to have at least eighty percent of the pets in the county protected against rabies. And to do that, she was going to have to hustle— which meant she didn't have time to worry about Thomas.

Dismissing him from her thoughts, she took a bath and dressed for work, then made sure she had everything she needed for the house calls she needed to make. Satisfied that she wouldn't run out of vaccine when she was halfway across the county, she had just dug her keys out of her purse and was on her way out the front door when a van bearing the logo of Ryan's Flowers pulled up in her drive.

Surprised, she greeted the delivery boy, Rebecca Ryan's son, with a smile. "Hi, Jimmy. Are you sure you've got the right house? I can't imagine who would be sending me flowers."

"Oh, no, it's no mistake, Ms. McBride," he said with a broad grin. "Mom said to get these to you first thing because it was a special order. She said they were your favorite." And sliding open the door to the van, he pulled out a bouquet of gardenias and white roses.

They were absolutely beautiful, and Merry couldn't deny that they had once been her favorite. But not anymore. Not since she'd held a bouquet of them at her wedding and waited for a groom who had never put in an appearance. Just the scent of them was enough to make her sick to her stomach.

That, however, wasn't Jimmy's fault, and with a tight smile, she took the bouquet from him. "Could you hang on just a minute, Jimmy, while I read the card?" she said when he waited expectantly for a tip. "I want to give you something for driving all the way out here and I may need you to do a favor for me, if you don't mind."

"Sure, Ms. McBride. I'm in no hurry."

Setting the arrangement on the library table in the entrance hall, Merry pulled the small card from the envelope. Just as she'd expected, the signature at the bottom was Thomas's. But it was the words he'd written above his name that had her seeing red.

Forgive me. I love you more than life itself and will never again do anything to hurt you. Please have dinner with me and let me make this up to you.

Did he really think it was that easy? That he could just send her flowers and an apology, then take her out to dinner and all would be forgotten and forgiven? He'd soon find out differently.

Crumbling the card, she tossed it on the table, then grabbed the flowers and shoved them back at a surprised Jimmy. "Take these to the hospital and deliver them to Mrs. Maxine Cooper's room, okay? She'll love them."

Confused, he frowned. "But they're for you. Don't you like them?"

"They're beautiful," she assured him, slipping a five-dollar bill into his shirt pocket. "But Mrs. Cooper's going through a rough time right now and she needs them more than I do. If you could write a new card and just put, *To Mom. Get well soon. Your loving son, Thomas.* I would really appreciate it."

She could tell from the look on his face that he thought she was nuts, but he didn't argue with her. "Okay, Ms. McBride, if you're sure that's what you want. I'll take them to the hospital right now."

"Thanks, Jimmy. Oh, and by the way," she said as he turned back to the van, "let's just keep this between us, okay?"

"Sure thing, Ms. McBride. No problem."

"Thanks. Mrs. Cooper would be hurt if she found out her son didn't think to send her flowers."

Understanding, he drove off with a wave, and Merry let out a sigh of relief. Thomas wouldn't be pleased when he walked into his mother's hospital room and discovered what she'd done, but she didn't want flowers or anything else from him. In fact, all she wanted was for him to just leave her alone.

Surprisingly, that's just what he did. Work kept her tied up for most of the day, and it was late when she finally got home. Half expecting to find a dozen hurt messages on her answering machine from Thomas, she was stunned when she discovered that he hadn't called once while she was gone.

She knew he had to know about the flowers—he was a good son and would have spent as much time with Maxine as the hospital would allow. In fact, he'd probably been right there in her room this morning when Jimmy delivered the gardenias and roses he'd originally ordered for her. He wouldn't have been happy about that. She knew him, knew how his mind worked, and now that he'd decided he wanted her back, he wouldn't take her reception of his peace offering lying down. But he still hadn't called. And she had to ask herself why. What was he up to?

She found out the next morning when Janey called her before she was even out of bed. "Have you looked at this morning's paper?"

Groggy, her eyes not even open yet, Merry groaned, "Are you kidding? It's barely six in the morning, Janey! Right now, I can't even tell you what my name is."

"Then you'd better read the back page of the paper," she quipped cryptically. "If Thomas has his way, in the not too distant future, it's going to be Mrs. Thomas Cooper."

"What?!"

"Read the paper," she retorted, and hung up.

Dread spilling into her stomach, Merry rolled out of bed and fumbled for her robe. She was still buttoning it when she stumbled outside and climbed into her Explorer. Unlike city folks, her paper wasn't thrown in her front yard every morning, but placed in her mailbox instead by some poor soul who no doubt started making deliveries at four in the morning. And her mailbox was on the highway at the ranch entrance, a half a mile from her house.

The newspaper was stuffed into the box, just as she'd known it would be, and she didn't even have to get out of her truck to retrieve it. Her heart in her throat, she pulled it out and unfolded it so that the back page was up. In the bright light of the early morning sun, she found herself looking down at a picture of herself and Thomas that had been taken just three weeks before what should have been their wedding day. They were in each other's arms and laughing into the camera. They looked happy and in love and didn't appear to have a care in the world.

It was one of her favorite pictures, but she didn't smile as she usually did whenever she saw it. Instead, her eyes dropped to the words written below it in large print for all the world to see.

Merry,
You have every right to hate me. What I did was wrong and I wouldn't blame you if you never spoke to me again. I couldn't tell you I was scared, and because I was such a coward, you were the one who was humiliated. I know I can never make up for that by just saying I'm sorry, so I'm publicly promising you that I will do whatever I have to win back your love and approval. I love you and want you to be my wife. Please give me a chance.

Shocked, Merry stared down at the message that blurred before her eyes, unable to believe she'd read it correctly. There had to be a mistake. Thomas wouldn't do this to her. He'd made her the town laughingstock once before. He wouldn't do it again by airing details about their relationship to whoever could afford the price of a newspaper.

But even as she tried to convince herself that this was just someone's idea of a bad joke, she knew there was no mistake. Once again, in the interest of getting what he wanted and not giving a thought to how the consequences of his actions might affect her, Thomas had set her up to be the brunt of countless jokes. She could hear them now: *Did you hear about the youngest McBride girl? She picked a real winner for a fiancé. First he stood her up at their wedding, and now he's courting her in the papers and asking her to marry him again. What kind of idiot would trust a man like that a second time? She must be really desperate to get married.*

She would kill him, she thought, fuming. She'd string him up by his ears and kill him!

It was barely seven in the morning when Merry pulled up before Maxine Cooper's house and cut the engine. Located two doors down from Myrtle Henderson and right in the middle of town, the house was contemporary in style and not the type of architecture Merry cared for. But Thomas had grown up there, and since he'd given up his apartment the week they'd planned to marry, he was, not surprisingly, staying there while his mother was in the hospital.

After Janey had called her, she'd changed into jeans and a T-shirt and had time to calm down during the drive into town, but one glance at the newspaper on the seat beside her, and she was steaming all over again. He wasn't, she promised herself furiously, going to get away with this. Clutching the paper in her fist, she stepped out of her truck and marched up to the front door.

In spite of the earliness of the hour, she knew he wasn't asleep. He was a morning person, just like she was, and had no doubt been up for hours. Punching the doorbell, she just dared him to keep her waiting. In the mood she was in, she wouldn't be responsible for her actions.

Just as she'd suspected, he was not only awake but dressed and shaved and thrilled to see her. ''Merry! This is a surprise! I wasn't expecting you this early.'' Beaming at the sight of her, he pulled the door open wider. ''Come in. I just brewed a pot of coffee and heated up some of Mother's banana bread. Would you like some?''

Manners dictated that she accept, but her instincts warned her that would be a drastic mistake. This wasn't a social visit. She was here for one reason and only one reason—to make him understand that she wasn't going to be courted, coerced, charmed or strong-armed into resuming their relationship. And the sooner he accepted that, the better.

''I'm not here for breakfast,'' she said stiffly as she stepped inside. ''We need to talk about *this.*''

Far from concerned when she waved the newspaper under his nose, he only grinned, thoroughly pleased with himself. ''You didn't accept my flowers so I had to do something else to get your attention. Were you surprised? I knew you would be. And it only cost me fifty bucks! Can you believe that? Talk about a steal! I bet I couldn't do that in Chicago for five times that amount.''

He rattled on about what a good deal he'd gotten, and Merry could only stare at him. Had she ever known this man? Ever understood who he was deep down inside? She was beginning to wonder.

"You just don't get it, do you?" she said, cutting in when he paused to take a breath. "I sent the flowers to your mother because I didn't want them. I don't want anything from you—"

"Oh, you don't mean that. You're just playing hard to get."

He was so cocky, so sure of himself, that it was all she could do not to throw the paper she still held right at his head. Why had she never noticed before how infuriatingly arrogant he could be? Seething, she dragged in a calming breath and tried to hold on to her temper, but it didn't help. Nothing did.

Narrowing her eyes at him, she said coldly, "Look at me, Thomas. Do I look like I'm playing hard to get?"

A blind man could have seen that she was deadly serious. His smile faltering, he lost a little of his cockiness, along with his tan. "No, of course you don't. I'm sorry. I don't know why I said that. I just love you so much—"

She stopped him before he could go any further. "If you loved me, you wouldn't have left me at the church and made it nearly impossible for me to face my friends and family. If you loved me, you wouldn't have humiliated me all over again with this," she said, pointedly holding up the newspaper. "If you really loved me, you'd leave me alone. Because that's all I want from you right now…to be left alone. After everything you've done to me, I don't think that's too much to ask."

She'd never been more serious in her life, and something in her eyes must have told him that he wasn't going to charm his way out of this one. And for the first time, he seemed to realize he was in real danger of losing her. Dropping any pretense of cheerfulness, he said humbly, "You're right. I apologize. I wasn't thinking. I'll do whatever you want. If you want me to back off and give you some space, you've got it.''

"What I want is no more gifts, Thomas. No more surprises, I mean it.''

"Whatever you say," he promised. "I just want you to be happy.''

If he'd truly wanted that for her, he'd have showed up at the church last month, she thought resentfully, but she kept that thought to herself. "Fine," she said stiffly. "As long as we understand each other. Now, if you'll excuse me, I've got to get to work.''

He opened his mouth to argue, only to think better of it when she shot him a warning look that had *Watch it!* written all over it. Holding his hands up before her like a man being held at gunpoint, he said, "Hey, don't let me get in your way. I've got to get to the hospital to check on Mother, anyway. I'll catch up with you later, okay?''

Frustrated, Merry wanted to shake him. What did it take to get through to him? She knew he wasn't so dense that he hadn't understood what she was saying. He was just playing games with her, pushing her buttons, and trying to get past her guard when she wasn't looking. And it wasn't going to happen. He wasn't catching up with her later or any other time.

"I don't think so," she said stiffly. "I plan to be on the run most of the day.''

Not giving him a chance to ask her where she would be, she hurried out before he could question her further, her only thought to get away. Men! she thought in exasperation. Why had she ever thought she needed one to call her own?

Still irritated, she left town behind and headed toward Wild Horse Canyon. It was a rough, remote area, but a number of people lived back in the hills, including Lester Allison. Ninety-eight if he was a day, Lester had stubbornly refused to go into a nursing home after his wife died, choosing instead to stay in the home he and Isabelle had shared for fifty-three years. Alone except for the five or six cats that kept him company on the property, he hadn't been into town in years. Neighbors brought him groceries, and whenever he wasn't feeling well, his doctor made a trip out to his place to see him. Even if he would have been capable of bringing his cats in for their shots, Merry doubted that he would have been able to catch them. From what she had heard, they were wild as March hares.

Her thoughts focused on how she was going to catch them, she didn't see the board lying in the road until it was too late. She instinctively tried to swerve, only to run over it anyway. Cursing herself, she immediately heard her right front tire blow as the nails that had been standing straight up in the board sank deep.

"Damn!"

Struggling to hang on to the wheel as it jerked under her hands, she lifted her foot from the accelerator and carefully eased her Explorer off the road and onto the shoulder. It wasn't until she came to a complete stop and turned off the ignition that she realized that she couldn't have picked a worse spot for a flat. Stuck on the side of a steep hill, she was perched on a whisper of a shoulder that fell sharply away to her right. The vehicle was already leaning—if she so much as shifted her weight wrong, she was afraid it would roll.

"Great, Merry," she muttered as she carefully set the emergency break. "This is just great!" Glancing out the passenger window, she felt her stomach clench sickeningly at the idea of trying to set up a jack on ground that slanted downhill at a forty-five degree angle. How was she going to do this?

"Block the tires," she said aloud. Joe and Zeke had drilled that into both her and Janey's heads from the time they were both old enough to sit behind the wheel. She might not be able to do anything to prevent the car from flipping if it chose to do so because of the uneven ground, but at least it wouldn't be able to roll back over her.

Suddenly realizing how absurd that thought was, she laid her head against the steering wheel and laughed helplessly. God, she was losing it. The car might roll all the way down the mountain the second she got out of it, and she was worried about getting run over! She had to have a screw loose. If she really wanted to worry about something, she should be worrying about how she was going to get out of this mess without help. She could call one of her brothers, but she really hated to do that. She'd always taken pride in the fact that she was self-sufficient, and she'd feel like a real sissy if she had to call someone just to change a simple flat.

She could do this, she told herself as she carefully pushed open the driver's door. All she had to do was take it slow and easy and not take any chances.

In theory, that sounded good, but as she eased from the truck to the ground, she found herself holding her breath. It wasn't until both feet were on the ground and she saw just how precariously the Explorer clung to the side of the mountain that her heart started to slam against her ribs. If she'd been going any faster when she hit that board in the road, she would have had a much more serious problem than just a flat tire. She could have lost control and gone careering down the mountain into the trees and killed herself.

Shaken, she removed the jack and spare from the truck

and had just blocked both back tires with rocks when another car approached from the south. Surprised—Wild
Horse Canyon was a remote area and there was little traffic
in and out of it—she turned in time to see Nick pull up
behind her and park with the lights on his light bar spinning. Anyone approaching from either direction would see
the lights and hopefully slow down as they passed.

She hadn't seen him since that evening at the diner, when
he'd told Thomas he wouldn't help him win her back because he was in love with her himself, and she'd secretly
thought it was for the best. She didn't know how to act
around him anymore, didn't know what to say. There was
an awkwardness between them that hadn't been there before and she didn't know how to deal with it.

But as he walked toward her with that deceptively lazy
gait of his, his long legs quickly eliminating the distance
between them, she realized just how much she'd missed
him. She didn't know if she'd ever be comfortable with his
feelings for her, but at least he was still in her life. Right
now, nothing else mattered.

"You always seem to show up when I need you," she
said with a smile, and it was nothing less than the truth.
They'd always had a sixth sense where each other was concerned. "How'd you know I was in trouble?"

"I didn't," he replied. "I was on my way over to Eth-
elda Dickerson's place—her cat's stuck on the roof and she
can't get him down—and just decided to drive through the
canyon instead of taking the interstate." Joining her at the
front of the car, he scowled down at the ruined front tire
on the passenger side. Flat as a pancake, it had thrown
rubber and would obviously never hold air again. "How'd
you do that?"

"I hit a board," she said with a grimace. "I know—I

should have seen it, but I was thinking instead of paying attention to my driving and was on it before I saw it."

"It could have been worse," he reassured her. "You could have thrown the board up into the motor and caused some serious trouble. Let's see about getting that jack set up." Squatting down to examine the ground where the jack needed to be assembled, he brushed gravel and loose dirt away and didn't like what he saw. "We're going to need a pretty good size rock to stabilize it. Something flat to level out the ground."

"There's one down here," she said, making her way carefully down the hill. "I saw it when I was looking for something to block the wheels."

She hadn't used it because it was too flat to effectively block anything, but it was just what they needed to set the jack on. Together, they moved it up the hill and into position, then Nick set the jack up.

Merry could have changed the flat herself and Nick knew it, but he enjoyed doing things for her when he could. So while she watched, he quickly loosened the lug nuts, exchanged the spare for the flat, and had the job finished in less than ten minutes. Only then did he realize that he should have taken longer so he'd have more time to spend with her.

Silently cursing his stupidity, he placed everything in the back of her Explorer and dusted off his hands. "There you go," he said as he wiped his hands on his handkerchief. "You want me to follow you back into town to make sure you don't have any more trouble?"

She hesitated, then shook her head. "No, that's okay. But thanks anyway. Mrs. Dickerson's probably already called the station a dozen times wondering where you are, and I need to get out to Lester Allison's place and vaccinate his cats."

He didn't like the idea of her driving around in such a remote area without a spare, but she was a grown woman, and an independent one, at that. She didn't need him telling her what to do. "All right. Call me on my mobile if you need me."

She had the number, so he expected her to head on out to the Allison place, but she just stood there, staring at him in puzzlement as if she'd never seen him before. Amused, he snapped his fingers in front of her nose. "Hello? Is anybody home? What's going on, Mer?"

Heat climbed into her cheeks, but she didn't look away. "Were you serious when you said you were in love with me?"

That was the last thing he expected from her. Since he'd told her how he felt, she'd gone out of her way to avoid him; and whenever she hadn't been able to do that, she'd acted as if that particular conversation had never happened. He knew she needed time to deal with the change in their relationship, but still, that had hurt.

"That's not something I would joke about," he said gruffly, his eyes searching hers. "Why do you ask?"

For a moment, he didn't think she was going to be able to answer him. She hesitated, only to blurt out, "It's just that you never show it like Thomas does, and I was wondering why."

The second the words were out of her mouth, Merry wanted to take them back. What in the world was she doing? Encouraging him to…to…what?

Unable to admit even to herself what she was asking for, she quickly took a step back. "Forget I said that. I don't know what got into me. I guess I'm just confused. Everything's so topsy-turvy right now. I think I must have been standing in the sun too long. I've got to go. Thanks for helping me with the flat—"

She should have known he wouldn't let her off the hook that easily. She turned back toward her truck, but before she'd taken two steps, he was there in front of her, blocking her path, his brown eyes glinting with frustration. "Don't think for a second that you're going to walk away after saying something like that," he growled. "You brought this up. Let's finish it."

"That's not necessary—"

"Oh, yes it is," he said silkily. "So you want me to be more like Thomas, do you? And how should I do that, Mer? By leaving you at the altar in front of the whole town? Or would you rather I make a commitment to you, then just walk out like it never happened? Is that what you want?"

Heat climbed into her cheeks. "No, of course not!"

"I know how I feel," he said, reaching for her. "But if you need an example, I'll be happy to give you one." And with no more warning than that, he pulled her into his arms.

Stunned, she didn't have time to do anything but gasp before his mouth swooped down and covered hers, and then she couldn't think of anything but Nick. She'd known him all her life, laughed with him, played with him, grown up with him and always loved him as a friend. But not once in all that time had she ever kissed him or even imagined what it would be like to be held in his arms. All her attention had always been focused on Thomas, instead. And because of that, she never even suspected that Nick could kiss like the devil himself.

Her head swimming and her thoughts blurring, she felt her bones begin to dissolve and could no more resist the sudden unexpected hunger he stirred in her than the tides could resist the lure of the moon. Lost to everything but the taste and heat and wonder of him, she melted against him.

Later, she didn't know how long the madness would

have lasted if the police radio in his patrol car hadn't crackled to life. In a daze, she suddenly realized she was standing on the side of the road in full view of anyone who chose to pass, kissing *Nick,* of all people, like there was no tomorrow! She had, she thought in growing horror, lost her mind!

Suddenly not sure of anything, least of all her own heart, she stumbled back out of his arms before he could stop her, panic urging her to run while she still could. "No!" she cried when he reached for her. "This is a mistake. I mean it, Nick! Just because I've broken things off with Thomas doesn't mean I'm looking for anyone else. I'm not. Please don't take this wrong, but after what he did to me, it'll be a long time—if ever—before I trust another man."

"I'm not Thomas," he retorted. "I would never hurt you."

She wanted to believe him, wanted to let down her guard, but she couldn't. The hurt was still too fresh, the wounds inflicted to her heart too raw. Her eyes blurring with tears, she choked, "I'm sorry. But I can't do this. Please…let's just forget this. We both have work to do."

Wiping her cheeks, she moved to step around him, and he let her go. Another man might have been discouraged when she drove away like she couldn't get away from him fast enough, but Nick stood in the middle of the road grinning like an idiot. God, she'd felt good in his arms! Even better than he'd dared let himself hope all these years. And he'd kissed her! He'd lost count of the number of times he'd fantasized about that, but nothing he'd ever imagined could have lived up to reality. And she hadn't pushed him away, at least not initially, and for no other reason than that, he felt encouraged. She might claim she didn't want another man in her life, but she wasn't immune to him. And that, at least, was a start.

* * *

Every year, the McBrides threw a birthday party and barbecue for Sara McBride's birthday and invited the whole county. Usually, it was an event Nick wouldn't have missed—Sara was like a second mother to him and he loved her dearly—but this year, he seriously considered not attending because of Merry. He didn't want to pressure her too much too soon, and it had only been two days since he'd kissed her. Now that she finally saw him as a man who was attracted to her and not just a friend, the last thing he wanted to do was scare her off.

But he hadn't seen or talked to her since he'd kissed her, though he hadn't needed to keep tabs on what was going on in her life. Everywhere he went, people were talking about Thomas and the different ways he was trying to win her back.

The gossips were thrilled—they thought Thomas's pursuit of Merry was the most romantic thing they'd ever heard of—but Nick knew that Thomas's grandiose gestures had nothing to do with love. Thomas never had liked to lose, and now that he knew Nick was interested in Merry, too, this was just a competition on his part. If he really loved Merry, he'd be grovelling at her feet for the way he'd humiliated her, begging her forgiveness, and trying to show her how he'd changed. Instead, he thought he could distract her with presents and public displays of affection so she'd forget what he'd done to her.

Merry wasn't that stupid, Nick assured himself. She knew Thomas as well as he did and wouldn't be taken in so easily. Nick could trust her to see their old friend for what he was. Still, he'd known Thomas would be at the party and would once again make a move on Merry. Nick knew she could take care of herself and more than handle Thomas, but every possessive instinct he had rebelled at the idea of leaving her there unprotected from the jerk's romantic shenanigans.

So at the last minute, he decided to go the party, which turned out to be a wise decision. As he made his way through the crowd on the back patio, it didn't take him long to find Merry. And Thomas. She was checking the bowls of food on the buffet table, making sure everything was set up to begin serving, and Thomas was right at her side, just as Nick had expected, hovering close and pretending to help while he joked and flirted with her.

Fury burned in Nick's gut at the sight of him standing so close that his shoulder actually brushed Merry's. To anyone else watching, she appeared to be enjoying herself, but Nick knew her better than most. Even from a distance, he could see the tightness of her smile and the irritation that set her blue eyes snapping. And in spite of his anger with Thomas, Nick couldn't help but grin. She was ticked off, and Thomas was too damn cocky to see it. If he didn't back off, he'd be lucky if she didn't serve him his head on a platter.

It was, however, her mother's birthday, Nick reminded himself, and she wouldn't want to cause a stink and ruin the party. So he'd do Thomas a favor and rescue his skinny neck—not because he gave a damn if Merry took him apart, but because she deserved to enjoy the party without having to worry about coming face to face with Thomas's mug every time she turned around.

Striding over to the buffet table, he ignored Thomas and said quietly, "I know you're busy, Mer, but I need to talk to you if you've got a minute. Do you think we could go out to the garden for a second?"

Relieved, Merry almost fell into his arms. "Yes, of course!" Turning to Thomas, she said, "Thanks for all your help, Thomas, but everything's ready. Would you find my mother for me and tell her we can eat whenever she's ready?''

"But I thought I'd go out to the garden with you and Nick," he whined.

"Sorry, buddy," Nick retorted and wasn't any such thing, "but this is official business. Why don't you go find Sara like the lady asked?" And without bothering to wait for his response, he took Merry's elbow and escorted her around him and out toward the rose garden at the side of the house.

Thomas had been so persistent that Merry half expected him to follow them, but something in the set of Nick's granite jaw must have convinced him that discretion really was the better part of valor. Resentment flashing in his eyes, he stormed off like a spoiled three-year-old, leaving her alone with Nick for the first time since he'd kissed her.

She'd thought of nothing else over the course of the last few days, dreamed of nothing else. And in spite of the fact that she couldn't help but feel awkward, she really was glad that he'd showed up for the party and come to her rescue. She had some things she needed to say to him, and they had to be said in private.

Reaching the garden, which emptied of guests when the dinner bell was rung, she turned and faced him like a sixteen-year-old facing her first beau. "Did you really have official business to discuss with me?"

Amused, he merely arched a brow at her. "What do you think?"

She laughed at how easily he'd outmaneuvered Thomas—it was no more than he deserved. "Thanks for the rescue. I tried every excuse I could think of to shake him, but he wasn't buying any of them."

"He always was tenacious as a bulldog. He doesn't give up easily."

"I know," she said as her smile faded. "I think that's why I could never see anyone but him. He was always so determined that I would be his. Not that I was completely blameless in all this," she quickly added. "I shouldn't have been so blind. I'm sorry about that," she said sincerely. "I never meant to hurt you. I just never realized that you looked at me that way. And when you did tell me how you felt, it scared the hell out of me. I was afraid if things changed between us, I would lose my best friend. After everything else that's happened, I don't think I could stand that."

She looked up at him with such worry in her eyes that it was all he could do not to take her into his arms in full view of everyone at the party. He understood her concerns and felt the same way—which was why he'd let years go by without telling her how he felt. He didn't want to lose her, either. But after that kiss in Wild Horse Canyon, he knew that wasn't going to happen.

"Nothing's going to put our friendship in danger," he assured her huskily. "Not if we don't let it. So let's make a pact. If you think we're in trouble, you tell me and I'll do the same, and we'll do whatever we have to to set things right. Okay? Have we got a deal?"

He could see the doubts reflected in her eyes, but she wanted to believe as much as he did that nothing could ever shake their friendship. Her smile misty, she took the hand he held out to her and shook it firmly. "Deal."

Chapter 8

Nothing has to change. We're the same as we've always been.

Over the course of the next few days, Merry clung to Nick's words at all hours of the day and night, whenever doubts hit her and she felt like she was losing control of her life. There were times when she actually convinced herself that he was right. After all, nothing really *had* changed. Nick had apparently loved her for years—she just hadn't known it. Now she did. That didn't mean life as she knew it was any different than it had ever been.

Nothing, however, was that simple. If she needed proof of that, she got it Wednesday night when she walked into Tiny's Pool Hall. She and a crowd of her friends met there every Wednesday night for the weekly pool tournament. It wasn't usually a serious competition but more of an excuse to get together, have some fun, and catch up on each other's lives. There was nothing structured or formal about it, no invitations or even calls to remind each other to come.

They'd all been doing it for years, and those who could make it, did. Those who couldn't, came whenever they could.

Unless Nick pulled the three to eleven shift at work, he was almost always there, and this time was no different. Merry saw him the second she walked through the door. Normally, she would have grinned and waved, then grabbed a drink before joining him and the others at their table, but not tonight. From across the room, his eyes met hers, and something in her heart seemed to shift. All around her, people were laughing and talking and she couldn't see anybody but Nick.

Why hadn't she ever noticed before how attractive he was? Oh, she'd always known he was good looking, but she couldn't ever remember noticing just how tall he was or how the corners of his eyes crinkled when he smiled. He had a sense of strength about him that was incredibly appealing, a quiet self-confidence that any woman with eyes in her head would find hard to resist. And a quick glance around the pool hall told her she wasn't the only one who'd noticed. More than a few of the ladies in the crowd were openly looking him over, and they all appeared to like what they saw. And he didn't see anyone but her.

The touch of his eyes was an almost physical caress, and without quite knowing how it happened, she was suddenly breathless. Flushing, she tried to look away, but she couldn't. Memories flashed between them…the touch of his hands on her, the wet heat of his mouth as he'd kissed her, the feel of his arms banded around her, holding her tight…and try though she might to ignore the sensations he stirred in her, all she could think of was that she wanted him to kiss her again. Right here. Right now.

Shocked, she stiffened and turned quickly away to the bar, desperately praying that he couldn't read her thoughts in her eyes. What in the world was wrong with her? she thought wildly. It hadn't been all that long ago that she'd been prepared to promise before God and her family and friends that she would love and honor Thomas all the days of her life. And now, just a little over a month later, she was already thinking about another man. And not just any man, but Nick, for heaven's sake! All because of a simple, innocent kiss.

There was nothing simple about that kiss and you know it, Merideth Sara McBride! a voice in her head retorted sternly. *If you want to pretend to Nick that you were un-affected so you can protect your heart, that's one thing, but don't you dare lie to yourself. If you'd been more honest with yourself about the kind of man Thomas was, instead of insisting on seeing him as the kind of man you wanted him to be, you'd have saved yourself a lot of heartache.*

Unable to deny the truth of that, she had no choice but to admit to herself that there'd been nothing innocent about the kiss she and Nick had shared. He'd rocked her world, and try though she might, she couldn't forget it. Or him. Without quite knowing how it had happened, he'd taken control of her every waking thought, and for the life of her, she didn't know what to do about it.

"Hey, there you are!" Stella spied her then and gave her a bear hug. "Where have you been? I stopped by the clinic a couple of times to see you, but you were always gone." Pulling back, she studied her worriedly. "Are you okay? The whole town's talking about Thomas and how he's try-ing to buy you back with flowers and pearls and fancy necklaces. You're not falling for that malarkey, are you? Because if you are, somebody needs to shake some sense into you, and I'm just the one to do it!"

Merry had to laugh. Stella had never had any trouble speaking her mind. The family usually ran for cover when they saw her coming, but Merry admired her honesty. You always knew where you stood with Stella. "I haven't seen any pearls or necklaces yet, but he did send me a bouquet just like the one I had for the wedding."

Outraged, Stella gasped, "Why, that insensitive clod! I hope you sent it back to him in pieces!"

"Well, actually, I sent it to his mother at the hospital," she admitted. "He wasn't too pleased."

"So tell him to get in line. You weren't too thrilled with him when he cut out on you at the wedding, either. The worm. I half expected him to be here tonight."

Merry had, too. Before Thomas had jilted her and run back to Chicago, he'd seldom missed a Wednesday night at Tiny's. He was a crackerjack pool player—but not as good as Nick. And that had always eaten at him. He'd never liked to lose, and every time Nick had walked in the door, Thomas had challenged him. And that was when he and Nick had been friends. He had even more reason to challenge him now.

But there was no sign of him, and Merry was glad of it. She just wanted a nice peaceful evening with no hassles. "He's probably at the hospital with his mother. I thought she'd be home by now, but apparently she's had a setback."

"Yeah, and it's named Thomas," Stella retorted, then had the grace to blush when Merry gave her a reproving look. "Okay, so that was tacky. I don't like him. I always thought he was spoiled and thoughtless and not good enough for you, and he proved me right. Now that I've said my piece, how about a game of eight-ball? I'll spot you five."

Anyone else would have been insulted by such a suggestion, but Merry knew her limits. She was notoriously bad at pool and seldom made a game of it if she was spotted less. "Five, huh?" she considered, grinning. "You're on."

Merry couldn't remember the last time she'd had such a good time. She actually beat Stella at eight-ball, then had the satisfaction of at least holding her own with Nick when he challenged her. She'd been afraid that he would somehow treat her differently in front of their friends now that he'd kissed her, but he was the same old Nick he'd always been. He teased her, but he teased all the women in the group, just as he always did, and no one seemed to notice anything out of the ordinary between them.

But he was as aware of her as she was of him, and without saying a word, they flirted with each other with their eyes, sending silent messages back and forth that no one but they could see. And she loved it. She'd never played that kind of game with him before, and she felt like she was sixteen again. She wanted to laugh, to flirt, to tempt him to do something outrageous, and part of the fun was that no one else knew. They were playing with fire and enjoying every second of it. She'd never had so much fun in her life.

Totally absorbed in each other, neither of them saw Thomas walk in. But Stella had eyes like a hawk and immediately stiffened. "Uh-oh, here comes trouble," she mumbled. "Damn! And we were having such a good time."

Alarmed, Merry lifted her head like a deer scenting danger and spied Thomas immediately. Already weaving through the crowd toward them, he looked like he'd had a rough day. His hair was mussed, his face unshaven, his cheeks flushed. But it was the belligerent set of his jaw and the unsteady way he walked that had dread spilling into her gut. Thomas didn't drink very often and seldom got drunk, but when he did, he almost always wanted to fight.

"He's been drinking," she told Nick quietly.

"If he thinks he's going to start a fight in here, he can think again," Nick said grimly as he handed her his pool cue. "Stay here. I'll handle this."

Merry would have liked nothing better than to stand back and play the helpless female to Nick's John Wayne, but she couldn't. That wasn't who she was. She didn't run from trouble, especially trouble that she felt partly responsible for. Thomas wouldn't be spoiling for a fight right now with Nick, who'd been his best friend for decades, if it hadn't been for her. So without a word, she handed both her pool cue and Nick's to Stella, and pushed her way through the crowd that was already starting to gather around Thomas and Nick.

"You backstabbing son of a bitch! You turned Merry against me."

"I didn't have to," Nick said quietly as someone pulled the plug on the jukebox and the entire pool hall went silent as a tomb. "You did that all by yourself. Now, why don't we take this outside—"

"The hell I will! I'm not going anywhere, damn you! *You* did this. You sweet-talked her and ran me down behind my back, and now you're trying to say it's *my* fault?! Some friend you are. I ought to beat the hell out of you—"

Fury transforming his face into that of a man Merry didn't recognize, he took a threatening step toward Nick, but that was as far as he got. Under the best of conditions, he had a tough time holding his own with Nick physically. Drunk, he didn't stand a chance. Before he could so much as blink, Nick grabbed him, spun him around and shoved his arm up between his shoulder blades. Helpless, Thomas could do nothing but stand there, cursing like a sailor.

Nick, to his credit, kept his temper under control. His jaw like granite, he leaned close and growled in his ear, ''You're not going to beat the hell out of anyone. You hear me? You so much as make a move toward me or anyone else in here and you'll spend the rest of the night cooling your heels in jail. Do I make myself clear?'' When Thomas only glared at him, he shoved his arm a little higher up his back. ''What was that? I didn't hear you.''

Standing at the edge of the crowd, her heart in her throat, Merry wanted to kick Thomas when he stubbornly clamped his teeth shut, refusing to say a word. ''Damn you, Thomas, try not to be any more of an idiot than you already are!'' she snapped. ''You can't win this one. Give it up.''

For a minute, she actually thought he was going to make Nick arrest him. He hesitated, defiance obvious in every line of his stiff body, refusing to back down so much as an inch. Then, just when Nick started to pull out his handcuffs, he reluctantly admitted defeat. ''All right,'' he said grudgingly. ''I won't cause any trouble.''

Nick slowly released him, but he didn't drop his guard so much as an inch. ''I think it'd be better for everyone if you left,'' he said curtly. ''Tiny's not going to serve you any beer since you're already drunk, and you're not in the mood for a friendly game of pool. There's nothing here for you.''

He had enough friends in the crowd that if he'd showed the least sign of remorse, someone would have stepped forward and suggested they let bygones be bygones. But in the tense silence, no one said a word in Thomas's defense, and he had no one to blame but himself. He'd acted like a jerk.

Still, he wasn't giving up without saying what he'd come there to say. ''I'll leave—for now. But don't make the mistake of thinking I'm going to go back to Chicago and leave you a clear field with Merry,'' he told Nick. "She's mine. She always has been and always will be. You stay away from her.''

All around them, people gasped, but Nick didn't so much as blink. "Merry's her own person and doesn't belong to anyone but herself. The only way I'll stay away from her is if *she* tells me to, and she's not doing that.'' His point made by Merry's very silence, he nodded toward the door. "Go on and get out of here. You've worn out your welcome.''

Fury blazing in his eyes, he left, but only because he had no other choice. The hard look he shot Nick before he stormed out, however, warned him that he may have won this round, but the fight was far from over.

For what seemed like an eternity, no one moved after the door slammed behind him. Mortified, Merry just stood there, heat climbing in her cheeks as all eyes seemed to turn on her. Then just when she thought she couldn't bear the speculative looks another moment, someone had the foresight—or kindness—to plug the jukebox back in. A Faith Hill song flooded the pool hall, breaking the spell that had fallen over the crowd with Thomas's first angry words. People turned back to their dancing and drinks and pool as if nothing had ever happened.

"Are you all right?'' Nick asked quietly.

Flanked by him on one side and Stella on the other, Merry couldn't remember the last time she'd been so embarrassed. "Oh, yeah,'' she retorted sarcastically. "Other than needing a hole to crawl into, I'm just peachy-keen. Dammit, I can't believe he did that!''

"I can,'' Stella retorted. "His mother spoiled him rotten and taught him to believe that he was entitled to anything he wanted. Now he's decided he wants you again, and you're not cooperating, so he's acting like a jackass.''

"He never could stand to lose," Nick added grimly. "At checkers or football or women."

They were describing a man Merry hadn't suspected existed, a selfish, self-centered egomaniac who treated life like it was a game. And if he couldn't win, he was going to sulk and pout and act like a bratty toddler until you let him have his way. "So I'm just another game to him," she said, hurt. "Is that what you're saying? That he pursued me because he just didn't want anyone else to have me?"

The truth hit her then, and before Nick could so much as open his mouth, she answered her own question. "Of course he didn't. That's why he didn't marry me. My God, that's it!" she said, stunned. "I was the prize, the trophy that he thought he wanted badly enough to marry. But when push came to shove, he couldn't bring himself to go quite that far. He quit the game and went home, but now that someone else is showing an interest, he wants to play again."

All this time, she'd thought it was her he loved, but the only things he'd really loved was the thrill of the win. And the win became all the sweeter if you could pull it off when your competitor was someone you respected and feared.

"I feel like a fool," she said hollowly. "I should have seen this years ago."

"You loved him," Stella replied simply. "And you believed in him. Don't beat yourself up for that. But now that you can see him for what he really is, don't let him worm his way into your good graces and hurt you again, either. He doesn't love anyone as much as he loves himself, and he never will. As long as you remember that, you'll be okay."

"You don't have to worry," Merry assured her grimly. "That's not going to happen."

* * *

After the fiasco at Tiny's, Merry promised herself she was going to avoid Thomas at all cost, but in a town the size of Liberty Hill, that proved to be next to impossible. Word had gotten out about the fight he tried to start with Nick, and everywhere Merry went over the course of the next few days, people could talk of nothing else. Some thought it was daring and romantic, and more than a few wanted to know when she was going to put that boy out of his misery and take him back. Appalled at the idea of discussing her private life in public, she was left with no choice but to squash that rumor in the bud. That, she assured anyone who asked, was never going to happen.

But Thomas seemed to be one step ahead of her with the rumors and told anyone who cared to listen that it was only a matter of time before she forgave him and took him back. Frustrated, she called his mother's house to tell him to back off, but all she got was the answering machine. Then she ran into Becca Ryan at the grocery store and learned that Thomas had called her to discuss flowers for their second wedding. What was left of her patience snapped. She was not going to let him do this to her!

More angry than she could ever remember being, she stormed over to the hospital, determined to wait outside his mother's room all day if she had to until he showed up so she could give him a piece of her mind. But when she reached Maxine Cooper's room, Thomas was already inside talking to his mother.

"Can you believe he cheated like that, Mother? Just took advantage of the fact that I was in Chicago and moved in on Merry like she was fair game?"

Stopping short at the sound of her name, Merry quickly stepped back out of sight in the hall. She knew she should have announced her presence—she'd never eavesdropped in her life—but she couldn't bring herself to do that. Not yet. After the way Thomas had acted at Tiny's and the things he was saying around town, she had a right to know what his next move was.

"I never was happy about your friendship with him," Maxine said in a superior voice that grated on Merry's nerves. "His father was nothing but a cowboy. Not that there's anything wrong with that," she quickly amended, "but breeding and education tell, and his parents didn't have either, God rest their souls. Which is why you can't expect him to play by the same rules a gentleman would. So you have to lower yourselves to his standards and fight fire with fire if you want Merry. That's the only thing people like Nick Kincaid understand."

"I do want her, Mother," he assured her grimly. "I don't care what I have to do, I won't lose her to Nick."

Her worst fears confirmed, Merry literally saw red. *How dare they!* Outraged, she wanted to storm inside and rake both Thomas and his mother over the coals, but Maxine, unfortunately, couldn't be held accountable for her own participation in this stupid game Thomas was playing. She was too ill and in no shape for any kind of confrontation. Thomas, however, was another matter. He had a lot to answer for.

Tempted to march in right then and there and demand an explanation, she had to force herself to draw in a deep breath and take a second to relax. She would *not,* she promised herself, lose her cool! If she was going to find a way to get through that thick head of Thomas's, she had to keep a tight rein on her temper and remain calm. She wasn't a violent woman. As much as she'd like the satisfaction of ripping into him, she couldn't take him apart at the seams. But oh, she wanted to!

When she walked through the door into Maxine's private room a few minutes later, she was totally in control of her emotions. But there was a hard promise of trouble in her blue eyes that anyone who knew her well would have recognized immediately. And Thomas knew her well.

Still whining to his mother, he glanced up, took one look at her, and paled. To his credit, he recovered quickly and turned to her with a delighted smile, but Merry wasn't fooled. She had him running scared, and it was no more than the rat deserved.

"Merry! I wasn't expecting to see you this afternoon. Mother and I were just talking about you."

"Were you really?" she said coolly. "So that's why my ears were burning."

Surprised, he laughed shakily. "Don't be silly, darling. It wasn't anything derogatory. Mother was just saying how much she hoped you would be her daughter-in-law one day. With her health the way it is, though, she's not sure that's ever going to happen. Which is why I think we should reschedule the wedding as quickly as possible," he continued smoothly. "It's crazy for us to be apart like this when we love each other."

Stunned, Merry couldn't believe his audacity. Did he really think that just because his mother was listening to every word that she was going to meekly fall into line and take him back? "I think it would be best if we talked about that in private," she retorted. "Now!"

"Oh, but Mother—"

"This won't take long," Merry assured Maxine. "You don't mind, do you? We really do need to talk and we haven't had much time alone."

Put that way, there was little the older woman could say, not after the way Thomas had just portrayed her. "Of course not," Maxine said with a grimace of a smile. "You two do need some time together. And I'll be fine by myself. It's been a tiring day and I need to rest."

Sold out by his mother, Thomas had no choice but to reluctantly follow Merry into the hall. "I can't be gone long," he began the second he pulled the door to his mother's room shut so they wouldn't disturb her. "Mother shouldn't be alone—"

"Trust me. This won't take a minute," Merry retorted in a low voice that wouldn't carry down the hospital corridor. "I heard you've been talking to Becca Ryan—"

"That was supposed to be a surprise!"

"Oh, it's a surprise, all right!" she hissed. "A very unpleasant one. And when were you going to tell me that we were getting married? A couple of hours before the wedding so I'd have time to make myself pretty for you?"

Pale, he winced as each word struck him like a dart. "C'mon, Merry, you know I'd never do that."

Unable to believe that he could say such a thing to her with a straight face, she could only look at him in amazement. "That's what I've been trying to tell you, dammit! I don't know you. I'm beginning to wonder if I ever did. The man I thought I knew and loved would have never left me standing at the altar, but that's exactly what you did."

"But I explained that! I was scared. But now that I've had time to put things into perspective, I know I really do love you."

"Oh, really? So this rush to marry me has nothing to do with the fact that someone else wants me?"

He bristled at that. "You've been listening to Nick again. That's why you really don't want to get married, isn't it? He's turned you against me."

Amazed at the way he refused to take any blame for his own actions, Merry could only marvel at his reasoning. Had he always been like this and she just hadn't noticed, or was this some new kind of defense mechanism he'd developed in order to cope with jilting her? "You know, I never thought I'd say this, but you really did me a favor that day you left me high and dry at the church. I don't love you, Thomas.''

"Don't say that! Nick—"

"No," she cut in sternly, "this has nothing to do with Nick. It never has. *You're* the one responsible for this. You're the one who showed me a side of yourself I'd never seen before, then gave me too much time alone to think. If you'd really cared about me, you would have at least considered what I was going through and called to make sure I was all right."

"I wanted to," he claimed, panicking as he sensed he was quickly losing her. "I thought of you all the time."

"And I thought about you," she admitted. "I was forced to face the fact that you didn't want to marry me, and as the days passed, I had to wonder if you'd ever really loved me. And if I wasn't sure of your feelings, I also had to question my own. The more I thought about it, it seemed like the answer had to be obvious. We weren't really in love—we'd just become a comfortable habit over the years—"

"No!"

"Everyone always expected us to get married, and once you came back to town last year and we started seeing each other again, we just got caught up in everyone else's expectations. When it came down to actually going through with the wedding, though, you couldn't do it.

"I'm not casting blame here," she said quickly when he once again tried to explain that he'd been scared. "It doesn't matter anymore. What's important is that we both realize that there was a reason we didn't get married. Let's accept that, wish each other luck, and go on with our lives before we end up hating each other."

For a moment, she thought he was going to cry. Regret

glistened in his eyes. "You're one of the best things that ever happened to me," he said huskily. 'I don't want to lose you."

"You already have," she said quietly. "You just didn't know it."

The news hit the streets almost immediately. A nurse passing in the hospital hallway heard Merry McBride tell Thomas Cooper that she didn't love him anymore and was never going to marry him. Within an hour, everyone in town was discussing the end of what most people had thought was a fairy-tale romance.

Nick heard the news from four different sources, each one hoping to be the first to tell him, and not surprisingly, the story had been distorted every time it was passed on. In one, Merry slapped Thomas, in another, she dumped a vase full of flowers on his head. But one thing remained constant in all four versions of the tale: Merry no longer loved Thomas.

It was the best news Nick had heard in months.

Heading out of town to check reports of a car broken down on the side of the road that cut through the Hawk River Valley, he couldn't seem to stop smiling. She'd finally realized she didn't love Thomas. There'd been a time when he'd thought this day would never come. Thank God he'd been wrong!

A cautious man, he tried to remind himself that this might not mean anything. Just because she didn't love Thomas didn't mean that she was willing to let herself love him. After everything that she'd been through, no one would blame her if she was gun-shy. Especially when it came to getting involved with someone she considered a friend. She'd tried that with Thomas, only to have it blow up in her face. She wouldn't be the first woman to swear off men after that.

He knew that, accepted that, and still felt like he'd just won the lottery. He had a chance, dammit, and that was something he hadn't had since the day he'd planned to ask her to the junior prom in high school. Before he could so much as open his mouth, she'd confided that she was in love with Thomas. If he lived to be a hundred, he would never forget the dreamy smile on her face and the stars in her eyes for another man. Nothing had ever been the same since. Until today.

Anxious to see her, he almost called her just to see how she was doing. But now that she was a free woman and his to pursue, he didn't want to ruin things but rushing her too soon. He'd give her some space and let her call him when she wanted to talk.

Resigned to waiting, he entered the Hawk River Valley and looked ahead down the long stretch of road that cut right through the middle of the valley. There was no sign of the car that someone had reported broken down on the side of the highway, but a hundred yards ahead, he caught a glimpse of something moving in the high grass at the edge of the shoulder. Frowning, he checked his rearview mirror to make sure no other traffic was following him closely, then turned on the lights of his patrol car and began to slow down.

What he thought was a wounded animal turned out to be a litter of red, shaggy-haired puppies that someone had apparently dumped on the side of the road. Nick took one look at them and didn't know if he wanted to laugh or curse. They were fat and healthy and playful, stumbling over their own feet and each other as they wrestled together in the grass. They couldn't have been there long, but as far as Nick was concerned, that was beside the point. What kind of monster would abandon four innocent puppies on the side of the road with no food or water? If he could have gotten his hands on them, he would have run them in for animal cruelty.

The biggest of the lot spied him as he got out of his car and immediately tried to play watchdog. Planting himself in front of his brothers and sisters, he bristled, yapping and wagging his tail at one and the same time.

Chuckling, Nick squatted down in front of him and held out his hand so he could sniff his fingers. "You're doing a good job, big guy, but you don't have to be afraid of me. I won't hurt you."

The puppy, figuring that out for himself, whined and licked his fingers. The others, obviously taking that as a sign of approval, launched themselves at him, happy to have company in the big, bad, lonely world they'd suddenly found themselves in.

Laughing, Nick scooped them all up in his arms at once. "I know, I know. But it's going to be okay now. I know just the place to take you."

Merry fell in love with them at first sight. "Oh, Nick, they're beautiful! Where did you get them?"

"On the side of the road."

"On the side…" In the process of taking the squirming puppies out of his arms, she stopped with the little watchdog in her arms and looked up at him with wide, shocked eyes. "Someone dumped them?" When he nodded, she started to swear.

Not surprised by her outrage, he said, "I couldn't believe it, either. They were out on the Hawk River Valley road. You think someone from around here did it?"

She couldn't, of course, know every dog in the area, but she took care of a large percentage of them. And, better yet, she knew their owners. And no one she knew would have ever dreamed of leaving one-month-old pups out in the country to fend for themselves.

"I don't think so. Why would they? Everyone knows that all they have to do is drop them off here and I'll find them a good home. It was probably someone from Crystal Lake. It's just down the road from the valley." Nuzzling the one Nick had nicknamed Tiger, she laughed when he licked her on the cheek. "Whoever they are, they deserve to be strung up by their thumbs, but at least no harm was done. They're precious!"

Watching the laughter that transformed her face as she played with the puppies, Nick felt love tug sharply at his heartstrings. Lord, she was beautiful! Over the course of their friendship, he'd seen her every way a man could see a woman—with makeup and without, with a smile on her face when she should have been crying, sick, and on top of the world—but he'd never seen her look more gorgeous than she did at that moment, with the puppies clamoring to get to her, delighting her.

"Have dinner with me tonight," he said impulsively, then wanted to kick himself. What the hell was he doing? He'd promised himself he was going to give her some time to adjust to the fact that she was a single, unattached woman again before he pushed her to get involved. She needed time, and so did he. Dean and George's last day had come and gone, and they'd left for their new jobs. Shorthanded until the two new men he'd hired reported for work next week, he was working double shifts with Harvey and spending just about every waking hour either at his office or in his patrol car. Considering all that, how could he possibly find time to date?

Just give me the chance, he thought, caressing her with his eyes. *I'll find the time.*

Surprised by the invitation, Merry glanced up from the puppies and almost said yes. And that shook her. She wasn't ready to date again. Not yet. Gossip about her and Thomas and Nick was already swirling around town, following her everywhere she went, and it was only going to get worse once she started dating again. Especially when people realized the new man in her life really was Nick. Just thinking about all the whispering and speculation, both behind her back and to her face, made her cringe.

But it was the thought of getting hurt again that scared her the most. She'd trusted Thomas and put her heart on the line without a thought, only to have him stomp on it and grind it into the ground. Nick wasn't like that, thank God—he was kind and caring and would cut off his right arm before he deliberately hurt her. She wanted to trust him, to see where a relationship between them might go, but sometimes people just got hurt, regardless of how careful they were. And that was something she never wanted to go through again.

"I want to," she said huskily, "but—"

"You're afraid," he guessed.

She nodded miserably, hating to disappoint him. "It's not you—you must know that. It's just such a big step and I don't know if I'm ready for that yet."

After everything she'd been through, Nick couldn't say he blamed her. Her trust in her own judgment had been destroyed, and that wasn't something she would rebuild easily. Still, in spite of that, he was far from discouraged. She wanted to go with him—that was a start. Now he just had to find a way to help her get past her fear.

"All right," he said. "Forget dinner. Let's try something else. What about the reunion?"

She didn't have to ask him which reunion. Signs announcing their fifteen year high school reunion had been posted all over town for weeks. A barbecue was scheduled, as well as a picnic so everyone could bring their families, but it was the big dance Saturday night in the high school gym that everyone was looking forward to. When she'd bought her tickets months ago, Merry had thought she'd be attending it with her new husband. Thomas would, no doubt, still attend, but not with her. Not in the party mood, she had, in fact, already decided not to go at all.

Wrinkling her nose, she said, "I don't think I'd be very good company, so I'll probably just stay home that night and watch TV."

"But you were really looking forward to this," he reminded her with a frown. "Jay Fischer's going to be there. And Betty Vaughn. They haven't been home in years. Don't you want to see them?"

Jay and Betty had both been on the debate team with her, and they'd been great friends all through high school. She kept up with them through e-mail and occasional phone calls, but that wasn't the same thing as meeting with them face-to-face. "Yes, of course," she began, "but—"

"Then go with me," he said quickly. "Not as a date, but a friend. Think about it. If you and Thomas had gotten married, the three of us would have gone together anyway. We can still go. Thomas just won't be with us."

Tempted, it was hard to argue with his logic. Especially when she really wanted to go. What harm could it do? she reasoned. They would just be going as friends—it wasn't as if they were dating or anything. And no one would be surprised to see them together—not when they'd been best buddies in high school. The questions would only begin if she *didn't* go with him.

"All right," she said, giving in. "As long as it's not a date."

Satisfied, he grinned,. "It's not. I promise. I'll pick you up at seven."

Chapter 9

The week preceding the reunion was one of those crazy weeks when everything went wrong. First, one of the patrol cars broke down, then Sheri, Nick's dispatcher, had to take time off when two of her kids got into some poison ivy. An electrical storm blew the computer system at the same time it knocked out telephone and power lines all over the county, and the ten-hour days Nick and Harvey were working turned into fifteen-hour. It was a grueling schedule. Nick hardly saw Merry, and every time he tried to call her, all he got was static because of the downed lines.

Exhausted, he knew he should cancel his "nondate" with Merry. What time he had off right then was limited, and he needed to spend it catching up on his sleep, not dancing the night away with a beautiful woman. But what he needed and wanted were two different things, and there was no way in hell he was passing up a chance to spend an evening with Merry. He'd sleep later.

Counting the hours until he could pick her up, he had

everything worked out for their first nondate. When Dean and George left, he'd started working from three in the afternoon until two in the morning, but he couldn't do that on Saturday, so Harvey had agreed to switch shifts with him. That meant he'd work his regular late shift Friday night, get off at three in the morning, grab an hour nap, then take Harvey's shift from four in the morning until three in the afternoon on Saturday. It would be a tough stretch, but he didn't expect the long hours to be a problem. He'd have the hour break between shifts, then time to catch a three-hour-nap Saturday before he had to pick up Merry at seven. That was enough sleep for anyone.

Friday afternoon, however, Nick discovered that even the best laid plans had a way of blowing up in your face. When Harvey showed up at his office an hour and a half after his shift ended at two, Nick didn't have to see the deep sorrow in his eyes to know that something was terribly wrong. "What is it?" he asked sharply. "What's wrong?"

"I just got word that my father had a heart attack. He's not expected to live. I've got to go, Nick."

"Of course you do. Oh, man, I'm sorry! I hope everything'll be all right." Frowning, he tried to recall what he knew about Harvey's dad other than he'd divorced his mother years ago and moved back east. "Your dad's in New York, isn't he?"

He nodded. "Yeah—Manhattan. I hate to abandon ship this way when you're shorthanded, but I don't know what else to do. He needs me—"

"Hey, don't worry about it," Nick said. "The new guys'll be in on Monday. I can handle things until then. In the meantime, you just worry about your dad and trying to get him well. When's your flight out? Can I drive you to the airport?"

Already in an emotional state, that just pushed Harvey

over the edge. Tears flooded his eyes. "Thanks, Nick. You don't know how much I appreciate this."

"I've been through it, man," he said simply, understanding. And he knew from personal experience just how difficult it was to lose a parent. He'd lost both of his by the time he was twenty-five, and unlike Harvey, he hadn't had a chance to say goodbye. "Stay as long as you need to," he told him. "Work'll wait. Your father might not be able to."

Single, with no one but himself to take care of, Harvey was already packed and ready to go. Nick drove him to the airport in Colorado Springs so he wouldn't have to leave his car in long-term parking, then waited with him until his flight was called. It wasn't until he'd seen the younger man off and started back to Liberty Hill that he realized that with Harvey gone, there was no one to switch shifts with him tomorrow evening so he could take Merry to the reunion.

"Damn!" Pounding on the steering wheel with the heal of his hand, he couldn't see that he had any choice but to cancel their date. Most of the people of Liberty Hill were decent, law-abiding citizens, but they weren't all saints. He had to deal with domestic disputes and drunk drivers and an occasional shoplifter. And on Saturday nights, especially during the summer when the teenagers were out of school and feeling their oats, it was important that he be out and about to discourage them from getting into trouble. And he couldn't do that if he was at the reunion dancing with Merry.

Resigned, he arrived back at his office in a foul mood, only to be greeted by Sheri the second he walked in the door. Hanging up the phone, she said, "Oh, good, there you are. Lincoln White is waiting to talk to you."

After a morning of disappointments, he didn't have to

ask why White would be calling at this late stage when he was scheduled to start work on Monday. The answer was obvious. "Well, that's just great! He's decided he doesn't want the job, after all, hasn't he? I should have known. What else can go wrong? No, don't tell me—I don't want to know. What line is he on?"

Patiently waiting for him to finish raging, Sheri smiled slightly, well understanding the strain he was under. "Actually, he's not on the phone. He's waiting for you in your office."

"What?! He's here?"

Grinning, she nodded. "He's arrived about thirty minutes ago."

Nick didn't wait to hear more. Striding into his office, he greeted Lincoln with a handshake and welcomed him to town. "I wasn't expecting you until Monday."

"I wrapped things up in Utah faster than I expected to, so I just decided to come on."

"Did you have any trouble finding a place to stay?"

"No, actually, I rented Dean Ziggler's place," he replied. "I would have bought it off him, but he's not sure he wants to sell yet."

"Good," Nick said. "That'll give you the entire weekend to get settled in."

"Oh, I already did that. Ziggler rented the house to me furnished, so all I had to do was bring my clothes and personal stuff right now, thank God. It made the move a lot easier."

"Then you're ready to go to work?"

"Sure, if you need me. When do you want me to start?"

There was, Nick decided, a god, after all. Grinning, he dropped down into the chair behind his desk. "How does tomorrow night sound to you?"

* * *

If Merry hadn't known better, she would have sworn she'd stepped back in time. Red-and-white crepe paper streamers hung from the rafters of the gym, jut as they had for every school dance she'd ever attended, and the song being belted out by the band had been number one on the charts the summer she graduated from high school. With Nick at her side, she only had to close her eyes, pretend Thomas flanked her on the other side, and she was back in high school.

But Thomas was nowhere in sight, she wasn't eighteen any more, and she wouldn't have gone back to that time in her life even if she could have. For too long, she'd held on to the past and the fairy-tale romance she'd had with Thomas when they were kids. When he'd come back into her life last year when his mother broke her hip, it was as if all the years since high school had never happened. They'd stepped right back into the puppy love they'd once shared and mistakenly assumed that it had grown into something stronger. It hadn't.

Never again, she promised herself. She didn't want to live in the past any more. Not when the present was so much more promising now that she'd finally admitted to herself that she didn't love Thomas. That was then, this was now, and now was really starting to get interesting.

Not surprisingly, people started talking the second they spied her with Nick, just as she'd known they would. She tried to ignore it, but some people made that impossible. "Oh, God, there's Winona Cobb," she groaned. "I haven't seen her since she moved to Denver eight years ago. And she's coming over. Damn!"

"C'mon, Mer, this is our chance to have some fun," Nick told her with a wicked grin. "Just play along with me, okay?"

She should have said no. Winona had always been the

biggest gossip in school, and Merry had never cared for her. The last thing she wanted to do was spend any time talking to her. But Nick had that glint in his eye that warned her he wasn't going to take no for an answer, so there was nothing she could do but grin and bear it as Winona rushed up and hugged her like she was a long-lost friend.

"Hi! My goodness, it's so good to see you! You look wonderful! Doesn't she look great, Nick? And so do you," she gushed, hugging him. "So how are you two? I hear you've been seeing each other—"

"Every chance we get," Nick assured her as he took Merry's hand and gazed into her eyes like a lovesick fool. "I'm trying to talk her into moving in with me."

If she hadn't been braced for something outrageous, Merry would have choked on a gasp. Instead, it was all she could do not to burst out laughing when Winona's jaw nearly dropped to the ground. Drawing Nick's hand to her cheek, she nuzzled against him. "I told you why I couldn't do that, honey-bunny. My brothers would come after you with a shotgun."

"B-but you and Thomas were going to get married just last month, weren't you?" Winona said, frowning in confusion. "And now you're thinking about moving in together. Aren't you rushing things a little?"

"I don't know how the hell you can say that," Nick retorted. "We've known each other all our lives."

"But she was in love with Thomas!"

"Well, yeah," he said with a shrug. "But that didn't work out, so I figured, what the hell. I've waited long enough. She's free now, and I don't ever plan on walking down the aisle for any woman, so why not live together? She was all prepared to live with Thomas, so why not me, right?"

Stunned, Winona looked back and forth between the two

of them, unable to believe that this was coming from two of the most conservative people in their graduating class. But she'd heard it with her own ears. Already anticipating people's reaction to this juicy tidbit of information, she started to tell them she'd see them both later, only to just then notice the mischief dancing in their eyes.

She froze, her gaze narrowing suspiciously. "Wait a minute. Is this some kind of joke?"

"No!" Nick retorted in pretended shock, making no attempt to hide his grin. "What was your first clue, Winona?"

In high school, she'd never responded well to teasing, and that, apparently, hadn't changed. Puffing up like a toad, she sniffed, "You always did have a sick sense of humor, Nick Kincaid! Go ahead and laugh. Enjoy yourself!" Steaming, she walked off in a huff.

Far from insulted, Nick mimicked, "Well, at least I *have* a sense of humor."

Beside him, Merry couldn't help but laugh. "You've done it now. You know how spiteful she is. Now she's going to tell everyone what you said and leave out the part that you were joking."

"Let her," he retorted with a grin. "We'll be the talk of the reunion."

They were already that—their classmates who still lived in Liberty Hill had already spread the word about Merry and Thomas's breakup—but no one believed Winona's vicious lies. Within minutes, they were surrounded by friends, and Winona was left alone to glare at them from across the gym.

When Thomas arrived, Merry's heart sank at the sight of him. She hadn't heard from him since she'd talked to him in the hallway outside his mother's hospital room, and she'd really started to hope that he'd finally accepted the

fact that she no longer loved him. But here he was, ready
to cause trouble once again.

She didn't say a word to Nick, but she didn't have to.
She felt him stiffen at her side and knew that he'd seen
Thomas, too. And he wasn't any happier about it than she
was.

Don't! she wanted to cry when Thomas finally spotted
them in the crowd and her eyes locked with his. *Don't do
this to us! Please, just let it go. Let* me *go!*

She didn't say anything, but she knew he heard every
word. From across the gym, she could see the pain in his
eyes, the longing he made no attempt to hide. And in spite
of the way he'd hurt her, she couldn't help but feel sorry
for him. Then he took a step toward her.

She stiffened—she couldn't help it—but she needn't
have worried. He didn't come any closer, but just stood
there for what seemed like an eternity, staring at her. It
wasn't until he gave her a silent salute, then turned and
walked out of the gym that she realized he was telling her
goodbye.

She was quiet on the way home, and Nick didn't push
her to talk. After Thomas had left, they'd both relaxed and
enjoyed the rest of the evening, but he'd been aware of the
fact that something was troubling her. And it didn't take a
genius to figure out that it was Thomas. She'd laughed and
smiled and joked with their classmates, but she hadn't been
the same after she'd spied Thomas in the gym. And that
had him worried. Did she regret breaking things off with
him?

Frowning, he pulled up before her house and cut the
engine, then walked her to her door. In the stark glare of
the porch light she'd left on, his face looked like it was

carved in stone as he watched her dig in her purse for her keys. "Have you changed your mind?"

Distracted, she glanced up. "About what?"

"Thomas. Have you decided you still love him, after all?"

"No!" Shocked, she nearly dropped her purse. "Why would you think that?"

"I saw your face when he left the gym tonight. For a minute there, I thought you were going to cry. What's going on, Mer?"

She hesitated, struggling to find the words to explain what she was feeling when she wasn't quite sure herself. "I haven't changed my mind, but I guess when he left tonight, we both realized that it was really over. And there's a part of me that's saddened by that. We had so much fun together, and now it's come to this. I know it's for the best, and I wouldn't go back to what we had before even if could, but I do regret the way things ended. We've been friends forever, Nick. And now we're not even talking."

"Sometimes you don't appreciate what you have until you lose it," he said huskily. "I'm sure that's what Thomas is going through right now. It can't be easy for him to see you with someone else—I know. I've been in his shoes. But that doesn't mean it's always going to be this way. He just needs some time to adjust to the change in the status quo."

She knew he was right—everything had changed and they were all still trying to get their bearings, she, most of all. Once, she would have hugged him for understanding and never given it a thought. But that was before she'd known that his feelings for her were much deeper than those of just a friend. Now, she didn't touch him, even in the old playful way they had in the past. She missed that and didn't have a clue how to get it back. She was afraid that if she said anything, he would think she was hinting that she wanted a more physical relationship. And while her heart pounded at the very memory of his kiss, she wasn't sure she was ready for that just yet.

"I know. It's just hard sometimes." Shaking off her melancholy, she forced a smile. "Anyway, I had a great time tonight. I'm glad you talked me into going."

"Maybe next time it can be a *real* date," he teased. Taking her keys from her, he unlocked her front door and pushed it open, then handed her back her keys. "I had a great time, too," he said huskily, and before she could guess his intentions, he leaned over and softly kissed her cheek. "Good night, Mer. I'll see you tomorrow."

Her heart thumping crazily, she stood in front of her open door and watched, dazed, as he drove away. And all she could think of was that she wished he'd kissed her on the mouth.

It was hours after Nick left before she finally fell asleep, and even then, her dreams were filled with images of him. Restless, she woke the next morning long after she normally did and was shocked to find herself reaching for him. How had this happened? she wondered wildly. They weren't even dating yct—not really—and she couldn't get him out of her head. What would it be like when they really did get involved?

Her pulse racing at the thought, she reminded herself that she wasn't jumping right back into a relationship with Nick or anyone else. Not when she was still coming to grips with her breakup with Thomas. He probably wouldn't like it, but she had to do what was right for her—and that meant she was going to move slow and not jump into the water without seeing how deep it was.

A sound outside caught her attention then, and she rose

from the bed, puzzled. It sounded like her lawnmower, she thought with a frown. But how could it be? She took care of her yard herself, and her mower wasn't one of those fancy electric ones that might, through some kind of electrical short, start by itself. It was the old-fashioned pull-cord kind, and not just anyone could start it. You had to set the throttle just right or it wouldn't do anything but groan. And only a few people knew that.

Thomas.

Her heart stopped at the thought, and with a muttered curse, she rolled out of bed and grabbed her robe. She'd given him too much credit last night, she fumed. She'd thought he'd finally realized he was beaten, but he'd just been biding his time, waiting for another chance to court her. Since flowers hadn't worked, he'd obviously hoped to get in her good graces by trying something else. And yard work had an advantage roses didn't—it couldn't be sent back.

This time, he'd gone too far, she told herself angrily as she marched to the front door. She'd tried to spare his feelings, to let him down as gently as possible, to be nice, dammit!—but he refused to get the message. And she was tired of it. This time, she'd be blunt, and if he didn't like it, that was too damn bad.

Yanking open the front door, she stormed outside, her robe flapping around her bare knees, hot words already tumbling off her tongue. "Damn you...Nick!"

Stunned, she stumbled to a stop, her eyes widening at the sight of Nick tinkering with the choke of her old, cantankerous lawnmower until it purred like a kitten. "What are you doing here?"

She had to raise her voice over the noise of the mower, but he heard her. "Mowing your grass," he said simply. "I noticed last night that it needed it and figured you didn't have time since you'd been working so hard on this rabies thing.''

''But don't you have to work today?''

''It's Sunday,'' he reminded her. And although he was on call all day, he had calls to the office forwarded to his cell phone and didn't go into work unless there was some kind of emergency. ''I guess I should have checked to see if you were awake first before I started the mower, but you're always such an early bird, I thought you'd be up. Sorry.''

His gaze dipped down to the robe that covered her from her neck to midcalf, then quickly shifted back to her eyes. Heat singeing her cheeks, Merry reminded herself that he'd seen her in her nightclothes before and it wasn't anything to get bent out of shape about. But this was different, and they both knew it. Then, she'd thought of him as a buddy, a pal, a psuedo brother, and she hadn't thought a thing of it. But there was an awareness between them now that set her pulse skipping anytime they were within a mile of each other, and try though she might, she couldn't ignore it. Especially when she wore nothing but a skimpy nightgown and robe.

Shaken, she stuttered, ''N-no. Don't apologize. I n-needed to get up, anyway. Have you eaten?''

''I had some coffee earlier, but that's it.''

In desperate need of a graceful exit, she sighed in relief. ''Good, then I'll get dressed and see what's in the refrigerator for breakfast. Come on inside when you're finished.''

Turning, she bolted inside, chiding herself all the while. What in the world was wrong with her? She wasn't a woman who got flustered when a man showed her attention. It wasn't that she took it as her due—she would never do that—but she did know how to handle herself. Or at least, she always had in the past. She'd never stuttered before, even with Thomas.

So what was it about Nick that shook her composure? she wondered as she hurriedly pulled on jean shorts and a blue T-shirt, then stepped into the kitchen. What was it about him that made her heart knock against her ribs? Why, after knowing him for years, did she get this silly grin on her face whenever she thought of him? She'd thought she'd loved Thomas with all her heart, but he'd never, ever, made her feel like this. Why? What was going on?

Not sure she was ready for the answer to that, she tried to distract herself with cooking breakfast, and for a while it worked. She loved to cook but didn't do it often because it wasn't any fun cooking for one. So she indulged herself by pulling out her mother's recipe for homemade biscuits, then made bacon and eggs and hash browns. Okay, she told herself with a grin as she pulled the biscuits out of the oven, she was going overboard with the cholesterol. Normally, she was very conscious about her diet, but sometimes, you just had to cut loose. If Nick complained, she'd take out the whole-grain cereal.

Setting the food on the table, she heard the back door open behind her and turned with a smile. "You timed that perfectly. I just pulled the biscuits out of the oven—"

That was as far as she got. She took one look at Nick and whatever she was going to say next flew right out of her head. It was a fairly cool morning, but humid, and he'd worked up a sweat pushing the mower around. Perspiration dampened his navy blue knit shirt, molding it to the hard wall of his chest, and his dark brown hair stood up in spikes from where he'd run his hands through it. Her fingers itching to smooth it into place, it was all she could do not to reach out and touch.

"Mmm. That smells fantastic," he said with a smile that

melted her heart. "Let me wash up and I'll be right with you."

Dazed, Merry nodded numbly, and expected him to head for the bathroom. Instead, he stepped over to the kitchen sink, whipped off his shirt, and began to splash water on his face and chest. She'd seen her brothers do the same thing countless times over the years and had never thought a thing of it, but her brothers weren't Nick. Fascinated, she felt her mouth go dry at the sight of him and couldn't have looked away if her life had depended on it.

When the phone rang, she reached for it blindly, never taking her eyes from him. "Hullo?"

"Merry! Thank God! Princess Leah's foaling and I think she's in trouble."

All her attention on Nick, it was a heartbeat later before the caller's words registered. Suddenly recognizing Harland Fitzgerald's worried voice, she stiffened and abruptly brought her attention back to work. Princess Leah was Harland's prize mare and pregnant with twins. And he had every right to be worried. Unlike other animals, horses didn't handle multiple births easily. In a large percentage of cases, one of the foals and sometimes the mother both died.

All business, she said, "Calm down, Harland. We're going to do everything for her we can. How long has she been in labor? How's her breathing? Is she in distress? How's she acting?"

An experienced horseman, he'd bred enough horses to know when one was in trouble, and as he hurriedly answered the questions Merry threw at him, it was apparent that the mare wasn't doing nearly as well as she could be. "I'll be right there," Merry assured him, worried herself. "Give me ten minutes."

Quickly hanging up the phone, her thoughts already

jumping ahead to all the things that could go wrong during the foaling, she whirled, only to stop short at the sight of Nick standing in front of her holding out a biscuit to her with a couple of pieces of bacon wedged in the middle. Only then did she remember the elaborate breakfast she'd cooked for them. "Oh, Nick, I'm sorry!"

"Don't be ridiculous," he chided with an easy smile. "Duty calls and you've got to go. Don't worry about anything here. I'll put the food away, then lock up on my way out."

He made it so easy for her that she wanted to cry. Why had it taken her all these years to see what a wonderful man he was? Taking the quick breakfast sandwich he'd prepared for her, she smiled tremulously. "Thanks. I wish I could stay—"

"But you can't," he finished for her. "Go. Harland's mare needs you." And with a quick kiss, he turned her toward the door to the garage and gave her a gentle push. Left with no choice, she went.

Nick had intended to leave after he ate his own breakfast, but as he started cleaning up the kitchen and putting things away, he couldn't help but notice the irritating drip of the kitchen faucet. It was, he knew, a new faucet that had been installed last year, when Merry had rebuilt her house after the fire. Still under warranty, it shouldn't have been dripping after only a year of use—unless it was defective.

There was no way of knowing that by just looking at it, however, so he turned off the water, grabbed some tools from the trunk of his car, and went to work. A few minutes later, he'd installed a new washer, just in case that was the problem, but the second he turned the water back on and tested the faucet, it started dripping again.

Another man might have left it at that point, and waited

to see what Merry wanted to do about it. And for all of two seconds, Nick considered that. After all, it wasn't like he didn't have things to do at his own house. And Merry hadn't asked him to do this for her. He could lock up and leave and she'd never even know he looked at it.

But she wasn't all that handy around the house, he reminded himself. There wasn't much she didn't know about animals, but when it came to tools, he doubted if she knew a pipe wrench from a pair of pliers. If she tried to fix it herself, she'd no doubt have water all over the kitchen floor and still end up having to call a plumber, who would charge her a fortune to drive all the way out to the ranch from town. Why should she have to do all that when he was right there and could do it for her?

The decision made, he turned off the water—again—and maneuvered his head and shoulders under the sink so he could disconnect the entire faucet. Five minutes later, he was headed for town and the hardware store.

Exhausted, Merry felt like she'd been through a war. She was dirty and tired, every bone in her body ached, and she didn't have to feel her hair to know that she had straw in it. And she couldn't stop smiling. She'd done it! She'd actually delivered two healthy foals and saved their mother, and no one knew better than she just how rare that was. She'd been practicing veterinary medicine for seven years and this was only the third time she'd encountered a multiple birth in horses. Each of the other times, one of the foals had died.

But not this time, she thought with a huge grin. Both foals were healthy and strong, and Harland was as thrilled as she was. When he'd realized that his precious Princess Leah and both her foals were going to make it, he'd enveloped Merry in a bear hug that had nearly cracked her ribs. In spite of the fact that it wasn't even noon, he'd pulled out the champagne he'd had on ice for the last three weeks in anticipation of the foaling and insisted Merry have a glass. In the mood to party, he'd been on the phone calling everyone he knew when she finally left.

Just thinking about the way he'd danced around the barn when he'd seen the beautiful twin foals brought a huge grin to her face. She was still smiling when she pulled into her driveway and saw Nick's car out front. Not even stopping to wonder what he was still doing there, she grabbed the bottle of champagne Harland had insisted she take home with her and rushed inside.

"Nick? Guess what? I just delivered twins!"

In the process of trying out the new faucet he'd just installed, Nick turned to see her bolt into the kitchen with a grin the size of Texas on her face. "Twins? You're kidding! And they're both okay?"

"They're fabulous! You should see them. They've got three white stockings and a little touch of white right in the middle of their chest..." Suddenly noticing the tools spread out on her kitchen counter, she frowned. "I was so excited, I didn't stop to think. What are you still doing here? I thought you left hours ago. My God, you fixed my faucet!"

Caught red-handed, he shrugged sheepishly. "Actually, it couldn't be fixed, so I got you a new one. I hope you don't mind."

"Mind?" she laughed. "Are you kidding? Every time the damn thing dripped, I promised myself I was going to call a plumber, but then I'd get busy and forget all about it. Gosh, this must be my red-letter day. Thank you!"

Delighted, she impulsively stepped forward to give him a hug, and just that easily they found themselves in each other's arms. For a startled moment, neither of them moved. Blue eyes, dark with awareness, stared into brown, and two hearts that had just moments before beat steadily now stumbled into a frantic, dizzy rhythm.

Nick told himself to let her go—it was the smart thing to do—but when she started to pull back, he found he couldn't. Not when he had her this close and he'd been thinking of nothing but her the entire time he'd worked on her faucet. With a murmur of need, he pulled her close and covered her mouth with his.

It was a whisper of a kiss, a promise of desire, a sweet entreaty of tenderness that was over almost before it had begun. Seduced, the roar of her blood loud in her ears, Merry gazed up at Nick with glazed eyes and couldn't for the life of her think of her own name. She couldn't have said how many times she'd been kissed since Thomas had first kissed her when she was fourteen, but no man had ever destroyed her so easily with just a languid brush of mouth against mouth.

Confused, unsure of the emotions he stirred in her so effortlessly, she stared up into his eyes searchingly. "Nick..."

"Have dinner with me,' he urged hoarsely. "We'll celebrate the birth of the twins."

She should have said no—somewhere in the back of her head, she knew that. She'd just been out with him last night, though she refused to think of that as a date, and she'd almost had breakfast with him this morning. If she was going to keep a handle on her emotions and not let things get out of control, she had to take things slow and easy. And there'd been nothing the least bit slow or easy about the kiss he'd just given her.

Knowing that, she should have thanked him and politely declined. After everything she'd been through, he would have understood. But that kiss that had set her heart thumping had also tempted her past bearing. How could she have known him all her life and never known that the man knew how to kiss like that? Fascinated, unable to resist the idea of going out with him on an honest-to-goodness-real-live date, she couldn't bring herself to turn him down.

"I'd love to," she said huskily. "What time would you like to pick me up?"

"Seven."

A slow smile curling the corners of her mouth, she nodded, "I'll be ready."

The clock on the nightstand beside her bed read 6:45, and Merry still hadn't decided what she was going to wear. Panicking, she looked from the pile of clothes she'd tried on, then pulled off and tossed on her bed, to the few dresses still hanging in her closet and realized she was quickly running out of choices.

"What are you doing, Merry?" she muttered aloud to herself. "You're not meeting the queen, for God's sake! It's just Nick. Pick something—*anything, dammit!*—before he gets here and finds you in your underwear!"

But she couldn't decide if she wanted to wear a dress or pants, and nothing seemed to fit right. And all the while, the clock continued to tick. *Please let him be late,* she prayed silently as she tugged on a pair of white slacks and a blue silk blouse. It was a nice outfit, but it just wasn't special enough, and with a muttered curse, she quickly unbuttoned the blouse.

When the doorbell rang at a few minutes to seven, she'd just wriggled out of the last dress in her closet and thrown it on the bed. "Oh, God!"

Glancing wildly around her bedroom, which looked like it had been hit by a tornado, she looked around for something else to put on. Everything she owned had been discarded on the bed, however, and she was left with nothing to wear but her robe. Mortified, she pulled it on and hastily buttoned it to the throat. In all the years she'd been dating, nothing like this had ever happened to her. He was going to think she was an idiot.

Color burning her cheeks, she hurried to the front door, all the while racking her brain for a reason for not being ready. In the end, all she could offer was the truth. "I'm sorry," she said the second she pulled open the door. "I couldn't decide what to wear."

He, on the other hand, had obviously had no such trouble. Dressed in khakis, a white shirt, and navy blue blazer, he looked wonderful. And, she noted, not the least bit nervous.

"No problem," he said easily. "Take your time."

With a nod, she quickly escaped to her bedroom and never saw Nick restlessly pace the length of her living room. Pulling at his tie, he knew exactly how she felt. He wasn't usually that particular about what he wore, but he'd changed ties three times and shaved twice before he'd finally been satisfied with his appearance.

He'd told himself there was no reason to be nervous— he was just going out to dinner with the woman he was crazy about. Then he'd seen her, and he'd realized that it didn't matter what they did tonight. They could have been going fishing or roller skating or up to her mother's to play dominoes, and he would have felt the same. It made no sense, but every instinct he had told him their entire future was riding on this one night. And it scared the hell out of him.

Chapter 10

He took her to Tony's, a country inn north of Eagle Ridge that was set high on the edge of a cliff and offered a commanding view of the mountains that surrounded it on all sides. Quiet and secluded, the inn was famous for its steaks and wine list and its outdoor patio, where couples could dine by candlelight and dance to the music of a live band on warm summer nights.

Merry had heard about the place for years, but she'd never been there, and as the maître d' escorted them to their table on the stone patio, she knew she was in for one of the most romantic evenings of her life when Nick seated her himself. Pulling out her chair for her, he waited until she was seated and she'd adjusted the full skirt of her aqua blue sundress, then he leaned down and pressed a gentle kiss to the back of her bare neck.

Shivers danced over her skin, drawing a soft gasp from her before she had a prayer of hiding her reaction from him. Her eyes wide with awareness, she watched as he came around the table to take his own seat across from her, but he only smiled and reached for her hand. Slowly, his thumb rubbed across the back of her knuckles, stealing the air from her lungs breath by breath. And just that easily, he pulled her into a fantasy, a fairy tale, a beautiful romantic dream unlike anything she'd ever experienced before.

It was a Sunday night, but the place was packed—all around them, other couples murmured quietly to each other, laughed and danced and enjoyed the evening, but Merry never noticed anyone but Nick. To the west, the sun slipped behind the mountains, painting the sky orange and magenta, while overhead, the stars came out one by one, but it was the heat in Nick's eyes that set her heart pounding in her breast. Fascinated, she couldn't look away.

"Would you like to dance before we order?"

Unable to resist the chance to be in his arms, she nodded, "I'd love to."

Music floated on the evening air, soft and dreamy and romantic, as Nick escorted her to the dance floor and turned her into his arms. Feeling as if she'd come home, Merry sighed in contentment and settled her head against his shoulder. With a will of their own, her feet fell into step with his, and with no effort whatsoever, they were dancing.

Later, she couldn't have named a single song the band played or said if the wine they drank with their meal was white or red. Time slowed to a crawl, the world and all its complications slipped away until only the two of them were left, lost in each other's eyes.

It was the most magical evening of Merry's life. Again and again, they returned to the dance floor. Dancing on air, she could have stayed right where she was the rest of the night, swaying to one love song after another in Nick's arms.

It couldn't, however, last. "Ladies and gentlemen," the lead singer of the band said as the last strains of "Mona Lisa" faded into silence, "we hope you've enjoyed your evening here at Tony's. It's time to call it a night, but not without one more song."

Blinking as if coming out of a daze, Merry looked around as other couples made preparations to leave. "Why is the band stopping so early?"

Chuckling, Nick took her hand and linked his fingers with hers. "It's nearly midnight, Cinderella. Time to get you home before we both turn into pumpkins."

"Midnight!" Stunned, she glanced at her watch in disbelief and discovered that it was, indeed, five till twelve. "I would have sworn it was barely nine o'clock. Did we have dessert?"

He'd had his every time he got to hold her in his arms, but that was something he kept to himself. Amusement dancing in his eyes, he couldn't help but grin at her as he settled the bill with their waiter. It was always amazing to him how she stayed so thin. The lady did love sweets. "No, I don't think we did. Would you like to stop at Ed's on the way home and get some chocolate pie?"

He didn't have to ask her twice. "Could we?"

Chuckling, he tugged her toward the closest exit. "We'll have to hurry. Ed closes at one."

They made it in record time, laughing and panting as they rushed into the diner just ten minutes before it closed. Ed, who seemed to always be there regardless of the time of day or night, took one look at Merry and turned away to dish her up a slice of pie. "What about you, Nick? You having the same?"

He nodded, grinning. "And coffee, Ed. Thanks."

"My reputation precedes me," Merry said with twinkling eyes as they slid into a booth.

Handling the small late-night crowd by himself, Ed delivered their food to their table almost immediately. When he set the largest slice of pie directly in front of her, then just stood there, his expression fierce as he waited for her to taste it, Merry didn't bat an eye.

Taking a generous bite, she sighed in delight as the creamy chocolate melted on her tongue. "Mmm. Delicious, Ed. The best so far."

They played the game every time she came in, and he knew his part as well as she did. His lips just barely twitching, he nodded somberly. "Damn straight," he growled, then ruined everything with a wink.

Chuckling, Merry watched him stalk off to check on the only other customer in the place. "Old softie."

"Only with the people he likes," Nick said as he, too, dug into his pie. "You're just lucky he happens to be crazy about you. Otherwise, *I* would have gotten the bigger piece. Damn, this is good!"

It was, in fact, the best pie that either of them had ever put a fork to. And given the chance, they would have lingered over every bite, savoring it as they talked and joked and put off ending the evening. Ed would have refilled their coffee cups as long as they sat there and never once mentioned that they were keeping him past closing, but they couldn't let him do that. Not when he had to be back in at six-thirty to open the diner for the breakfast crowd. So by mutual agreement, they refused refills on coffee, finished the last mouthwatering bite of their pie, and rose to leave only five minutes past Ed's normal closing time.

Up until then, Merry hadn't given much thought to what would happen once they reached her house. But now, as Nick opened the passenger door of his car for her and waited for her to buckle up before shutting the door and coming around to slide behind the wheel, she only had to look at his face to know that he intended to kiss her good-night once they reached her house. And he wouldn't, she knew, give her an innocent peck on the cheek this time. He'd kiss her the way a man kissed the woman he was in love with. Just thinking about it made her heart start to pound in anticipation.

So what was all that baloney earlier about taking things slow and easy? a caustic voice taunted in her head. *Or did you forget that?*

She hadn't—she'd just been having so much fun that she hadn't thought that far ahead. But now as they left town behind and headed for the ranch, nervousness twisted her stomach in knots. After spending hours dancing in his arms, she readily admitted that she wanted him to kiss her—more than once. And that was what worried her. She didn't seem to have any control where he was concerned, and if she didn't do something fast, she was going to be in serious trouble in about ten minutes flat.

Just barely resisting the need to twist her hands together like a nervous virgin, she blurted out, "We need to talk."

Not taking his eyes off the road in case a deer or elk ran out in front of him, Nick said, "What about?"

"Sex."

That got his attention. His eyes shooting to hers in the darkness for all of two seconds, he immediately brought his gaze back to the road. "An interesting topic," he murmured dryly. "What about it?"

He was laughing at her—she was sure of it when she saw his lips twitch in the glow of the dash lights—but she'd never been more serious about anything in her life. "I won't pretend I'm not attracted to you," she said huskily. "I am, and it scares me to death."

"Why?"

The rough timbre of his voice wrapped around her in the dark, soothing her, encouraging her to confide in him, and before she knew it, she found herself opening her heart to him. "I don't know what to do with all these emotions you stir in me," she said thickly as her eyes started to sting with tears. "I want you to kiss me, to hold me, but then I remember Thomas, and I feel like there's something wrong with me. I'm not supposed to feel this way so soon! And certainly not with you!"

"Why not me?"

"Because..." How could she explain it to him when she didn't understand it herself? "I don't know," she said helplessly. "I've gone over it in my head a hundred times and the only thing that comes to mind is that you're Nick. You're my best friend. You were the one who taught me to parallel park and got me through geometry. You were there when my father died...and made me laugh when Thomas made me cry. You're like a brother—but you're not. And that's the problem. I don't know where you fit in my life anymore. And until I do...."

When she hesitated, he shot her another quick, sharp glance. "Until you do...what? Go ahead. You've come this far. Don't chicken out on me now."

She'd never run from anything in her life—she didn't intend to start tonight. Lifting her chin, she said, "I think it would be best if we left sex out of our relationship. That would only complicate things more than they already are."

She expected him to argue, to at least try to change her mind, but he surprised her by completely agreeing with her. "We're both adults," he said in that deep, raspy voice that she loved. "That shouldn't be a problem."

Taken aback, she arched a brow at him. "So you don't mind?"

"I'm not a Neanderthal," he assured her. "I can control my baser instincts."

Not sure if she was relieved or disappointed, she didn't know if she wanted to laugh or cry. "Well," she huffed, "I'm glad we got that settled."

Hiding a smile at her irritated tone, Nick drove through the ranch entrance, and within minutes, he was pulling up before her house. She'd left a light burning both inside and out, and without a word, he took her keys from her and opened her front door for her. When she made a move to step inside, however, he stopped her with just a touch on her arm. He liked to think his self-control was rock solid, but the romance of the evening had worked its magic on him, too.

"I think it would be better if we said goodnight right here," he said huskily. "It's late, and we both have to work tomorrow."

"Oh…yes, of course!" Turning back to him, she smiled shyly and had no idea how much she looked like the girl he'd known at sixteen. "I had a wonderful time tonight. Thank you."

"So did I," he murmured, and reached for her. "Come here."

Her eyes wide, she stuttered, "B-but you agreed to n-no s-sex."

"True," he replied consideringly. "I just wanted a kiss, Mer, but if you want to take it further—"

"No. No!" Suddenly seeing the mischief dancing in his eyes, she wanted to shake him. "You rat! I thought you were serious!"

Chuckling, he snatched her into his arms and was still laughing when his mouth covered hers. Between one heartbeat and another, however, the kiss turned dark and sensuous. He knew he should have let her go then, but he just couldn't bring himself to do that. Not yet. Not after he'd spent the evening in a perpetual state of arousal, aching for her.

With a murmur of need, he drew her closer, then closer still. Dear God, how he wanted her! But the feel of her against him, warm and giving in his arms, her mouth hot and hungry under his, went straight to his head. One kiss led to another, then another. Caught up in the wonder of her, he never felt his good intentions slip. Then, without quite realizing how it happened, he was reaching for the zipper of her dress.

Suddenly realizing what he was doing, he froze, cursing himself. What the hell was he doing? He'd just promised her that he wasn't going to do anything but kiss her, and the next thing he knew, he was peeling her clothes off of her! And on her front porch, no less! Swearing, his body hard with need, he clenched his jaw on an oath and carefully pulled her zipper back up with fingers that weren't quite steady.

Looking up at him with eyes that were dark with desire, she swayed toward him. "Nick…"

He moved like lightning then because if he hadn't, he would have snatched her up and carried her inside, and she wasn't ready for that yet. Setting her away from him, he took a quick step back, then another. "I've got to go," he rasped. "Dammit, Merry, don't look at me like that! I've only got so much self-control. If you don't want to find out what my limits are, you'd better get your sweet little butt inside while you still can. I mean it. Go on!"

She didn't, to her credit, hesitate. Whirling, she rushed inside and slammed the door after her as if the devil himself was after her. Standing right where he was, Nick waited for her to throw the dead bolt, then sighed in relief when it clicked into place. That, he told himself grimly, had been too damn close.

Merry had to give Nick credit. Over the course of the next few days, he held firm to his promise to keep sex out of their relationship. They talked several times a day, and now that he had two new deputies to help with the work-load, he had more time off so they could see each other, and not once during any of the conversation they had did Nick make a reference to the kisses they'd shared on her doorstep. He treated her just as he always had in the past, as a friend and nothing more, and she did the same. If his heart, like hers, stumbled into a frantic rhythm every time their eyes met, he didn't mention it and neither did she.

They were, however, both aware of the heated attraction between them. With each passing day, it became more dif-ficult to stick to the terms of their agreement, and to her chagrin, Merry knew she had no one to blame but herself. She was the one who'd done this to herself. She'd laid down the ground rules, insisted that they just be friends, and now she didn't think that was what she wanted at all.

More confused than ever, she needed some time to think, to get her head on straight, but when Nick showed up at her clinic one afternoon and offered to help check the traps she'd set in the woods for foxes and coyotes that might be responsible for helping spread the rabies epidemic, she couldn't pass up the chance to be alone with him.

"I set some new traps at the Hoffsteader place and up in Wild Horse Canyon yesterday," she told him as they headed west in her truck. "Martha Hoffsteader called me the other day to tell me that a pack of coyotes that lives in Wild Horse Canyon has been running wild through her ranch every evening after sunset, tearing up everything in their path. Her sons killed a couple of the more aggressive ones, but she's still having a problem.''

''Do you think they're rabid?''

She shrugged. ''It's certainly possible, especially since there've been a number of cases reported south and east of there. But coyotes are unpredictable at the best of times. During a drought like the one we've been in for the last few years, when water and food supplies dry up, they can get desperate. They might just be hungry, but I'm not taking any chances.''

Especially now that she had the epidemic pretty much under control. Until Martha Hoffsteader had called, there'd been no new reports of any possible rabies cases in nearly two weeks, and vaccination of the pet population in the county was virtually complete. Once she was able to clean up Wild Horse Canyon, she'd hopefully have the problem beaten.

They went to the Hoffsteader ranch first and checked the wire cages Merry had set up in strategic places. All of them were empty but two, and those held young coyotes that appeared to be fine except for the fact that they were frightened and didn't like being caged up. That didn't, however, mean that they hadn't already been infected with rabies. In the beginning stages of the disease, there were no outward signs that anything was wrong.

''I'll take them back to the clinic and watch them,'' she told Nick as he helped her hoist the caged animals into the back of her truck. ''If they've got rabies, it'll show up soon enough. C'mon. Let's go check out the canyon and see what we find there.''

Wild Horse Canyon was a deep, twisting canyon on the southern edge of the Rockies that was composed of a series of gorges that snaked off into dozens of different directions. Too rugged and remote for ranching, it wasn't, even under the best of conditions, the kind of place anyone should venture into alone. On a day when dark storm clouds were gathering angrily overhead, it looked downright dangerous.

Following Merry on foot into the canyon to the spot where she'd left one of the traps, Nick frowned as he noted just how secluded the area was. They'd had to leave the car a half a mile back, and civilization seemed a thousand miles away. "You came up here yesterday all by yourself?"

Finding the trap empty and the food she'd bated it with gone, she pulled a small slab of raw beef from the cooler she'd brought with her and tied it in place in the trap. "It's really not as deserted as it looks," she told Nick absently, her gaze focused on her work. "There's a line cabin over in those trees to the right that hunters use during hunting season, and you can run into hikers up here just about any time of the year. It's perfectly safe."

Nick knew she was right—the area was popular with outdoorsmen at certain times of the year—but he still didn't like the idea of her traipsing around the canyon alone. She might have experience hiking in the mountains—you couldn't grow up in that area of Colorado and not love hiking—but accidents could still happen. Especially when the terrain was steep and rugged and not fit for anything but goats. One slip and she could fall and seriously hurt herself, then be trapped there for hours, maybe days, before anyone found her.

Just thinking about it twisted his stomach in knots. "The next time you need to come out here, call me and I'll go with you," he growled. "I don't like the idea of you being out here all by yourself."

Touched, she grinned and pressed a hand to her heart. "My hero!" she sighed dreamily.

Amused in spite of himself, he reached over and tugged

at her hair. It was the first time he'd touched her in days. "You're damn straight, woman. I don't go anywhere without my Superman suit. I've got it on under my clothes right now."

"Really?"

"Oh, yeah," he assured her when she arched a brow at him over dancing eyes. "You get in the least bit of trouble, and I'm ready to fly to your rescue."

"Be still my heart!"

Laughing, Nick would have liked nothing more than to pull her into his arms then and kiss the stuffing out of her, but he'd given her his word. Reluctantly, he dropped his hand from her hair before he forgot his good intentions and forced a smile that didn't come as easily as he would have liked. "So where's the next trap?"

"Another half mile down the trail," she said as she started to hoist the backpack containing her supplies. "I—"

Whatever she was going to say next was lost by the crack of thunder that suddenly broke over their heads. Startled, they both flinched and glanced up to discover that while they'd been talking, the clouds gathering overhead had darkened ominously. Black and swollen, they churned angrily, trapped within the peaks of the surrounding mountains.

Frowning, Nick said, "I think we're going to have to skip the other trap for now. I don't like the look of that sky."

Lightning came out of nowhere just then, streaking in a jagged line straight toward a tree fifty yards to the north of them. In the roar of thunder that followed, Nick had to yell just to be heard. "C'mon, we're getting the hell out of here!"

He took her backpack from her and turned to run back the way they had come, but they'd waited five minutes too long. The skies opened up before they could take two steps, and in a matter of moments they were soaked to the skin.

It wasn't, however, the rain that Nick was worried about. The red dirt of the trail underfoot was dangerous enough in dry weather. In wet, it turned slick as glass. Blinded by the heavy downpour, if they took one misstep, they could find themselves at the bottom of a ravine and never know what hit them.

"We'll never make it to the truck," he roared.

Then, just when he thought conditions couldn't get any worse, mother nature proved him wrong. It started to hail.

Crying out in alarm, Merry ducked as hail rained down upon them. "The cabin," she yelled, pulling him with her into the trees. "It's up here."

Slipping and sliding, they crashed through the underbrush, dodging vines and low-lying branches as they climbed up the steep mountainside, searching for the cabin among the thick trees. The storm had brought an early twilight, and in the near darkness, it was nearly impossible to see. Finally, just when they both thought they must have missed it, they came across it quite by accident, nearly hidden among the trees.

The door was unlocked, and with a sigh of relief, they stumbled inside just as the storm abruptly intensified. Lightning flashed sharply like bombs exploding in the darkness, while thunder boomed, shaking the cabin to its very foundation. Overhead, hail pounded against the tin roof, producing a deafening roar while the wind gusted to twenty-five miles an hour, tearing at trees and shutters and door latches, threatening to tear the screens themselves from the windows. To anyone who didn't know better, it sounded like a hurricane was roaring through the mountains, destroying everything in its sight.

Soaked to the skin, Merry stood shivering just inside the

cabin's front door, peering into the darkness for some kind of light. Considering the cabin's remoteness, she wasn't surprised that it didn't have electricity or any other modern convenience, but there had to be a lantern or candle or oil lamp around there somewhere. It was an unwritten law among hunters and hikers that whenever they used a line cabin, they always replaced any supplies they used during their stay. The problem was finding a light source in the dark.

Obviously thinking the same thing, Nick moved cautiously in the thickening shadows to a cabinet near the fireplace. Feeling around blindly inside, searching the shelves, he grunted in approval when his fingers closed over a box of matches and a thick candle. "Here we go," he told Merry. And with a strike of a match, they had light.

In a single glance, he took in the contents of the one room cabin, noting the rough-hewn table in the middle of the room, the simple iron bed in the corner, the cabinet where he'd found the candle. There was a fireplace against one wall, a pile of firewood neatly stacked next to it, and a few kitchen tools and an iron skillet hanging on hooks nearby. That was it. No kitchen or bathroom, no stove or water, other than the stream outside that ran behind the cabin.

It wasn't the kind of place where Nick would have wanted to spend his vacation, but it was sturdy and dry and would do in a pinch. Especially when it was raining cats and dogs outside and the car was over a half mile away.

Satisfied, he turned back to Merry. "Not bad," he began as the thunder of the hail on the roof began to ease. Then he got a good look at her in the candlelight and his mouth went dry at the sight of her.

She was soaked to the skin and literally standing in a puddle of her own making. Her hair hung in limp curls to her shoulders, giving her the appearance of a drowned rat, but it wasn't her hair Nick was looking at. It was the thin pink shirt and equally thin white cotton pants that were plastered to every inch of her breasts and hips.

His heart slamming against his ribs, he watched goose bumps rise on her skin and realized she was cold. The sudden rain and high winds had dropped the temperature at least fifteen degrees in the last few moments, and they were both wearing wet clothes. Swearing at his thoughtlessness, he looked around for something to cover her with and could find nothing but a rough towel hanging on a peg.

Grabbing it, he strode over to her and gently wrapped it around her wet shoulders. "I'll light a fire," he said roughly, turning away. "Give me a second and I'll warm things up in here in no time."

He'd already done that just by folding the towel around her, but Merry couldn't find the words to tell him. Her pulse pounding, she watched him go down on one knee in front of the fireplace and wondered if he had any idea what he did to her every time they were alone together. And never had she been more aware of their solitude than she was now. The rest of the world could have blown away in the storm outside the cabin's front door, and she wouldn't have noticed anything but the ripple of muscles across Nick's strong back as he placed logs in the fireplace and lit the fire. The clean, woodsy scent of him tugged at her senses, tantalizing her, teasing her until all she could think of was him. The feel of him, the taste of him, the aching need she had for him.

Sitting back on his heels, he watched the fire as it caught and started to burn, and Merry couldn't help but watch him in return. In the glow of the fire, his angular jaw was carved in stone, his cheeks and blade of a nose sculpted by the firelight. He looked hard and primitive and incredibly appealing.

When he suddenly glanced up at her without warning, there was no time to school her expression, no time to look away. He saw the need in her eyes, the desire she couldn't hide, and his own eyes darkened in response. His gaze never leaving hers, he rose slowly to his feet.

Her heart started to pound when he reached for her. "I want you," he rasped as his hands closed over her shoulders. "I know we had an agreement, but you need to know that if I kiss you now, I don't think I'll be able to stop."

It was her call. If she insisted on sticking to the terms of their agreement, she knew he would respect that. He'd back off, keep his hands and kisses to himself, and not touch her again, regardless of how long the storm lasted. Her common sense told her that was the wise thing to do. She was still adjusting to the fact that she was attracted to him—it was way too soon for a physical relationship. Her heart knew that, accepted that, and didn't give a damn. She wanted him and nothing else mattered.

Anticipation setting her pulse thundering, she said huskily, "It's still cold in here. I think we should both get out of these wet clothes."

His gaze narrowed sharply. "There can't be any misunderstandings here, Merry. Tell me what you want."

That was easy. "You," she answered simply, and slid her arms around his neck to pull his mouth down to hers.

He couldn't have resisted her then if the devil himself had been pounding on the door, demanding to get in. Not when he finally had her all to himself and she wanted him as much as he wanted her. With a low groan that seemed to come all the way from his soul, he pulled her close and kissed her the way he'd been dying to for years.

He'd lost count of the times he'd dreamed of this, ached

for it, for *her,* and he wasn't going to rush it. Not this first time. Slowly, gently, he kissed her as if he had all the time in the world, then kissed her again, this time taking the kiss deeper, letting her feel what she did to him. Caught up in the taste of her, he didn't remember reaching for the buttons of her blouse, but suddenly he was peeling the wet garment from her shoulders. An instant later, her bra joined it on the floor.

Her skin was golden in the firelight, her breasts full and pert and beautiful. Cupping her in his hands, he groaned at the feel of her. ''You're so pretty,'' he rasped, and leaned down to explore her with his mouth.

Moaning softly, Merry clung to him, her senses spinning. Nothing had ever felt like this before, and he'd hardly touched her. When he finally brought his mouth back to hers, she was breathless, needy, desperate to touch him, too. ''My turn,'' she whispered huskily, and lifted her hands to the buttons of his shirt.

One by one, she unbuttoned them, slowly trailing her fingers down the middle of his chest, teasing him even as she teased herself. And with every brush of her fingers, with every button that slowly parted, the anticipation built. When the shirt finally hung open, giving her a glimpse of the hard wall of his chest, her breath caught in her throat as she slowly pushed it off his shoulders until he, too, was bare to the waist.

He'd looked much the same that morning in her kitchen after he'd mowed her lawn, but she hadn't gotten to touch him then. Giving into impulse, she lifted her hands to his shoulders and ran her fingers over him, tracing every hard muscle, loving the strength she found there. He was a man she could always depend on, she thought, leaning forward to kiss the spot where his heart beat beneath her hand. Why had it taken her so long to realize that? All these years, he'd been right there in front of her nose, and she'd never seen him.

Watching the emotions flickering in her eyes, Nick cupped her face in his hands. "Hey," he growled softly. "What's going on in that head of yours?"

Tears came out of nowhere to cling to the ends of her lashes. "I can't believe that all this time I couldn't see you for Thomas. You're such a better man."

"Everything happens for a reason," he said softly, leaning down to kiss her tears away. "The past got us to where we are today. Nothing else matters but now."

And now, she had to admit, was pretty incredible. Murmuring to her reassuringly, he dropped kisses on her cheeks, the tip of her nose, the corner of her mouth, and she forget all about Thomas and the past. There was only Nick and the feel of him, the taste of him, the heat of his mouth on hers. With one long, slow kiss after another, he seduced her with a tenderness that melted her bones, until she was achy and vulnerable and desperate for more.

Restless, she moaned when he started to put her away from him, but his hands were there to soothe, his voice rough as he murmured, "It's okay, sweetheart. I'm just getting rid of the rest of these wet clothes."

He stripped them both of their wet pants and underwear, then, ignoring the bed in the corner, carried her down to the floor and the towel he quickly spread out before the fireplace. Heat lapped at them from the crackling fire, but it was the flames that licked at Nick from the inside out that turned his body hot and hard and hungry as he came down into her waiting arms. At the feel of her under him, her body cradling his, he very nearly lost it.

Sucking in a sharp breath, he struggled for control, but she didn't make it easy for him. Her hands roamed over him, stroking and teasing and driving him wild, and just that easily, she brought the storm inside. With a low growl, he captured her fingers and anchored them on the floor by her head.

"Nick!"

"Easy, love," he murmured, kissing his way down her body. "We're going to take this nice and easy."

He meant to drive them both slowly out of their minds, until they both burned so badly for the other that they forgot their own names, but he hadn't counted on Merry's determination. Tangling her legs with his, she moved under him, rubbing against him as he kissed her breasts, her waist, the curve of her hip, her soft moans calling to his own need as nothing else could.

Fire licking at him, his body tight, he released her hands, but only to fumble for his jeans and the condom in his wallet. When his fingers shook, he cursed, unable to remember the name of any woman who'd ever made him burn this hot. But there'd never been any woman for him quite like Merry. She pushed his hands aside, took care of the necessary precautions herself, then she was pulling him down to her, into her, and the pleasure was almost more than he could bear.

A groan ripped from his throat when she moved with him, her rhythm matching his so perfectly that if he hadn't known better, he would have sworn they'd been together like this for lifetimes. Nothing had ever felt so right, so perfect, so natural. He wanted to tell her, but his mind blurred, his senses swam, and all he could think of was that he wanted this time with her to last forever. That was all he wanted. Forever.

But his body and heart had different ideas, and with every stroke, every urgent lift of her hips, every dark, hungry kiss, the fire burned brighter, hotter, until it flared out

of control. With a hoarse cry, she shuddered in his arms
and just that easily, he was lost to everything but his driving
need for her. Her name torn from his throat, he followed
her over the edge and into the flames.

Chapter 11

"I love you."

He'd never meant to say the words so quickly—after everything that she'd been through, it was too soon—but lying there on the cabin floor with her cradled in his arms as the storm slowly passed outside, emotions that had been bottled up in his heart for years clamored to be spoken. He loved her and wanted to spend the rest of his life with her. Right or wrong, ready or not, she had to know that.

Running his hand soothingly down the silken skin of her bare back, he said huskily, "I know you're probably not ready to hear this, but I've been waiting years to tell you how I feel, and I can't put it off any longer."

"Nick—"

"No," he said quickly, even as he heard the protest in her voice. "Just listen. I love you—I can't remember a time when I didn't. I know Thomas told you the same thing, but I mean it with all my heart. I want to marry you."

That was as far as he got. Before he could say another

word, she pressed her hand to his mouth, stopping him in his tracks. "Don't!" she cried softly, her eyes dark with distress. "Not yet. It's too soon. That doesn't mean I'm turning you down," she assured him when he stiffened. "But I can't say yes, either. Not yet."

She'd hurt him and she knew it, but she didn't know what else to do. He'd touched her heart in a way Thomas never had, but panic raced through her veins just at the thought of making a commitment to him or anyone else at this point in her life. "Please, can't things just stay the way they are for a while?" she pleaded, sliding her hand from his mouth to cup his cheek gently. "We've just found each other. Let's enjoy that for now and not worry about the future."

He wanted to argue—she could see it in his eyes—and she couldn't say she blamed him. He'd had to stand for years and watch her with Thomas, and he, no doubt, felt like he'd waited long enough. But he had to understand that she'd just escaped a mistake by the skin of her teeth. She needed time—time to recover, time to get her head on straight, time to learn to trust her own feelings again. Until she could do that, she could never go forward with plans for the future.

"I'm not turning you down," she repeated quietly. "I just don't want to rush into anything. I did that when Thomas came back to town last year, and look what a disaster that turned out to be. If I'd just waited and given us some time, I would have realized that he didn't love me the way I needed to be loved by the man I planned to marry, and my feelings for him weren't much stronger.

"And no, I'm not saying that's going to happen to us," she said when he started to frown. "I just want time to be sure, Nick. This has all happened so fast. We need to slow things down and give ourselves some time."

"How much time?" he growled.

He sounded like a sullen little boy who was going to pout now that he hadn't gotten his way. Biting back a smile, she suggested, "Why don't we take it one day at a time and see how things go? We'll both know when we're ready to take the next step."

It wasn't what he wanted, but they both knew it was the wise thing to do. They hadn't waited this long to find each other only to mess things up by rushing. "All right," he said grudgingly. "We'll do it your way—for now. But you should know I'm not a very patient man."

If that had been the case, he would have given up on her a long time ago, but that was a thought Merry wisely kept to herself. "I'll try to remember that," she said solemnly, her blue eyes twinkling. "Now that we've got that settled, is there anything else you'd like to discuss? It's still raining outside, so it looks like we're not going anywhere fast. Maybe you'd like to talk about the stock market or global warming or—"

He shushed her simply by leaning down and pressing a lingering kiss to her breast, just above her heart. "The only warming I want to talk about is the way your body catches fire whenever I kiss you right here," he said huskily. "And here." Trailing his lips up the side of her neck, he kissed her just below the ear and smiled when she softly moaned. "So what do you say? Do you think we can talk about that until it stops raining?"

"Oh, yes," she purred, her smile sultry as he brought his mouth to hers for a slow, languid, kiss. "And if I have my way, it's going to rain for a long, long time."

It did, in fact, rain all afternoon, but they couldn't hide away in the cabin forever. Left with no choice, they carefully hiked back to where they'd left Merry's truck, and in the process, got soaked all over again. Still, neither of them could regret it. Driving back to the clinic in the rain, they held hands all the way.

The weather system that brought the storm that trapped them in the cabin didn't move on as expected, but settled in over the southwestern part of the state instead, and stayed a solid week. Day after day, storms rolled across the sky, dropping rain on parched land that hadn't seen any significant rainfall in over two years. Streams and ponds filled to capacity, then overflowed, and the drought that had hurt ranchers all over Colorado was finally broken.

But with the much needed rainfall came all sorts of problems for Nick and his deputies. Because of the slick roads, there were more wrecks in one week than there had been in a year, and that didn't include the number of drivers who drowned out their vehicles when they tried to drive across low-lying streams that had overrun their banks. Then there were the elderly folks around the county who got stuck in the mud or needed help with a leaking roof or couldn't get out to check on their pets or cattle or summer wheat crop. At least three or four calls came in an hour, sometimes more, and Nick and his deputies answered every one of them regardless of the time of day or night.

It was exhausting work that kept Nick running all over the county, and there were times when it seemed as if the rain would never end. He managed to find a way to see Merry every night, either at her house or his, even if it was just to watch TV together, but he had to let the rest of his life slide. Then one day, he came home after working ten hours straight to find a letter from the FBI in his mailbox. For the first time in weeks, he remembered the resume and application he'd sent to Howard Quinn at the Bureau.

Howard had promised to do what he could for him, but since he hadn't heard from him, Nick had assumed that there were no openings at the moment or he didn't have the qualifications for the job. Setting down at the kitchen table to go through his mail, Nick tore open the envelope, figuring this was just formal notification thanking him for applying and wishing him luck elsewhere.

Dear Sir:
After considering your application for employment, I am happy to inform you that you have been accepted into the Federal Bureau of Investigation's agent school at Quantico, Virginia....

Stunned, Nick almost dropped the letter. He'd been accepted to Quantico! Elation shot through him. Hot damn! He couldn't believe it ! It was the job offer of a lifetime, a chance he'd really thought he'd never get, even when Howard had assured him he had all the qualifications the Bureau was looking for in agents. The FBI. Dear God, it was every law enforcement officer's dream!

Quickly reading the rest of the letter, he lifted a brow at the day he was to report to work in Virginia. He had six weeks. Damn, he had to get busy! He'd have to make a weekend trip to Virginia to find a place to live, and call Tina Adams to discuss lowering the asking price of his house. He'd finished the last of the touchup repairs and still hadn't had any offers, so obviously the price was too high. But first, he had to give the mayor his notice and discuss hiring his replacement. And then there was Merry—

Suddenly stopping in his tracks, he swore. What the hell was he doing? He couldn't take this job, not if it meant leaving Merry. And what else could it mean? Her family was here, her clinic. She'd spent years building up her business, putting her heart and soul into it. How could he ask her to give that all up and walk away from her family to move across the country with him? Especially when she hadn't even accepted his proposal yet?

Torn, he frowned, swearing at the dilemma he found himself trapped in. He didn't need the job with the Bureau to be happy—all he needed was Merry. He loved her, and if she married him, he'd be perfectly content to spend the rest of his life in Liberty Hill. But if she couldn't bring herself to consider trying marriage again, if she just wanted to continue on the way they were indefinitely, living separate lives and seeing each other when they could, he knew he couldn't stay there, not and only have part of her. He was willing to give her some time, but in the end, he wanted all or nothing.

The question was...could he really walk away?

Not sure himself what the answer to that was, he frowned down at the letter from the Bureau and was still searching for an answer when the phone rang. Tossing the letter down with the rest of his mail on the kitchen table, he rose to answer it. "Hello?"

"I hate to bother you when you're off duty," Sheri said, "but we've got a problem."

After all the other problems that had cropped up due to the weather over the course of the week, Nick didn't bat an eye. "What now?"

"There's been a three-car pileup with a truck in the median on the Eagle Ridge Highway out by Walker's Point, and Rick and Lincoln are already out on other calls."

"So where the hell's Harvey?"

"Getting towed in from Gunnison. It looks like the transmission finally went out on his patrol car."

Of course, Nick thought, swearing. Things didn't go wrong when it was convenient. What was the fun of that? Disasters were much more interesting for the powers that be if they happened when everything else was falling apart.

"I'll be right there," he growled. "I just have to change into a clean uniform."

In the end, it would have been better if he hadn't taken time to change into clean clothes. The clean ones only got dirty again when he had to wade into the mud to investigate the accident, which was a mess. The semi had been carrying a load of live chickens, and now dead ones were strewn all over the highway. Soggy feathers were everywhere, and in spite of the fact that two witnesses claimed the truck driver was at fault, three more said it was one of the accident victims who'd been weaving in and out of traffic in a little red sports car who'd really caused all the trouble.

Resigned, Nick calculated the time it would take to clear the mess up and do the paperwork and swore. Merry was meeting him at his house in two hours for pizza and a Martin and Lewis film festival on TNT. He'd have to hurry if he wasn't going to be late.

The pizza was cold and the first movie in the film festival half over when Nick finally walked through his front door three hours later. He'd called Merry to tell her about the accident and that he was going to be late, so she hadn't really been worried about him, but she had started to get concerned when another storm had moved through the area and he still hadn't made it home.

Pushing up from the couch in the den at the first sound of his footstep in the hall, she turned to greet him with a smile of relief, only to wince at the sight of him. She'd never seen a more miserable—or irritated—man in her life. He'd obviously got caught out in the storm. His uniform was soaked through and splattered with mud. But it was the feathers that clung to his hair and wet clothes—and the furious set of his jaw—that was nearly her undoing. She'd never seen such a comical combination in her life.

She didn't, however, dare laugh—because once she started, she didn't think she'd be able to stop—but Lord, it was hard. Biting her lip to hold back the giggle bubbling in her throat, she choked, "Are you all right?"

He just glared at her. "What do you think?"

"Dumb question," she agreed, trying and failing to hide the grin that kept turning up the corners of her mouth. "Why don't I heat up the pizza while you take a shower? Would you like some feathers—I mean, a salad!—with that?"

He had to laugh—he couldn't help himself. "Damn you," he chuckled. "A salad sounds great, but hold the feathers, okay? I'm cutting back on my fat intake."

Grinning, Merry watched him head for the bathroom and called after him, "Don't forget to wash behind your ears, Chicken Little. It looks like you're growing wings back there."

For an answer, he shot her a rude hand gesture over his shoulder and disappeared into the bathroom. Chuckling, Merry stepped into the kitchen to reheat the pizza and make a salad. Five minutes later, she was up to her wrists in lettuce when the phone rang.

Normally, she would have let the answering machine take it, but with the weather conditions as bad as they were, she thought one of Nick's deputies might be calling about another wreck. "Not again," she said with a frown as she quickly wiped her hands and reached for the phone. It was so nasty out, and he was only just now changing into dry clothes. Surely he wouldn't have to go out again before he even had supper!

"Kincaid residence," she said in a less than welcoming voice. "This is Merry."

"Hi, Merry, this is Sonny York." A retired teacher who now spent his days dabbling in the stock market, Sonny regularly discussed the ups and downs of the market and the occasional stock tip he got from friends on the Internet with Nick. "Is Nick in?"

"Yes, he is, Sonny, but he's in the shower right now. Can he call you back?"

He hesitated. "Actually, I'm leaving in just a second for Colorado Springs, and I won't be back for a week. I've been trying to get in touch with him all day with some info on a stock he asked me to check out, but I keep missing him. If you could just give him the numbers for me—"

"Of course," she said quickly. Looking around for something to write with, she found a pen on the kitchen table, along with a pile of what looked like discarded mail. "Just a minute," she told him as she searched for a piece of scratch paper. "I need some paper. This should do. I—"

"...you have been accepted into the Federal Bureau of Investigation's agent program at Quantico, Virginia...report August 15..."

The words fairly leapt off the page at Merry, slapping her right in the face. Stunned, she hardly heard Sonny as he rattled off the name, cost, and projected earnings of a stock she'd never heard of. He was leaving. She'd thought he'd given up the idea of applying with the FBI, but not only had he sent in an application, he'd been hired. And he'd never said a word to her.

"Did you get all that?"

Lost in the sudden pain that squeezed her heart, it was a long moment before Sonny's words registered. "What?" Glancing down at the numbers she jotted down without even being aware of it, she said distractedly, "Oh, yes, I got it. Thank you, Sonny. I'll make sure he gets this."

She hung up without wishing him a safe trip, her

thoughts in a turmoil as they jumped right back to Nick. The FBI. He was moving to Virginia to become an FBI agent, she thought numbly. She should have been happy for him. The Bureau's reputation may have taken a few hits over the last few years, but it was still one of the top law enforcement agencies in the world. Nick had to be thrilled. And who wouldn't be? Only the best were accepted into the Bureau's elite ranks.

And Nick was the best. Why had it taken her so long to realize just how special he was? She'd only just recently started seeing him for the man he really was, and now she was losing him. Just like she'd lost Thomas.

No, she thought, correcting herself. The pain she'd felt when Thomas had humiliated her in front of the entire town was nothing, *nothing,* compared to what she felt now. She was devastated. And furious. She'd stood by and let Thomas walk out on her and that turned out to be the best thing she could have ever done. Although she hadn't realized it at the time, marriage between the two of them would have never worked. She accepted that now. But her feelings for Nick were so much deeper and more complicated than anything she'd ever felt for Thomas. He was her best friend, her confidant, her lover. He'd become so special to her, and now she was going to lose him? She didn't think so!

Steaming mad, she completely forgot about the salad she'd been making when Sonny called and read the letter from the Bureau over again, instead. But she didn't like its contents any more the second time than she had the first, and almost threw it in the trash. It wasn't hers to throw away, however, and with a muttered oath, she tossed it back down on the table.

"Mmm! That pizza smells good," Nick said as he stepped into the kitchen with a broad smile creasing his face. "When do we eat?"

Angry words already building up on her tongue, she whirled on him...and temporarily forgetting what she was going to say. No man had a right to clean up so well, she fumed. Dressed in jeans and a blue and white T-shirt, he'd shaved and washed his hair, and even from where she stood across the room, Merry could smell the tantalizing scent of his cologne. It was, she silently acknowledged, a scent that was far too tempting for her current peace of mind.

Irritated that she'd even noticed, she glared at him. "To be perfectly honest, I've lost my appetite. Why didn't you tell me you were still pursuing the job with the FBI?"

His eyes immediately flew to the mail on the table and the letter that lay in clear view on top. Swearing under his breath, he took a step toward her. "Look, I was going to tell you, but I forgot about it myself until today—"

She snorted in disbelief. "You forgot that you applied with the FBI?"

"No, of course not," he retorted. "It just slipped my mind. There's been a lot going on, and I really didn't expect to get accepted."

She wanted to believe him, but she couldn't forget Thomas, couldn't forget the way he'd walked out on her without a word of warning. "So when were you going to tell me you were leaving? Or were you? Thomas didn't."

"Is that what this is about?" he asked sharply. "Thomas? I told you before, Mer, don't compare me to him. I'm nothing like him."

He was right. It wasn't fair of her to lump him in the same category as Thomas. They were two different men and just because Thomas had betrayed her didn't necessarily mean that Nick would, too. "No, you're not," she agreed quietly. "You're ten times the man he is. I'm just hurt. I won't lose you the way I did him. I won't go through that again."

His brows snapping together in a scowl, Nick didn't like the direction the conversation was going one little bit. "What do you mean...you won't go through *that* again?" he demanded. "If you're saying you don't want me to leave just because everyone knows we've been seeing each other and you don't want to be humiliated in front of the whole town again, you'd better know right now that's not good enough. I need a hell of a better reason than that to stay."

Stunned, she blinked at him in confusion. "Humiliated? What are you talking about? You think I don't want you to leave because people will *talk?*"

"What else am I supposed to think? You just said that you wouldn't lose me the way you lost Thomas, that you wouldn't go through that again."

Stunned that he would misunderstand her so completely, she cried, "But I wasn't talking about being stood up at the altar! Granted, that's not something I would wish on anyone, but in my case, it was a blessing in disguise. I would never regret that."

"Then what are you so bent out of shape about?" he said, frowning. "I don't understand."

"It's you," she replied. "I don't want to lose *you.* That's why I was so shook up when I saw that damn letter. I couldn't bear the thought of losing someone I loved a second time."

Something flared in his eyes at that, something that set her heart thumping in her breast. And just that quickly, she realized that in her rush to make him understand that she refused to let him walk out on her, she hadn't said the one thing that needed to be said above all others.

"I love you." The words came so easily, as if they'd always been there, right on the tip of her tongue, waiting to be said. All this time, she'd loved him, she thought, stunned. And she'd never even suspected it.

Tears glistening in her eyes, her throat tight with emotion, she stepped toward him, reaching for him, needing the strength of his arms around her. "I love you," she said again, "and I'm not going to lose you. If you're going to Virginia, so am I."

She couldn't have surprised him more if she'd stripped naked and run right through the middle of the town square. "But everything you love is here...your family, the ranch, your work."

She couldn't deny it—he knew her too well. "I'll come home and visit the family when I can, but I'm going with you...." Suddenly realizing that she may have misinterpreted his intentions, she broke off in chagrin. Unsure of herself, she said stiffly, "I'm sorry. I'm jumping to conclusions here, aren't I? I assumed that you would want me to go with you. You did ask me to marry you. But maybe you've changed your mind..."

"Don't be ridiculous," he growled, and pulled her into his arms.

She loved him! Over and over again, the words echoed in his head like a song, until he could have shouted with joy. He wanted to ask her when, how, for how long, but he couldn't stop kissing her. Not now. Not when he had her in his arms, next to his heart, and she'd finally said the words. Nothing else mattered but that. Just the two of them, together at last.

Laughing, she struggled to get her breath as he suddenly swept her up in his arms and started for his bedroom. "Nick! Wait! The pizza—"

"To hell with the pizza," he muttered against her mouth, and retraced his steps into the kitchen to turn off the oven. Seconds later, supper forgotten, he strode into his bedroom with her still in his arms and did a free fall with her onto the bed.

"Nick!"

"Merry!" he mimicked, chuckling as he rolled across the mattress with her and stopped when she came up on top. "Tell me again."

She didn't have to ask what he meant—she knew. She needed to say it as much as he needed to hear it. Her smile turning soft and tender, she stared down into his beloved face and saw him, really saw him, for the first time. Fascinated, she traced the manly slant of his dark brows, the straight line of his nose, the sensuous, inviting curve of his mouth, and all she could think of was that he was hers. Forever. Because if she knew anything about Nick Kincaid, it was that when he gave his love, it was forever.

"I love you." The words came straight from her soul. "More than I ever thought it was possible to love anyone— including Thomas. I know I probably shouldn't bring up his name at a time like this, but we can't pretend that he was never a part of my life. I did have feelings for him, and for a long time, I thought those feelings were love. But the difference between what I felt for him and what I feel for you is like day and night. I just needed you to know that."

But telling him and showing him were two different things, and showing was so much more enjoyable. With a murmur of need, she leaned down to kiss him, and all she could think of was how easily she could have lost him if fate hadn't stepped in and taken a hand. If Thomas hadn't chickened out at their wedding, if two of Nick's deputies hadn't quit, making it impossible for him to leave town to find another job when he'd wanted to, she wouldn't even have known that he loved her, let alone had the chance to fall in love with him herself.

So close, she thought, shaken. She didn't want to ever come that close to losing him again. "I need you, Nick," she whispered huskily in his ear. "More than I thought I could need anyone. Don't ever leave me."

"Never," he promised in a rough growl, burying his hands in her hair to pull her down for a fierce kiss. "I love you. I'm not going anywhere without you."

Reassured, that was all she needed to hear. Her heart expanding with love, she gave herself up to his kiss and the longing that had settled like an ache deep inside her. Her hands rushed over him, claiming him, savoring the feel of his lean, hard body, and with every touch, her mind silently shouted, "Mine."

Hot pleasure rippling through him, Nick groaned and told himself he was going to take charge of their loving any second now. Well, maybe in another hour or two. After he'd stood the bliss as long as he could. In the meantime, he'd just lay there and let the lady do whatever made her happy. After all, she seemed so bent on having her way with him. He wouldn't want to disappoint her.

But he wasn't nearly as strong as he thought he was, not when it came to Merry. Her smile teasing and seductive, she stripped him out of his clothes before he knew what she was about, then shed her own. Between one heartbeat and the next, bare skin rubbed against bare skin and he was hot and hard and desperate for her. Growling low in his throat, he rolled her under him, settled between her thighs, and slid into her with an ease that rocked them both.

In the sudden, hushed silence of the darkened bedroom, their eyes met in a silent communication that was nearly Nick's undoing. If she hadn't told him that she loved him before that moment, he would have known it then. It was there shining in her eyes for all the world to see—love, tenderness, happiness, desire—in a wild mix of exhilarating emotions that went as deep as her soul. And in that instant, Nick knew beyond a shadow of a doubt that any feelings she'd once had for Thomas had faded into oblivion and were gone forever. *He* was the one she loved, the one she wanted to be with, the one she intended to spend her life with.

Impossibly moved, he leaned down and brushed her lips with his. Once, twice, in a caress as soft as a feather floating on a summer breeze, he kissed her, convinced he needed nothing more from her at that moment than just that.

Then she moved.

It was just a slight movement, a tiny adjustment of her hips that might not have even been noticed—if it hadn't brought him deeper inside her. His breath hissed between his teeth, her eyes darkened with desire, and suddenly the fire that always seemed to spark between them lately was hot and intense and seemed to singe the very air they breathed.

''Do that again,'' he rasped. ''I dare you.''

The youngest of four children, she wasn't one to refuse a dare. Especially one that could only bring them both a great deal of pleasure. Her smile slow and sultry, she sensuously tightened her muscles around him—and just that easily, almost made him whimper in delight.

''Uncle! Aunt! Great Grandma Sally Ann!'' he groaned in defeat as he fought the need to move himself. ''I surrender, sweetheart. You win! Stop before you push me over the edge.''

That, however, was exactly what she wanted, and she had no intention of stopping. ''Make me,'' she said huskily, and lifted her hips invitingly to his.

She set a rhythm that he found impossible to resist, teasing him with the seductive dance of her hips, stroking him slowly, intimately, until he thought he would die from the pleasure of it. Need fisted inside him, heat licking at his nerve endings. Unable to bear the sensual torment a second longer, he drove deep, up to the hilt, and nearly shattered them both.

"Nick!"

"I know, honey," he groaned, loving the feel of her, hot and moist, around him. "It feels good, doesn't it?"

It felt wonderful! Caught up in the magic of it, they surged together, increasing the pace, instinctively knowing what the other needed without saying a word. A tender touch, a lingering kiss, a murmured endearment whispered in the night, and two hearts beat as one.

Enchanted, Merry could have stayed just that way, with him buried deep inside her, their bodies moving to a throbbing beat as old as time itself, for the rest of the night. But her heart was already thundering, desire clawing at her, tearing at her until she could focus on nothing but the ache of it. Then Nick, sensing her need, kissed his way up the side of her neck, using lips and teeth and tongue to tease the sensitive spot right below her ear, and her breath caught on a sob as her body suddenly tightened in response. Clinging to him, to the moment, she tried to draw it out, but it was too late. Capturing her hips in his hands, he changed the angle of their union just a fraction, and she felt his touch all the way to her heart. Lightning flared in her blood like liquid gold, and in the next instant, his name a cry on her lips, she shattered.

"Nick!"

Never had he heard her call his name in just that way, with such love, as if he was all she'd ever wanted or needed. Just that simply, she destroyed him. His breath tearing through his lungs, the roar of his blood loud in his ears, he surged into her, his hips pumping madly. Release was, he knew, just out of his reach in the darkness. Then, with no warning, he was on it in a rush. Before he could do anything but groan, it took him like a storm, swallowing him whole, consuming him. And for the first time in his life, he discovered the true meaning of ecstasy.

Later, Merry couldn't have said how long they lay there in each others arms, savoring the touch and feel and wonder of each other and the intimacy of what they had just shared. It could have been minutes, hours, days. Time had no meaning, no place. It was just the two of them, alone, together in bed. More content than she'd ever been in her life, she couldn't think of anywhere else she'd rather be.

"I was serious when I said I would go with you to Virginia," she said quietly. "Nothing is more important to me than being with you. You know that, don't you? I love you."

"And I love you," he replied huskily, tightening his arms around her. "Which is why I'm not going anywhere."

Surprised, she pulled back just enough so that she could see his face in the light that filtered down the hall from the living room into his bedroom. "You're not taking the job with the Bureau? Why not? If it's because of me—"

"It's because of us," he cut in, shushing her. "This is where we belong, sweetheart. Where we've always belonged. I admit that working in D.C. sounded like something out of a dream, but that's not really who I am. I like being a small-town sheriff and knowing everyone in town. I want us to live here, raise our kids here…"

Her heart turning over in her breast, Merry arched a brow at him. "And what kids would that be?"

"The ones that we're going to have after we're married," he replied without batting an eye. "You are going to marry me, aren't you?"

He asked in an almost casual way, as if it was an afterthought and her answer a given, but he didn't fool Merry for a second. She felt the sudden tension in the arms that cradled her close, and under the hand she rested on his chest, his heartbeat was anything but steady. He was all but holding his breath, and, no doubt, expected her to turn him down like she had before.

Tenderness flooding her, she stretched up and pressed a gentle kiss to his mouth. "Yes, I'll marry you," she said huskily.

"In church?"

Somehow, deep inside, she'd known that's what he would want...a church wedding in front of the whole town. Just like the wedding she'd planned with Thomas. Just thinking about putting herself through that again sent dread spilling into her stomach. How could she set herself up for that kind of disaster a second time?

"Oh, God, I don't know. Nick, please—"

"It won't be like before," he assured her. "I'm not Thomas. I know what I want—I've always known what I wanted. You, sweetheart. Just you. So when I tell you you can count on me to be waiting for you when you walk down that aisle, you know I'll be there. I wouldn't miss it for the world."

There was no doubting his sincerity or the fact that he meant every word. Come rain or shine, hell or high water, sickness or anything else short of death, he would be there for her. She could count on him. All she had to do was trust him.

There'd been a time, just weeks ago, when she would have run at the very idea of trusting a man, any man, ever again. But that was when her heart was still battered and bruised and hurting. Now that she'd given herself time to heal, to feel again, to love, she knew she had nothing to fear. Not from Nick. Even when she'd been prepared to marry another man, he'd been there for her, thinking of her happiness before his own. He loved her. The last thing he would ever do was hurt her.

He was so special. And she'd almost missed him. Tears welling in her eyes at the thought, she blinked them hurriedly back before he could misunderstand and took his hand, linking his fingers with hers. "Yes, I'll marry you," she whispered huskily, the smile that spread across her face slow and beautiful and filled with love. "In church or the middle of Main Street or on the town square if that's what you want. Just tell me the date and time, and I'll be there."

He didn't hesitate. "One month from today, your church, ten o'clock in the morning. How does that sound to you?"

"Perfect," she said, her eyes shining with love. "It looks like you've got yourself a deal, Sheriff Kincaid. Shall we shake on it?"

"I've got a better idea," he growled, and sealed the proposal with a kiss.

Chapter 12

He gave her one month to plan a wedding. He refused to wait another second more than that to make her his wife. He'd already waited thirty-two years. That was his limit.

Given the choice, he would have liked something simple and old-fashioned, and Merry thankfully agreed. She'd already planned one elaborate wedding, not because she'd wanted all the pomp and circumstance, but because Thomas—and his mother—tended to be snobs when it came to that kind of thing. They'd both insisted that nothing less than the most sophisticated wedding the town had ever seen would do for a prominent lawyer and the daughter of one of the biggest ranching families in the state. So for the sake of peace and unity, Merry had given up her dream of a simple wedding and gone along with them, only to have the whole thing blow up in her face.

Never again, she promised herself. Like Nick, she just wanted the two of them to get married. She didn't need expensive flowers flown in from California or ten attendants in designer dresses. All she needed to make her happy was Nick standing at the altar, waiting for her as she walked down the aisle.

He would be there for her. Deep in her heart, she knew she could count on him, but the closer they drew to their wedding day, the more anxious she became. A knot of nerves tightened in her stomach, and every time the phone rang, she jumped, afraid it was Nick calling to tell her he'd changed his mind. He had no intention of doing such a thing, of course—she knew that, dammit!—but she was helpless to control her fears. She had a horrible feeling history was going to repeat itself, and if it did, she didn't think she would be able to bear it.

Feeling guilty for doubting Nick even for a second, she tried to hide her fears from him, but he knew her too well. He didn't say anything, but she saw the understanding in his eyes. And with every passing day, he made a point to spend as much time with her as possible to alleviate her fears.

The week before their wedding, however, she was a basket case. Thankfully, there were hundreds of last-minute details left to take care of and only so many hours in the day. Rushing around trying to get everything taken care of before the big day on Saturday, she had little time to worry about whether Nick would be a no-show.

Then, before she knew it, it was Friday night, time for the rehearsal dinner, and she couldn't help but think about Thomas. He'd been sick at their rehearsal dinner, unable to appreciate the gourmet meal his mother had had catered, and at the time, Merry had been afraid he was coming down with some kind of stomach bug. Now, in hindsight, she realized that even then, he'd known he wasn't going to go through with the ceremony. And he'd never said a word.

Her second rehearsal dinner, however, was nothing like

the first. There was no caterer, no huge wedding party, no wine or long-winded toasts. It was just her and Nick and her family at Ed's, enjoying his Friday night special of fried fish, French fries, and hush puppies. Anyone who came into the diner for dinner and cared to join them was welcome, and before too long, everyone in the place was celebrating their upcoming wedding with them.

And Nick loved it. Merry watched him laughing and talking with her brothers and some of the unexpected guests, and she didn't think she'd ever seen him more relaxed or happy. Every chance he got, he touched her or nudged her foot under the table just to let her know he was close by. And when it came time for dessert, his eyes met hers over Ed's fantastic chocolate pie, and she knew that he, too, was thinking of the night of their first real date, when he'd taken her dancing under the stars at Tony's, then brought her to Ed's for dessert. When he'd finally taken her home, he'd kissed the stuffing out of her on her front porch, and she'd been walking on air ever since.

Her eyes darkening at the memory, she smiled at him and rubbed her foot against his under the table. Grinning, he rubbed back and started to lean over to whisper something in his ear when he suddenly glanced past her to the diner entrance and stiffened. Between one second and the next, his expression turned stony as all around them, people abruptly seemed to forget what they were talking about.

Her heart sinking, Merry didn't have to ask him what was wrong. Only one person could bring that look to his face and turn an entire diner full of people silent as a tomb. Thomas. Her back to the entrance, she knew the exact moment he found her and Nick in the crowd and started toward them.

What was he doing here? she wondered wildly as she felt him draw closer. He'd left town right after word of her and Nick's engagement had hit the streets, and they hadn't heard from him since. And they hadn't really expected to. In spite of the fact that they'd been friends forever, she'd felt it would have been in poor taste to include him in the wedding, so she hadn't sent an invitation to either him or his mother. It was the last break of ties that went back to childhood.

Considering that, there was no reason for him to come back to town the exact same weekend of her and Nick's wedding—unless he meant to cause trouble.

Nick, reaching that same conclusion, ground his teeth on a oath and said grimly, "I'll handle this." Giving her hand a reassuring squeeze, he rose to his feet just as Thomas reached their table. "I don't know what you're doing here," he told him coldly, "but this is a private party, Thomas. I don't want to be ugly, but you're not wanted here."

Braced for a scene, Merry half expected him to bristle and tell Nick to go to hell, but surprisingly, he didn't. Instead, he was unusually meek when he said, "I know I'm intruding, and I'm sorry about that. But I'd like to apologize to you and Merry if you have time to talk to me for a few minutes."

There'd been times in the not-too-distant past when Thomas would have said just the same thing and not meant a word of it. A born charmer, he knew when to be humble and just what to say to get people to drop their guard when they were angry with him. Over the course of their friendship, Merry had seen him do it more times than she could remember. He'd apologize with all the sincerity of a monk, act contrite, and worm his way back into the good graces of whomever he'd offended. And all without feeling even a touch of remorse.

But studying him now, Merry couldn't believe he was

pulling some kind of ruse. His eyes were direct, his face flushed with embarrassment, and there was no question that he was uncomfortable apologizing in front of an entire diner full of people who had been in the church three months ago when he'd left Merry literally at the altar. He had no friends there, no sympathetic ears, no voice to champion him, and he knew it. Still, he stood there, humbling himself in front of a hostile crowd, in order to apologize.

After what he'd done to her, Merry had never expected to feel a lick of sympathy for him ever again, but at that moment, she truly felt sorry for him. Pushing to her feet, she took Nick's hand. "Why don't we go outside and discuss this? Excuse us, everyone."

Not waiting for Nick's reaction, she pulled him outside with her and turned to face a very grateful Thomas. "Thank you, Merry," he said huskily. "I know I have no reason to expect any kind of consideration from you, but I appreciate that. I really wanted to talk to the two of you in private."

"So why didn't you call ahead of time and set something up?" Nick retorted. "You didn't have to do this tonight of all nights. Though I guess we should be grateful for small favors, shouldn't we? You could have shown up at the church tomorrow."

"I wouldn't have done that," he said stiffly, "but I can't blame you for thinking I would. I acted like an ass, and you both have every right to hate my guts."

He sounded so disgusted with himself that Merry flinched. "Thomas—"

"No, let me finish," he insisted. "This isn't easy for me to say, but I've had a lot of time over the last month to think about the three of us and my behavior, and I've got a lot to answer for."

His voice hoarse with a rare show of emotion, he swallowed thickly. "I did this to the three of us. I destroyed our friendship. I'm ashamed to admit it, but I knew all along how Nick felt about you, Merry, and suspected that my feelings for you weren't strong enough for marriage."

Nick cursed, and at his side, Merry did the same thing. "Then why didn't you say something?" she demanded. "Why did you humiliate me in front of the whole town?"

"Believe me, that wasn't what I wanted to do! It just happened. The plans for the wedding took on a life of their own, and before I knew it, you were waiting at the church for me. I meant to tell you weeks before that I couldn't go through with it, but I knew if I did, Nick would step forward and tell you how he felt."

"And then you would lose her to me and you couldn't stand the thought of that, could you?" Nick said, challenging him angrily.

To his credit, Thomas didn't try to deny it. "There'd always been a special closeness between the two of you, and yes, I had a feeling that once I was out of the picture, Merry would see that and fall in love with you. I'm not proud of myself for that," he said stiffly, "or any of the other things I did. I was wrong. And if you never speak to me again, it's no more than I deserve. But I had to let you know before you got married that I really do wish you both all the happiness in the world."

If he was lying, the man was a sociopath. There was true regret in his eyes and a sincerity that not even a charmer like Thomas could fake. Touched, Merry really felt sorry for him. If he hadn't inflicted such pain on her and Nick, an apology might have been all they needed to let bygones be bygones. But he'd destroyed so much trust, and that wasn't something that could be rebuilt with just a few simple words. He'd have to work hard to earn that back.

He was, however, making an effort to mend fences, and Merry was grateful for that. He'd been a part of their lives for too long for either one of them to write off his friendship for good. "Thank you, Thomas," she said huskily.

For a minute, she didn't think Nick was going to cut him any slack, but he obviously thought better of that and unbent enough to offer his hand. "Thanks, man. This took guts."

Relieved, Thomas shook his hand and very nearly cried. It wasn't world peace, but it was a start.

What a difference a few months made, Merry thought, as she checked her appearance in the dressing-room mirror. For her first wedding, the one that never came to pass, she'd arrived at the church in a limo. For her wedding to Nick, she rode with Janey and her mother in Janey's Jeep. In June, she'd had an elaborate wedding dress that had to be specially ordered and cost the earth; now she wore a simple princess design that she'd bought off the rack right there in town. Comparing the two in her mind, she had to admit, simple was better.

But it wasn't just her dress and transportation that had changed—everything was different. This time, she'd gone with spring flowers instead of white roses and gardenias; and instead of mailing out elaborate engraved invitations, she and Nick had sent out handwritten notes to just about everyone in town.

The biggest difference, however, was in herself. Before, while everyone else was frantically getting ready and worrying about Thomas's tardiness, she'd stupidly been as calm as the proverbial cucumber, sure he would be there any second. Obviously, he'd never put in an appearance, which was just one more reason why she shouldn't have wasted a single second worrying about whether Nick was going to show up or not today. He was honest and dependable, and she could count on him to be there for her. A man of his word, he'd promised to meet her at the altar, and there wasn't a doubt in her mind that he would do exactly that.

So why, then, was she a nervous wreck?

Cursing her doubts, she thought she hid them well—until Janey teased, "Is something wrong with your watch, Mer? You keep checking it."

Caught red-handed, she grinned sheepishly. "Okay, so I'm a little nervous. Can you blame me? Wait till your wedding day, and we'll see how calm you are, missy."

Janey, who at thirty-six had never had a real romantic relationship, had long since given up hope that Prince Charming was going to come riding into town for her. Some things just weren't meant to be. "Me? Get married?" she laughed, truly amused. "Yeah, right. Maybe in my next lifetime."

"Don't be too sure of that," her mother said gently. "None of us knows what life has in store for us."

"That's right," Merry agreed. "Who would have thought last Christmas, when Thomas and I announced our engagement, that nine months later I'd be marrying Nick instead? If he shows up," she added under her breath.

"Stop that," her mother scolded, hugging her. "You're tying yourself in knots for nothing. Nick's never let you down in his life, honey. He's not going to start now. He loves you. You have to have faith that he'll be here."

It sounded so easy. *Have a little faith.* With the logical part of her brain, she did. But logic couldn't stifle the feeling of déjà vu that pulled at her like a riptide. Unable to resist, she glanced at her watch again. In fifteen minutes, the ceremony was scheduled to start. What was she going to do if history repeated itself?

* * *

"Is Merry okay? Has anyone checked on her?" Nick asked worriedly as he adjusted the bow tie of his tux. "She didn't eat much last night—"

"What are you talking about?" Zeke laughed. "She had *two* slices of pie! And did Ed let anyone else have seconds? No! I know because I asked and he told me he was saving what he had left for Merry to take home with her in case she had an attack of nerves in the middle of the night and needed a chocolate fix to calm her down. The old goat— he always did have a soft spot for her."

"Jealousy rears its ugly head," Joe retorted, his brown eyes glinting with humor. "If I remember correctly, little brother, you could have used a little chocolate yourself the night before you married Lizzie. I don't even think you slept that night, did you?"

Zeke couldn't deny it—there were too many witnesses. "Okay, so I was a little nervous—"

"A *little?*"

"All right, I was a basket case—"

"Hey, guys," Nick cut in, "we're talking about Merry, remember? How was she this morning? Did she look like she slept last night? When I talked to her on the phone earlier, she said she was fine, but this has got to be hard for her. Everything's just like before. It's spooky."

Joe couldn't argue with that—he'd been looking over his shoulder for Thomas ever since they got to the church— but that wasn't something the best man told the groom on his wedding day. "It just seems that way because it's the same church and the same crowd of friends and family out front," he said. "But what happened before was a mistake, Nick. Everyone knows that. It was the right bride but the wrong groom. This time, everything's right, and Merry knows that. I'm sure she's fine."

"She has your cell phone number, doesn't she?" Zeke asked. "She'd call you if she was really worried."

Nick wanted to believe them, after all, they were her brothers and unlike him, they'd seen her this morning. They knew her state of mind. But he knew how uncomfortable Merry had been at the idea of arranging another church wedding. Once she agreed to marry him, she'd planned everything with her usual enthusiasm, but he'd known that deep down inside, she'd been afraid he was going to pull a disappearing act on her, just like Thomas. He'd done everything he could to reassure her that that wasn't going to happen, but actions spoke louder than words. The only way she would believe they were actually getting married was when she saw for herself that he was really there at the church.

"I've got to see her," he announced.

"You will in fifteen minutes," Zeke retorted. "When she walks down the aisle to you."

"No, I mean right now."

"Whoa!" Joe exclaimed, stepping in front of him when he turned toward the door. "You can't do that. What are you trying to do? Jinx this marriage before you even say, *I do?* C'mon, Nick, be reasonable. It's only fifteen minutes."

"We can even move the time up if everybody's ready," Zeke suggested. "Why don't I go check with Reverend Peters—"

"*I'll* go check," Nick said stubbornly, "on Merry. Don't try to stop me, guys. I know I'm going against tradition, but this is the most important day of our lives and I want her to enjoy every single part of it, including the anticipation of walking down the aisle. The only way she's going to do that is if I tell her I'm here."

"So call her."

"A call can be made from anywhere. She needs to see me."

"We'll tell her we just saw you—"

"I'd rather do it myself," he insisted. Without another word, he stepped around Joe, pulled open the door, and went in search of Merry.

Merry can relax. He's here! Someone tell the organist to get ready. This time, there really is going to be a wedding.

The second Nick stepped into the church vestibule, the whispers started and spread through the crowd like wildfire. Everyone who was anyone had turned up to see if he was anything like Thomas, and Nick couldn't say he blamed them. When a woman was jilted in full view of the rest of the town, it was no surprise that the next man who got involved with her would find himself the center of all eyes. And when the woman was someone like Merry, who was held in so much affection by just about everyone, that same townful of people was going to expect him to prove himself. He didn't have a problem with that.

"Hey, Nick, good to see you. Glad you could make it!"

"Me, too," he chuckled, accepting a handshake from Martha Hoffsteader's youngest son, Lance, who'd just arrived. "I wouldn't have missed it for the world." Glancing into church, which was already overflowing, he grinned. "Hope you can find a seat—it looks like we've got a full house."

"Nobody deserves it more," Lance assured him. "How's Merry holding up?"

"I'm just about to find out," Nick replied, and excused himself to knock on the door of the choir's dressing room.

Janey answered his knock, took one look at him, and immediately moved to shut the door before he could see

Merry. "Just what do you think you're doing, Nick Kincaid?" she hissed through what was little more than a crack in the door. "Have you lost your mind? You can't come in here."

"Yes, I can," he replied. "Open up. I need to talk to Merry."

"Do it after you're married."

"No. I'll do it now, Janey."

She hesitated, surveying him with a scowl through the inch-wide gap she'd left in the door. In spite of the fact that she'd never dated a man in her life, she was a die-hard romantic who believed in happily-ever-after. And Nick's appearance at the door to her sister's dressing room on her wedding day totally bucked the rules set down in the fairy tales. She wanted to send him packing, but something in his expression warned her he'd never let her get away with that.

Giving in, she reluctantly stepped back. "All right," she grumbled. "Come in, if you must. But I think you're making a mistake."

So did Sara McBride. As protective as a mother hen with ruffled feathers, she frowned disapprovingly at the sight of him. "This is not at all proper, Nick," she scolded. "Merry's in the rest room putting the last finishing touches on her hair. You have to leave before she comes out."

"I just need to see her for a second—"

"You will, dear. Just as soon as the wedding starts."

He might have talked his way around Janey, but Sara McBride was a whole different matter. Her gaze steady and unblinking, she stood between Nick and the door that led to Merry, as immovable as the Rock of Gibraltar. With nothing more than a look, she stopped him in his tracks.

"C'mon, Sara. I just want to tell her I'm here—"

"I'll tell her—"

Behind her, the door to the rest room abruptly opened. ''I'm sorry. I know I shouldn't worry,'' Merry began, only to stop abruptly at the sight of Nick. ''Nick! You're here!''

The relief in her voice was all the encouragement he needed. Lifting a brow at Sara, silently asking her permission, he waited until a wry smile curled the corners of her mouth before he quickly stepped around her. In the next instant, he had Merry in his arms.

He hadn't meant to touch her—he'd come just to assure her that he was there, in the church, and would be waiting for her at the altar. But she looked so beautiful in her wedding dress, and when her face lit up at the sight of him, all his good intentions went right out the window. He reached for her, desperate to hold her.

''I love you.''

''I love you.''

They spoke at the same time, saying with three little words everything that needed to be said, and never saw Janey and Sara smile. The whole world could have been watching and they wouldn't have noticed. They saw nothing but each other, heard nothing but their own soft sighs when they went into each other's arms, felt nothing but the love that filled their hearts as brown eyes locked with blue.

He swore he wasn't going to kiss her, not until the minister said he could kiss the bride, but Merry had other ideas. Ignoring her mother and Janey, she stood on tiptoe, lifted her mouth to his, and kissed him.

Emotions poured through him…love, joy, tenderness, passion…clogging his throat and squeezing his heart, and with a quiet murmur, he pulled her closer. His arms banding her tight, he was sure he could never let her go long enough to let her walk down the aisle to him. But then her mother quietly sniffed, wordlessly reminding them that they had a whole church full of people waiting for them, and with a groan, he slowly, reluctantly, ended the kiss.

Her blue eyes sparkling like diamonds, Merry smiled up at him happily. "Now that we've got that settled, shall we meet at the front of the church in say...ten minutes?"

"Make it five," he said with a grin, giving her another quick kiss. "I don't think I can wait any longer than that."

Beaming, she watched him walk out and couldn't stop smiling. When the door shut behind him and she turned to find her mother and Janey grinning at her in understanding, she had to hug them both. "I can't believe I was worried," she laughed. "This is going to be wonderful!"

Overflowing with love, her heart thumping crazily, Merry gathered in the foyer of the church with her family and fought the sudden need to cry. She'd pictured this moment a thousand times in her head, sure she knew exactly how it would be. But nothing in her imagination could have prepared her for the absolute perfection of the moment.

The church couldn't have been more beautiful. Just as the organist started playing "Precious and Few," sunlight streamed through the stained glass windows, setting a rainbow of pastel colors cascading across the altar and the spring flowers that decorated it. The crowd caught its breath with a nearly silent, reverent gasp. In the sudden hush, Merry would have sworn she could hear a choir of angels singing with joy.

"Mom, look," she whispered, tears welling in her eyes as Nick and Joe, who was his best man, came through a side door and crossed to a spot in front of the altar. Both dressed in black tuxes and looking incredibly handsome, they stood framed in the sparkling sunlight like two heavenly beings from above.

Her face alight with love, Sara hugged her close. "*This*

is why Thomas didn't show up in June," she said softly, her own eyes bright with tears. "He wasn't the one you were supposed to be with. Nick is."

Merry didn't doubt that for a minute. Unable to take her eyes off Nick, she felt her heart swell with love. How long, she wondered, had she loved him without even knowing it? It must have been always.

"The organist is waiting for our signal to start the wedding march," Janey reminded her quietly. "If you're ready, Zeke can escort Mom to her seat, then we can get started." Her smile crooked, she nodded to the front of the church, where Nick was watching their every move. "Nick is already impatient. If we take any longer to get this thing started, we may have a kidnapping on our hands."

Chuckling, Sara gave Merry one last hug, then stepped back. "We wouldn't want that. The poor boy's waited long enough, as it is. Zeke, let me have your arm, dear."

When they had rehearsed the wedding the night before, it had all seemed so simple. It was a small wedding party, made up of only her family and Nick, so everyone knew their duties. Once Nick and Joe took their places at the front of the church, Zeke would escort their mother to her seat, then return to the foyer so that he could give Merry away. The organist would start the music, Janey would precede them down the aisle, and the wedding would begin.

But as Zeke started to offer their mother his arm, Merry realized that the wedding she'd thought was going to be so perfect wouldn't be everything that she wanted it to be if she didn't make an immediate change. "Wait!" she cried softly.

Surprised, Zeke stopped in his tracks, arching a dark brow at her as her mother and Janey turned back to her with a frown of concern. "What is it, honey?" her mother asked. "What's wrong? You haven't changed your mind, have you?"

"Yes! I mean, no!" she corrected quickly when she realized how that sounded. "Not about Nick," she assured her mother. "You know how much I love him, Mom. This is the right thing for us. It's walking down the aisle I want to change."

Frowning, Zeke tried to understand. "You don't want to walk down the aisle? Then how are you going to get married? Check her pulse, Janey. I think she's having some kind of breakdown."

"No, I'm not," she laughed. "Stop that. I just want to make a few adjustments to the original plans."

"What kind of adjustments?" Janey asked. "The minister's waiting, Mer. And so is Nick."

Glancing down the length of the church to where Nick waited for her in front of the altar, she saw his sudden frown and smiled reassuringly at him. When she glanced back at her family, fresh tears glistened in her eyes as she reached for Zeke's hand first, then her mother's. "I know you're standing in for Dad," she told her brother huskily, "and I'm happy about that. But I have another parent, and I want her to give me away, to."

Her smile hesitant, she glanced at her mother. "Mom? Is that okay with you? Would you walk down the aisle with me and Zeke and help give me away?"

Caught off guard, Sara McBride gasped softly, sudden, unexpected tears welling in her eyes and spilling over her lashes. She'd known she would cry later during the ceremony, but she'd never expected this. Touched, her beautiful smile the exact replica of Merry's, she squeezed her hand. "Oh, honey, you know I will if that's what you want," she choked. "This is your day. I want it to be perfect for you."

''That's what I want, too, Mom,'' she said huskily. ''And it will be if you and Zeke both give me away.''

She didn't have to ask twice. Beaming, her mother said, ''I'd love to.''

His own voice suspiciously gruff, Zeke growled, ''Thank God that's settled! Can we start the wedding now?''

For an answer, Merry signaled to the organist, who immediately broke into broad grin and began the wedding march. Janey, quickly stepping into place in front of her mother, Zeke, and Merry, smiled serenely and started down the aisle.

Her heart thumping madly, Merry stood between her mother and brother and waited for the nerves to hit. She was about to take the biggest step of her life—anybody in their right mind would have to be nervous at this point. But as her gaze slipped past Janey to where Nick stood waiting for her with the minister and Joe, a peacefulness unlike anything she'd ever known settled over her and her heart slowed to a sure, steady beat. This was the man she loved, the man she wanted to spend the rest of her life with. How could she be nervous when the one thing she wanted most in the world was to be with him?

Her right arm looped through his left, Zeke held her close and looked down at her with brotherly affection. ''They're playing your song, Mer,'' he said as Janey reached the front of the church and the organist broke into a loud, rousing rendition of the wedding march. ''You've waited a long time for this. Let's give everybody a show.''

Laughing, she glanced at her mother, who only grinned and winked. Together, the three of them started down the aisle.

Standing at the altar, feeling as if he were standing on air, Nick watched Merry walk toward him with her mother and brother on each side of her and couldn't stop smiling. Lord, she was something! He'd waited a lifetime for her, but at the moment in time, as images of her at six and sixteen and twenty-eight flashed before his mind's eye, it seemed like only seconds had passed between the first time he'd laid eyes on her and now. And all he could think of was that he wanted more. More laughter, more tears, more time to hold her and love her and make love with her. He'd never realized how much until now. She was the other part of his soul, and he didn't just want to spend the rest of his life with her. He wanted eternity.

Did she know how much he loved her? Too late, he realized he'd never explained his feelings in just that way to her, and that was something that every woman longed to hear from the man she'd promised to spend the rest of her life with. He should have told her—she needed to know.

But there was no time. She stopped before him at that moment, turned to kiss her mother and Zeke, then stepped to his side. A hushed silence fell over the church as the music faded to a whisper, then a memory. In the quiet stillness, he took her hand, their fingers entwined, and her eyes, shining with love, lifted to his. And just that easily, he knew she knew exactly how much he adored her. Because everything he was feeling was right there in her eyes.

They smiled at each other, totally oblivious to the friends and family members who smiled with them, sharing their joy. Then hand in hand, they turned to face the minister and heard the words they'd been waiting a lifetime to hear.

"Dearly beloved, we are gathered here today…"

* * * * *

COMING NEXT MONTH

If you enjoyed what you just read,
then we've got an offer you can't resist!

Take 2 bestselling love stories FREE!
Plus get a FREE surprise gift!

MONTANA MAVERICKS

Montana Mavericks: Wed in Whitehorn
Stories that capture living and loving beneath the
Big Sky, where legends live on and love lasts forever!

Silhouette® brings you a BRAND-NEW program that includes
12 incredible stories that will take you to Whitehorn,
Montana, where love and mystery are always in the air!

Watch for the first book in June 2000 at
your favorite retail outlet.

LONE STALLION'S LADY
by **Lisa Jackson**

Use this coupon on any Montana Mavericks title
and receive $1 off.

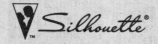

Visit Silhouette at www.eHarlequin.com   MM100CAN

MONTANA MAVERICKS

Montana Mavericks: Wed in Whitehorn
*Stories that capture living and loving beneath the
Big Sky, where legends live on and love lasts forever!*

Silhouette® brings you a BRAND-NEW program that includes
12 incredible stories that will take you to Whitehorn,
Montana, where love and mystery are always in the air!

*Watch for the first book in June 2000 at
your favorite retail outlet.*

LONE STALLION'S LADY
by **Lisa Jackson**

Use this coupon on any Montana Mavericks title
and receive $1 off.

$1 OFF!
the purchase of any **MONTANA MAVERICKS** title

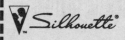

5 65373 00076 2   (8100) 1 06536
